Keith Brooke is a youn ... se
short fiction has ap ...
anthology *Othe* ...
is his first ...
available i ...

'A gripping story ... nge and skin-of-the-teeth survival, but ... also much more: an anti-war testament with a direct power that requires no preaching'
FAREN MILLER, *LOCUS*

'It has been several years since a first novel grabbed me the way Keith Brooke's *Keeper of the Peace* did'
TOM WHITMORE, *LOCUS*

KEEPERS OF THE PEACE

Keith Brooke

CORGI BOOKS

KEEPERS OF THE PEACE

A CORGI BOOK 0 552 13724 3

Originally published in Great Britain by Victor Gollancz Ltd

PRINTING HISTORY
Gollancz edition published 1990
Corgi edition published 1991

This book is set in 11/12pt Times
by Kestrel Data, Exeter

Corgi Books are published by Transworld Publishers Ltd,
61–63 Uxbridge Road, Ealing, London W5 5SA, in Australia by Transworld Publishers (Australia) Pty. Ltd, 15–23 Helles Avenue, Moorebank, NSW 2170, and in New Zealand by Transworld Publishers (N.Z.) Ltd, Cnr Moselle and Waipareira Avenues, Henderson, Auckland.

Made and printed in Great Britain by
BPCC Hazell Books
Aylesbury, Bucks, England
Member of BPCC Ltd

KEEPERS OF THE PEACE

Chapter One

20 June 2084

Most of the people down here call us aliens. I guess that's to be expected: Extraterran Peacekeeping Force is too much of a mouthful, and EP sounds too friendly. But we're still at least as human as they are.

We just call them shit.

Back in the lobby of the Dallas airport building a piece of shit in a blue CivAir uniform smiled at me over a narrow plastic counter. 'Can I see your ID please, sir?' she said.

I put down my shoulder bag, fumbled in the inside pocket of my jacket. Along with my ticket, there was a small card with some writing and a bad photograph of me on it. 'Here you are,' I said, handing over the card.

There was one main building left at Dallas Airport. From the outside it looked like an old aircraft hangar and that illusion didn't change much when I got to see it from the inside. The lobby was a big open area cut off by partitions about two metres high. Above that was a huge volume of air before the inside of a corrugated metal roof closed us in.

'Where are you headed?' asked the girl in the uniform.

I smiled. 'With only one flight scheduled to leave here in the next fifteen hours,' I said, '*you* tell *me* where I'm headed.'

She scowled, said, 'Let's see your ticket, then.' My hand went back to my pocket and withdrew the flimsy green ticket. When I handed it over she smiled and said, 'Ah! You're going to *Reno.* So's the plane.'

But I wasn't paying attention to the girl. Instead I surveyed the lobby. More crowded than I'd expected. Not many people can afford to travel by air, these days.

I looked back at the girl. 'I'm afraid you'll have to see an inspector,' she said. 'Nothing to worry about. It's all just part of the procedure.' She smiled her company-policy smile. 'If you'll just remain in the reception area. You'll be called soon.'

Conscious of my every movement, I gathered up the ID and ticket and stooped for my bag. As I straightened, I looked around. 'You look ill,' said the girl. 'Maybe you should have some coffee.'

I followed the wave of her hand and saw a refreshments stall. 'Yeah,' I said. 'I think I might do that.'

Another calming breath then I limped my way over to the stall. 'Coffee,' I said, and paid for it. I sat on a bench, plastic cup in hand, and stared blankly ahead of me. This was my first mission behind enemy lines and I had been chipping down since entering the airport building, keeping my adrenalin down to manageable levels. Mustn't look too tense.

Why the inspector? What was wrong? There were three possibilities. First, they could have inside information. Somebody had told them about our mission. Told them to look out for a coloured guy with a leg brace going under the name of Trudeau. If that was the case, the mission was over; Jed Brindle missing in action, June '84.

Not quite so bad was the possibility that the girl on the desk had spotted something odd about my act. The ticket was genuine but the ID was printed by an intelligence unit back in Grand Union. Maybe she'd spotted something. I'd only been on Earth seven and a half months. Back on Lejeune – *any*where in the colonies – the whole system of body language is different. Gestures, behaviour, mannerisms. Any of these could have made the girl suspicious. Still, if this was the case the mission was probably over, for me at least; Jed Brindle missing in action, June '84.

Or maybe it was 'just part of the procedure'. They get so few air travellers, they could probably take the time to check out most, if not all, of the passengers before letting them on the plane. Then Jed Brindle would have to keep his cool and try very hard *not* to end up missing in action, June '84.

Looking around again, I began to notice why there were so many people around. Only a quarter of them could be passengers, the rest were traders, pickpockets, beggars. Anybody who'd realized that the one place rich people will gather is the airport. I spotted Jacobi over at a cigarette vendor. I looked away again.

When the girl had told me to wait to be called I had chipped hard, kept my juices low. Mustn't panic. A side effect of that sort of use is the tranquil feeling you get after a time. Sitting on my bench, the coffee burning my hand through the plastic cup, I felt like I was floating. I watched a piece of paper dancing in the gusts of wind from the doors as they opened and closed, opened and closed.

'*Would Mr Trudeau please make his way to Room G. Room G is by Gate D. Thank you.*' The announcement startled me, brought me to awareness. The shock gave me the kick of adrenalin I needed, so I didn't chip any more. I rose from my seat and limped towards Room G.

A door with the correct letter printed on it was set into one of the partitions. It was open halfway. I walked in.

A little fat guy sat behind a desk, a bristly beard

covering loose jowls, his white collar fastened too tightly. He was wearing a CivAir uniform. The sound of the door reached his ears and he looked up with a start. 'Huh? Oh, er, come in, Mr Trudeau,' he said, stumbling to his feet. 'It *is* Mr Trudeau, is it not?'

I stared at him. 'Yeah, that's me,' I said. I decided on the appropriate gesture and offered him my hand to shake.

He looked at it curiously. Then he seemed to realize what it was for and shook it with his own clammy little hand. 'The name's Pabby Alvarez,' he said. 'This won't take long.'

I looked around the bare room, one wall lined with tall grey lockers and filing cabinets, the others stuck up with calendars, wall-charts, pieces of paper with scrawled messages. The room felt bigger than it was. A narrow desk had a single sheet of paper on it. Even after more than seven months I sometimes found it strange getting used to how primitive everything was on Earth. The shortages, I guess. If this office was on the moon or in Lagrangia there would be at least a monitor and an assortment of shunt-leads. Almost certainly there would be a holo-projector, a manual console, maybe a wall screen. I sometimes wondered if Grand Union was really worth protecting from its primitive neighbours.

The room had no top and, looking up to the high ceiling of the building, I realized why I felt so exposed. It was because it sounded just like I was out in the lobby, the sounds of people and daily life swirling around us like leaves on the wind.

'Take a seat,' said Alvarez, retaking his own. 'Just a few formalities, Mr Trudeau. New regulations we have to follow. The war with the aliens, you know.'

'Sure,' I said. 'Hey, I hope this isn't going to make me miss the flight.'

'No. Like I say: it won't take long. It's all timed to fit into the schedule, you know.'

'Yeah, I know,' I said. Alvarez wasn't going to be much of a challenge, I decided. I just had to avoid any intimate search. There were no metals or explosives for them to detect, my interfaces were disguised but not inaccessible. But an intimate search would find that my clothes weren't all they appeared. Under the outer layers I was wearing an isothermal body-suit. In case of emergencies. But to get my clothes off I would have to remove my leg brace and I was relying on sympathy for my handicap to protect me. There were two zaps tucked into the brace, little hand lasers that look and feel like toy guns, hence the name. Weak but effective at short range, they were the best we could hope to smuggle safely onto the plane.

'Are you going to Reno on business, sir?'

'And pleasure, yes,' I said with a casual grin.

'Can I check your ID and ticket, sir?'

'Yeah, here they are,' I said, handing them over. 'I had them out ready.'

The little man glanced at the ticket and then looked at the ID more closely. 'You work in recycling in Brownwood,' he said.

Not sure if it was a question, I said, 'Plastic bottles.' He looked up. 'Plastic bottle tops, too.' I grinned and he flickered a smile at the corners of his bristly little mouth.

'Divorced,' he said, continuing on his way down the list of details on my ID. I kept quiet this time. 'No children. Disabled travel assistance.' He glanced down at my strapped-up leg. 'Environmental?' he asked.

'The leg?' I said. 'Yeah. Been like it since I was a kid. The bones are weak, the skin peels and cracks. I have to mop up the fluid every so often.' I made as if to reach for my leg but he flinched and shook his head.

There were a lot of unpleasant environmental diseases and abnormalities around on Earth, although none on my leg. It made me think of my little sister, Triona, in her prosthetic suit. At least it was more use to her than these shitty braces would be. I'd used my suboccipital chip to hypnotize a convincing limp into my walk.

'You're a citizen of CalTex,' he said. 'Strange accent for a Callie, if you don't mind the comment.'

'*La République*,' I said in my best high-school French accent.

'Huh?' said Alvarez. 'Quebec? Is that what you're saying?'

Good, he hadn't caught me on the pronunciation. 'Yeah, the People's Republic,' I said. 'I've been living down here nine years now, but I guess the accent is still hanging in there.'

'Say,' said the man. 'I've got relatives up there. Aunt, uncle, cousins. I used to go up there every year when I was a kid.'

Shit. Chip down on the juices. Relax. Let the breath flow nice and even. You're smarter than this little jerk in his deep blue uniform. 'Yeah?' I said, cracking my face with a grin. He was smiling, waiting for more. *When I was a kid.* Twenty-five, thirty years ago. A kid.

'Hey, do you know, Montreal?' I said. 'Ever been to Genevieve's on Thirty-Fourth?' Of course you haven't, jerk. I just made it up.

He looked confused for a moment, then said, '*Yeah.* Sure. Used to slide away from my folks sometimes and go there for a joint and some hard liquor.'

Jerk.

I had been worried for an instant, back there. But then I saw that he was making it up as fast as I was. Playing the Big Man About Town when he was only a small fat jerk with bristles covering his small fat face.

I smiled pleasantly. 'At Genevieve's?' I said, still smiling. 'Hey, I didn't know they *did* that kind of thing there. I used to go for the Fauré and crusted port. You know?' My smile broadened.

He flushed behind his beard and he spluttered and said, 'Oh. Did you say *Genevieve's*? Shoot, I thought you were talking about another place I used to go.' He grinned an embarrassed grin. 'Wires crossed, you know?'

'Yeah,' I said. 'I know.'

He looked awkwardly down at his sheet of paper, and I let my smile slowly subside. 'One last formality,' he said and rose from his chair. He came around the desk and stood before me. My eyes were level with the top button of his too tight jacket. 'If you would be so kind as to tip your head forward, Mr Trudeau.'

The final obstacle. The true test of whether or not I was an 'alien'. I leaned forward. With his left hand he parted the hair at the back of my head and with his right he fumbled around at my scalp. I'd grown my hair longer for the mission, lost the army cut. Nothing was visible of my suboxy, the medics had speed-grown a flap of flesh over it before I left. I wouldn't be needing to use any suboccipital shunts until I found my way back to Grand Union. The little guy's hand ran over the hollow at the base of my skull. The hollow that contained my suboxy, my suboccipital neural interface chip, to give it its full title. His finger ran over where the jack-sockets lay, millimetres below his touch. His finger ran higher up my skull and lingered on a natural lump, before continuing on its journey. I held back a sigh of relief. He had come close.

His hand moved back down again and I tensed. His finger caught on something, a flap of skin, the hard lump that it concealed. He frowned. His breath was hot on my face, smelt of old coffee grounds. *Chip down*, but it was no good, his finger was still there, pressing at my suboxy. Split second dragging out into infinity.

I stared into his eyes, read each flickering change of expression as understanding slowly filtered through. Sweat broke on his forehead, his cheeks, his upper lip. He flinched and I chipped up hard, felt the adrenalin surging through my body.

My hands were on his neck, thumbs crushing his windpipe, before he had time to believe what his senses had tried to tell him. *Alien.*

Within seconds he was slumping, his weight dragging at my arms. Still, I hung on to his throat, my thumbs pressing hard until his pulse had been still for over a minute. Standard technique.

I stepped back, looked around the room, fought the urge to flee. Solid floor, flimsy partition-walls, one door, no windows. *Lockers.* The first one opened easily. One-fifty high, it held a coat and an old pair of jeans. I went over to Alvarez, dragged him across by the feet. Pushed up against the locker he was too broad, too tall. But I coped with that, I'm strong.

I made him fit.

'Thank you very much, sir,' I said, as I backed out of the interview room, closing the door gently behind me. I shouldered my bag and limped through a turnstile, flashing my ticket and a cheery grin at the girl on the desk. She smiled back.

I found myself in another large lobby area, less crowded than the last. It was only passengers this time, not the traders and other street trash. I found a seat and sank into it, fingering the locker key in my pocket. Twenty-five minutes to take-off. I closed my eyes.

*

We have lots of names for the people down here. Shit is only one of them. Frags is the name we tended to use back on Lejeune and in the training camps. It comes from The Fragmented States of America, a nickname for the state the USA has gotten itself into since it split up into CalTex, Grand Union and the smaller debris of states and counties. The range of names suddenly expanded when we arrived in Grand Union. Duds, boonies, rubes, momsers, blood claats.

Plain old *shit* will do for me.

I opened my eyes to see a grey-haired shit standing over me. Cords and a light grey jacket hung loosely from his thin body. He had a narrow pinched face, tiny rectangular sunglasses perched on the tip of his sharp nose. A piercing blue gaze.

I closed my eyes again. This was Cohen. Luke Cohen, Northern California's State Rep. on the CalTex Alignment. Holds the government portfolio of Strategic Military Planner.

The target of the whole mission.

And he was standing looking straight at me. A mind-image of Alvarez, crushed into his locker, made me open my eyes again. None of this seemed real. I shook my head, chipped down on my nerves.

Cohen was still staring at me. Standing behind him and to one side was a huge muscle-clad woman. She was dark with long fluffy hair and a thin black moustache. She must have stood nearly two metres high.

'Mind if we join you on the bench, son?' said Cohen. 'It's been a long wait for the plane.'

I looked back at the small grey man. Shit, he was average height, but he *looked* small, next to his hulk of a bodyguard. Anybody would. 'Sure,' I said. 'Help yourself.' I chipped down on some of the apprehension and closed my eyes again. I started to count off the time until I could move away from Cohen and head for the plane.

'It's a terrible thing, the mess we've made of our world, isn't it, son?'

I opened my eyes again and he was still looking at me.

'The diseases,' he said and nodded at my braced leg. 'The effects on our climate, our economy. On our way of life. I remember when things were only beginning to get bad and I hope to see a time when we can change them back for the better. Eh, son?'

I seized the opening. 'Look, if this is an election speech, I don't want to hear it,' I said, chipping some juice to add authenticity to my display of anger. I stood and limped a few paces, then turned. 'And I'm not your son, mister.' I walked away as fast as my brace could carry me, thankful that I had taken the opportunity to get away and hoping I had carried it off well enough.

I went and stood at a window, passing Jacobi on the way. He sent a burst of Comtac tingling in my abdomen – what he called a 'belly laugh' – and smiled at me. I ignored him. We weren't supposed to make contact until we had boarded the plane.

I looked out of the window for a short while, watched a maintenance crew beetling around the plane that I assumed was ours. A Boeing 245, not as big as the military transport planes, but sleek and powerful, all the same. It was like some giant cat, waiting to pounce. A cat with over one hundred luxury seats lining its bowels. Reflected in the glass I could see the line of admin cubicles, rooms A through to K.

I forced myself to look around and immediately spotted Jacobi again, smoking a cigarette and chatting to a stewardess. Glancing aimlessly around the waiting area, I eventually spotted Amagat reading a poster by the exit. Her mousy hair was tied in a tail behind her head, drawn tightly away from a strong face. Her pale, green eyes seemed to betray a weakness that was out of place. She was scared.

My casual look around failed to locate Lohmann but I stopped looking, not wanting to give myself away. As I returned my gaze to the window, Cohen tried to catch my eye.

I ignored him and concentrated on the Boeing.

A look at a clock, a short time later, and I knew Lohmann was cutting it fine. There were any number of things that could have cut him off before he reached the airport.

Before he even reached Dallas.

Almost one-fifty kay-ems of travelling in CalTex territory to go wrong in. I looked around the waiting area again to make sure I hadn't just missed him. I hadn't. Amagat was anxiously looking around. I sent out a burst of Comtac. *Chip down*, it told her. *Chip down.*

I glanced in her direction a few seconds later and she had calmed herself. Our eyes met and I felt a flutter of acknowledgement. There are three Comtac electrodes implanted into an EPs abdominal wall. A weak radio signal can be chipped out to stimulate the 'trodes in a number of coded patterns. It seems to be the ideal solution to squad communication. Proper radio equipment needs more conscious control, and they say it leads to confusion, anyway. Too much distraction. It can also be detected rather easily. I hardly have to think to chip a message to anyone within the range of twenty metres or so. Hardly have to think to read a return message either.

Where was Lohmann? I caught myself looking around again and chipped down on my juices. Have to stay cool. If Gil had blown, the three of us could still pull it off.

'Would passengers for Civic Airlines Flight 304 to Reno, via Cheyenne, please assemble outside the airfield exit. Thank you.'

The announcement momentarily set my pulse racing. I tore myself away from the window and followed the crowd out of a door marked AIRFIELD EXIT. We waited outside. A last look back into the building failed to reveal Lohmann.

After a minute or two a man in CivAir blue appeared from a small STAFF ONLY door and said, 'Right now, folks. If you'll just follow me out to the plane, the flight will leave in a little over ten minutes. Thank you.'

We walked out on to the airfield, following our guide. A short distance away, I saw a cart being pulled by two huge horses. Grey blinkers shielding their eyes, shining brass buckles, great shaggy hooves. They looked prehistoric. The cart was loaded with cases and I realized it was the luggage being taken to the plane. I fingered the strap of my shoulder bag, somehow relieved that I was travelling light.

Maybe fifty metres from the building. No sign of Lohmann.

A few paces later I realized that Cohen was at my elbow, the bodyguard at his. My leg twinged in its brace. Sometimes autohypnosis can be a little *too* realistic. I had to slow down and let Cohen pull level. 'Listen, son,' he said. 'I'm sorry about what I said earlier. Maybe it was a bit insensitive of me to go up to a stranger and talk about his impediments. It's just that you reminded me of someone I used to know. Will you accept my apology?'

I looked at him and was transfixed by his sharp gaze. 'Yeah,' I said, looking away. 'I guess I was a little hard on you, too.'

Cohen settled into his stride next to me and I began

to want to get away from him again. Why did he have to pick on *me*? The guy who was planning to kidnap a whole plane just to get this little jerk over to Grand Union. We were halfway to the plane.

'Hey! Don't let it go without me!'

I looked around, fighting panic.

And there was a man clad in a fashionable beige jump-suit running out of the airport building, waving his bag in the air. A figure in a CivAir uniform emerged after him but gave up the chase after only a moment or two.

'Wait for me!' cried the man, but we were waiting anyway. The whole group of a hundred of us was fixed to the airstrip, watching the approaching figure of Private Gilbert Lohmann. He joined us and we continued on our march to the plane. His cheeks were flushed and his eyes heavily glazed. He beamed around at anyone who cared to look.

The exertion, I thought. But no. That look in his eyes. I couldn't kid myself for long. Gil had stoked up on drugs to see him through the trip. He'd always been a light user, but since coming to Earth he'd gone deeper and deeper.

And now he was stoked to the eyeballs on a mission that had a high probability that we would all end up dead unless we worked pretty damned hard at it. Gil smiled at me and I looked away.

Chip down, I Comtacked. The best we could hope for was just to keep him quiet for the trip. Maybe keep us all alive.

We reached the steps that led up to the plane's entrance.

'If you'll all just go on up,' said our guide. 'You'll find the seat numbers marked clearly on your tickets and on the seats.' Then he moved over to Lohmann at the edge of the group and said, 'If you'd just spare me a moment, sir, we'll check your documents. There appeared to be some irregularity back at the terminus.' He had a firm hand on Gil's left arm as the rest of us entered the plane.

The seats reserved for the squad were scattered towards the front. Close to the pilot's cabin. I sat in mine and glanced casually over at Jacobi, one row forward and on the opposite side of the aisle. He was looking back at the entrance. Waiting for Gil.

I gave myself a couple of gentle downs with my chip. Calm myself. A patter in my abdomen and I was being told to chip down. Amagat. She was the only one that would be stating such an obvious precaution.

At that moment that dragged into minutes, the whole plan rested on Gil not giving us away. It was out of my hands, so I closed my eyes and chipped right down. Get some rest.

The plan. The flight was due to leave in ten minutes. Taking the roundabout route to Reno, via Cheyenne up in Wyoming; avoiding the trouble-spots that a direct route over New Mexico would put us above. After ninety-five minutes we would be within fifty kay-ems of Grand Union's border with CalTex. After those ninety-five minutes we would take over the plane, somewhere over Amarillo, Texas.

Simple. But already things were falling out of place. There was the new airport 'security' – a brief flash of Alvarez crammed into that locker – and then there was Cohen picking me out for some reason. And now there was Gil, getting stoked up on some hash or other. Terran drugs are much more potent than homegrown. I guess we're not used to them. They're a lot less refined, too. Can have nasty effects, sometimes.

Comtac flickered in my belly. *Alert.* I looked around

and saw Gil weaving his way down the aisle towards the front of the plane, the steward helping him along from behind. As they passed I heard the steward say in a quiet voice, '. . . time, sir, it might be wise to take your medication *after* you get on the plane. Then the side-effects can wear off during the . . .'

They passed out of the range of my ears and the steward helped Gil into his seat. 'Thank you, my man,' he said as he settled down for the flight.

The plane's engines burst into life, running through the motions before take-off. The plane shuddered and then settled again, the sound of the engines dimmed until my mind dismissed it as part of the background noise.

I moved awkwardly, stretched my uncomfortable braced leg. I sank lower into the padded luxury of my seat and began to chip the counter-instruction. I had to have my leg in a more usable state by the time it came for action.

In ninety-five minutes. The engines had taken on a new tone and I saw that we were moving, accelerating, lifting away from the airstrip. I put aside the fear of someone discovering Alvarez's body, closed my eyes again, chipped down.

Things had been threatening to go wrong even earlier than at the airport. Right back to even before we had set out on the mission.

I was in the squad with Jacobi and Lohmann long before we were posted to Earth. Right after initial training we were put into the four-man squad – *Plato's* squad – and we finished our training together. Then we spent seven months being shuttled from city to city in Grand Union. Policing at first, but more and more it had been raids on guerrilla bases. Safe houses, weapons caches, any terrorist stronghold. We earned something of a reputation, found ourselves thrown into worse and worse troublespots.

Then two things happened almost simultaneously: Plato was withdrawn from command of the squad and we were withdrawn from what we had expected to be our rôle in the fighting until the end of our round of duty.

Plato had always been a great guy to be around and he was a great leader of the squad. He knew us so well that he could play us off against each other, strengths and weaknesses working together to make us one of the top fighting units on Earth. And on top of that, he managed to be a fine friend to us all. That's a rare combination, and it didn't last. Plato took to acting strangely. Then, when we were on leave in Kansas City, I asked him if he was going to come out with the squad. He just ignored me and rushed out.

I never saw him again. There were all sorts of rumours about what had happened to him. People were bound to be interested, Plato was some kind of *hero* to the other EPs.

There were endless wild stories about defection, mental breakdown, desertion. Someone even said he had jumped off Broadway Bridge. There were a lot of reports that he had been seen drinking in the basement district. Maybe he was picked up by angry kids. There's a lot of hard feelings against EPs even in Grand Union.

Of course the official version was that Plato was recalled to an off-Earth station. Intelligence work, or something like. Hell, if there's one thing I've learnt in my year in the Army, it's not to know what to believe. And when you *do* settle on a belief, don't hold it too strongly. Sometimes the Army's views may clash with your own and it'd be a fool who disagreed with the Army.

So there we were: a four-man squad, cut down to three, and singled out for what they tell us is a highly important mission behind enemy lines. Step forward Sublieutenant Margot Amagat. Fresh on Earth, but one of the generals has faith in her so she finds herself in charge of the three of us.

But we were broken. We weren't *the squad* without Plato. We were a completely new squad, with a new leader. And they were breaking in the new squad on this bastard of a mission.

Amagat just didn't click with the squad like Plato did. There was a great big something missing. She was too rigid, too keen on her own leadership. Too inexperienced. We were with her for a five-day briefing and training session, then we were dumped on the border near Gainesville for a rendezvous in four days on the aeroplane.

And in that time Lohmann somehow managed to stoke his brain out and threaten the whole mission.

It was weird, hiking down the crumbling remains of Interstate 35. Picking up lifts in horse-drawn wagons. My own home-colony, a little Bernal sphere at L5, is an agricultural museum, but we don't have *horses.* Maybe one or two holograms, but not the real thing. Down on Earth they use horses a lot. Fuel shortages, I guess. I was surprised that I wasn't challenged by anybody but they all seemed quite happy to accept that I had fled Grand Union because of the aliens. I'd expected more suspicion in war-time, but I guess there's also a good deal more acceptance of the unusual, too.

On the outskirts of Dallas I changed out of my travelling clothes, stout boots and a jump-suit that was by then dirty and torn. I washed and shaved in a little stream that I first checked to see the water wasn't what they call 'grey' – poisoned with any of a huge variety of pollutants. Then I put on a lightweight business suit, more appropriate for a Mr Trudeau. I rigged the brace, loaded it with the zaps and the panhalothol capsules we would be using on the plane. Then I dumped what I didn't need and made my way into Dallas on a hot, dry morning. Five hours later I was sunk into a seat on the plane as it banked in a wide sweep around the city of Dallas and levelled its course on Cheyenne.

I opened my eyes and looked slowly around the plane. Double seats on either side of a narrow aisle, weak yellow lighting. I was on an aisle seat. Easy to get out of in a hurry.

Amagat was in one of the front seats, opposite side to me. Lohmann was three rows behind her, chatting away to an old lady in the seat next to him. Drug-induced nonsense, I hoped. Jacobi was behind Lohmann, all I could see of him were two brown stubs of ears and his oily black hair.

I glanced over my shoulder and saw Cohen and his bodyguard about halfway down the plane, opposite side to me. He noticed my look and winked in my direction. I looked away.

'*Welcome to Flight 304, folks.*' The intercom crackled with the pilot's voice. '*This is your pilot speaking. In-flight refreshments will be around in a few minutes, but first I have an announcement to make.*'

I sat up, alert now.

'*I'm delighted to be the one to inform you that the dispute with our Mexican neighbours has reached settlement. New Mexico is once again a safe part of the Alignment, so I can announce a change in our flight plan. We can now fly to Reno via Santa Barbara, missing out Cheyenne. Passengers for Cheyenne will be put on a connecting flight at Reno and will still arrive there ahead of schedule.*'

I felt an urgent patter of Comtac. *Chip down. Chip down.* But I didn't need to be told.

'*I'll just repeat that,*' broke in the pilot. '*This flight will now fly to Reno via Santa Barbara. No stop-over at Cheyenne. Now I'm sure you'd like to know about the wide range of refreshments available from your CivAir stewardesses . . .*'

I slumped down in my seat, my eyes closed. If only someone could wipe those few short words.

Chapter Two

Extracts from the diary of Jed Brindle, 6 March 2083 – 31 March 2083.

6 MARCH 2083

'*Jed Brindle, Austin Whitney and Soriya Keele to a radio shunt*,' said the announcement and I guess it was those words that changed my whole life. All it takes is a few words. It makes things seem very fragile, somehow.

Hey, I guess I'd better start this thing properly, you know?

I haven't kept a diary since school, like the one the tutor wants. Only the tutor makes you shunt into *it* so it can suss your head. Hell, it doesn't exactly encourage free expression when you know everything you write is going to be torn apart so they can map your mind.

Anyway, when I was given my draft notice I just had to rush back here and get down what I feel. A crazy whirl of emotions and I guess if I put it down somehow, give it an existence outside of my own head, I might make some sense of it all.

But the spark has died. Cut that: the spark was *extinguished.* Pa saw to that.

But I'm letting it all get away from me, it's not making any more sense than it did in my mind. Hell, I haven't made much of 'starting it properly', have I?

I'm lying on my bunk, dictating direct from my brain

on to a Sanyo data bubble shunted into my suboxy. I'm getting all this down out of stubbornness. I guess it's out of loyalty to that earlier, overwhelming desire to record it all. Hey, maybe they'll use this as the basis of the hee-vee feature they make of my soldiering: *The Battles of Brindle* or something like.

OK, deep breath, focus the mind and back to the story. (Make a note: this is going to take some *heavy* editing.)

We were raking hay on the Penn strip when the announcement came. Maybe ten of us and not one geek (that's what we call tourists here on Lejeune). But geeks or not the work has to be done.

Lejeune's a small place if you ignore the Growers, just a simple little Bernal hanging in L5. We're slightly apart from the dense clusters formed by the larger colonies; cylinders, spheres, tori, so dense they've taken to calling that part of L5 the Lagropolis.

Our main *raison d'être* is the food. The vast zero-gee growers hang around our little sphere like junkies around a lysergine tab. But since Pa wired up there hasn't been much work. He has direct links to all the growing equipment and his drones deal with anything he isn't directly jacked into. There's only room for a few ag-techs on top of that.

But Lejeune's also a museum. Farming through the ages. Hack and burn, strip cultivation, twentieth-century chemigrow (sealed off for hygiene), we do it all. By traditional methods.

So there we were, raking hay on the Penn strip. My trad smock was itching me and the work was hard. Lying here, my muscles are aching yet I feel that I enjoyed it.

Stin was aping, imitating, one of Pa's drones and asking himself if robots have wet dreams. I leaned back on a fence post and rubbed spit into my sore, dry hands.

'Hey, Stin,' I said. 'Don't you think he can hear you?' But Stin didn't care, none of us did.

'*Jed Brindle, Austin Whitney and Soriya Keele to a radio shunt*,' said the announcement. '*Jed Brindle, Austin . . .*' As it began to repeat itself the three of us dropped our tools and headed for the van where there would be shunt leads. Stin, Soriya and I were all about the same age and, considering recent rumours, I should have guessed the reason for the call but I didn't. Stin said later that he knew right away but, Hell, he's always saying things like that, and I guess he always will.

The van was down on its pads on the magstrip, a Rockwell De-sting bee bouncing off the windscreen. Stin reached through an open side window and hooked out three shunt cables. I raked aside the wiry hair at the back of my head and plugged the radio lead into my suboxy.

And I was given my draft notice. Jed Brindle until the 31st and then it'll be *Private* Brindle.

How did I feel? I guess I was overtaken by Stin and Soriya in what I felt. They were wild, excited, overflowing. How could they last until next month, they wanted to know.

We hugged each other, we did a crazy dance by the van. Hell, I almost think Stin had one of those wet dreams he attributed to the drones. The noise brought the rest of the team over from the field and we were all excited. We quit our work and headed for Simpson, the main town on Lejeune.

I leapt off the moving van just before Simpson and Hell as near broke my spine. That would have been a fine way to blow my draft. I guess I didn't know quite what to expect from my parents, but, as I went into the house and hollered, it occurred to me that they might not share the excitement.

After a short time Pa's home drone came out. That's

the one he uses for socializing. It's not a humanoid: that would be an act of hypocrisy, he says. (He's very high on his morals, is my Pa.) The home drone is a waist-high plastic cylinder. It's bigger than necessary for its circuits and voice synthesizer and the other bits it needs, but Pa says that's so people have something to address. The drone floated in on a cushion of air and said 'Hello' in a resigned sort of a way.

'Hey, I've been drafted,' I said. 'They called me up!'

'Yeah,' said the drone. 'I relayed some security mail. High encryption. I guessed they were draft notices. They've called up Mia and Lacey, too.'

My sisters. The army wouldn't be wanting Triona, my youngest sister, because of her disabilities. Crippling seizures, peeling skin, muscles that would waste away if it wasn't for regular biostim shunts. There were lots like that. Some put it down to hereditary problems dating back to Earthside pollution. Others blamed it on cosmic rays and poor shielding. I guess I don't really have an opinion on that. Triona was in training to be wired up, to follow after Pa. Then she would actually be in control of something more than her own wasted body.

There was something behind Pa's words but it was lost by the drone – I guess you can't read any expression on a block of plastic. Sure, he can *tell* you, but there's no way you can see for yourself. Some people hold that against him, but not me. I guess Triona must have taught me that. She can't walk, she talks through a synthesizer, she's apart from the rest of us. But she can *feel.* The way I see it Pa's the same. His only contact with the world is through his drones, no-one can be pals with him any more. But that doesn't mean he doesn't feel, that he's not human.

So I tried to ignore the lack of feeling in the drone's

words as Pa told me that three of his four children were joining the army. 'What do they say?' I asked.

'I don't know, they're somewhere in Simpson,' said the drone. It settled down on its plastic haunches. 'But I'll say to them what I'm going to say to you: Don't do it. Be a conshy. There's no way they can enforce a draft notice, the colonies are too scattered. No real government anyway. They can't force you—'

'But—'

'—to go if you don't—'

'Pa!' I shouted to break his flow. 'Will you just hold it for a minute?' I took a long breath in the ensuing silence. 'Hell, will you just leave it? I've been called up – they *want* me – and I'm going.' That's the first time I've argued with him, the first real time I've crossed him, but I had to do it. I have to run my own life.

'Jed,' said the drone, 'Jed.' That was he first time I'd noticed him squeeze something resembling emotion into one of his voices. 'Jed, I'm not trying to tell you. It's just . . . the Army changes people. It's important.'

But I was angry and I didn't want to say anything more when I was in that frame of mind. Hell, I've got less than a month left on Lejeune and I don't want to leave with things in a bad way.

'Jed, it's not our fight. We don't have to get involved. There's . . .' His voice disappeared as the door whisked shut behind me. I didn't want to hear.

Looking back on that little scene I've found a new respect for Pa. He's a wily old coot. I think he knows exactly how people react to him and his drones and he plays on it. Of course he can't show his feelings through his expressions, his actions, but I think he uses that. He can vary the loudness of the drone's voice, maybe introduce a bit of vibrato; the drone can impose itself or hang back. Yes, he can show feelings, but he's subtle.

It didn't work on me though. Maybe *duty* is an old-fashioned word, but I feel I've still got to give it some attention. I don't know what it'll be like in the Army and I don't know how I'd cope if it came to action. But there's one thing I know and that is that I couldn't live with being a conshy.

They say it'll never come to action anyway. We've only got a few thousand troops down in the Grand Union and it's not going to grow.

Yes, my mind's made up. I'm going to go.

28 MARCH 2083

I guess I'm just as bad at this diary business as I was at school. Three weeks since I last shunted my news. So what's been happening?

Pa's not happy and Ma's worried his mood might affect the coffee crop. The reactions of the people of Lejeune have been mixed. The draft wants to take 120 young people from a population of a little under five thousand, so there are a lot of families that will be broken up for a time.

But there's a lot of excitement too. The Lagrangian media have been whipping up support for months and now our own little Lejeune hee-vee station has joined in. The 'gung-ho spirit' they call it. Of course we have our conshies, but the hee-vees say Lejeune has one of the highest acceptance rates. Amongst the few to refuse the draft were Mia and Lacey. I guess Pa must have more influence over them. Mia promptly decided that she was pregnant and would soon marry her long-time partner (who had avoided the draft by being too old). Lacey just wired 'Fuck off' in her acknowledgement call. Still, it means Triona will have some company.

A few days ago I went for my medical. A huge military

transport docked on to Lejeune and all the draftees had to file onboard. After waiting for what seemed like hours I reached the front of the queue and walked into the first free compartment. Prompted by a synth voice I said my name aloud and plugged a lead into my suboxy. Body scans, psyche probes – I don't know what followed but they must have found me acceptable. I left with an ID card. It had an old-fashioned magnetic strip on it and a flat picture of me. The only words on it were: *Private J. B. Brindle. F Division.*

The museum work has Hell as near come to a standstill since the 6th. Most of the young folk have been drafted and they're making the most of their last month of freedom, as they see it.

But that's not for me. I've just gone on the way I always have. I guess I'm not much of a one for excitement (good prospects for a soldier!), and anyway there's work to be done. The less we do now the harder it's going to be to get back in shape again once things calm down. So I've worked the strips, smiled at the geeks and even played the village idiot for them. They pay their money.

Ma dug me out at the Penn strip on the day after my medical, said she wanted to speak with me. The sharp lines under her eyes have always given her a drawn look, but this time she looked positively haggard. 'You don't have to do it, Jed,' she said, in a tired voice.

'Please, Ma, don't give me any more of that.'

'No, I guess you've had as much persuading as anybody should rightly have to take,' she said. She straightened her shoulders and suddenly seemed twenty years younger. 'I just want to make sure you keep in touch. Let us know how you're doing. Your father does care – he cares a lot – it's just . . .' Her voice trailed away.

'Yeah,' I said. Hell, it felt like we were saying goodbye already. I didn't want a whole week of farewells.

Ma sagged again and looked around the field. 'Nothing will ever be like it is now, will it, Jed? It all changes.'

Uncomfortable, I followed her gaze around the field and said nothing.

'It's just . . .' She paused and tried to pull words out of the dry, dusty air. 'I'm scared for you, I'm scared for us *all*. I'm scared this might all just blow up in our faces. We're not big enough to take on the Earth again.'

'We're not taking them on, Ma, it's just a small force in a broken up little country. And they did ask for help. And about *me*.' I kicked at some straw on the hard dirt. 'Hell, I'll probably never even *see* the Earth from closer than the moon.'

'Yes, but the implant surgery.'

This was it, the Number One Worry. Surgery. I ran my hand down the course of my scar, the line of my left jaw. I guess that's something I do when things are difficult for me, trace the line of damage. People say the scar gives me the look of a fighter but, Hell, it was just an accident when I was fourteen. Old farm tools have none of the safeties of the real thing.

'They'll change you, you'll be a different person, Jed.' She ran a hand through her hair. 'Like your father.'

That was enough for me. She had finally said what she had clearly been wanting to say for a long time. She wished Pa still had the use of his body. Well, like I say, I don't see as how it's fair to discriminate against people because of their bodies. It's just not right. I threw down my hay-rake and left on a Scoot, scared of what I might say.

I'm not doing very well at leaving people with good

feelings, it seems. Hell, the surgery's nothing to worry about. All it will be is an extra shunt or two and some improvements to my suboxy. Sure, there are rumours, but one thing we have lots of out here in Lagrangia are rumours. So many colonies and stations, you have to expect rumours about what goes on in them all. But you live with it.

Oh yeah, before I deshunt I'll add a little more.

I'm not so sure about never seeing Earth, now. I guess it was just about the time I was talking with Ma that things developed. The Callies have burnt out some of our Reconn satellites. Expanded hostilities from the Earth's surface. From all of the press reports before I thought they just didn't have that sort of firepower. I guess there's a lot we didn't know.

And I guess somebody must have anticipated some of this. Whoever issued the drafts must have known that things would get worse and we'd be needed down there. *Some*body knows what's going on.

31 MARCH 2083

I left Lejeune today. I'm now sitting on the shuttle with the other local conscripts. There's lots of excitement, lots of nervous chatter, lots of people staying apart. I guess I'm one of the last group. I'm holding myself back to see what comes and I decided to take the opportunity to keep up with my diary. Only three days since the last update: getting better, huh?

I'm putting this on my chip's memory and I'll have to remember to shunt it on to a bubble later. If I ever get the time.

My last three days on Lejeune were quiet, no more family rows. This morning I said my goodbyes at the family house.

The atmosphere was strained, to say the absolute minimum. Lacey and Triona were there. Mia with her fiancé – I think his name's something cute and old-fashioned like 'Garry' – and of course Ma was there, forcing her hand to rest lightly on the top of Pa's home drone.

As so often happens in that sort of tight atmosphere, we all tried too hard. Fixed grins, forced conversation, bursts of ridiculous tense laughter. I wanted to leave but I also wanted to stay a little longer, to try to patch up some of what had been said over the past month. But, following the others, I tried too hard and things were awkward.

Pa didn't help at all, in fact I think he deliberately tried to make me feel bad. What came across was his overwhelming pride in his two good daughters. They did well by him. Hell, if people still inherited things, I think I'd have been struck off the old wirehead's will. 'We're all looking forward to the wedding,' he told Garry. 'I'm thinking of having a humanoid drone made for the occasion.' (The old hypocrite.) 'Of course, we can't *all* be there,' he added, twitching the drone slightly and letting its voice trail away into the awkward silence of the room. There was a lot of that.

Ma was OK, Lacey and Mia and even Garry were quite friendly, if a little superficial. Shortly before I left, Triona drew me aside and led me out on to the leafy back veranda. Following her, her hand pulling lightly at mine, I noticed for the thousandth time the smooth artifice of her walk, the hard outline given by her Glidewalk.

Halting in her locked-upright position, she looked me in the eye. 'Don't let them get at you, Jed,' she said through the voice synthesizer built into her throat. I didn't know who she meant, the family or the Army, but from Triona I would have accepted either. Looking back, I think she might have meant both. 'Keep in touch,' she said.

She was going to leave it at that, avoiding the physical contact that some find repulsive. I said, 'Hey, *Triona*. It's your big brother.' I leaned forward and kissed her flaky cheek and hugged her in her hard mechanical suit. After a short time of silence, Triona glided out of the veranda and left on her Scoot.

Shortly afterwards I left the family home and walked alone into Simpson, regretting the tension, the bad feelings, the *good* feelings. Hell, I was confused by the whole situation.

Simpson was festive. Streamers, noise, dancing lasers, the smell of drink and drugs and celebrations. And for a moment, on top of it all, I thought I could smell the salty tang of tears.

Magstrip coach from Simpson for the short trip to the Station and pretty soon we were loading ourselves into the Extraterran Army shuttle that I'm now sitting inside. It's a small place for over a hundred young people, the seats are firm and small and we had to strap in tightly to protect ourselves from the sudden bursts of gees. I've only left Lejeune a handful of times and then only to visit other places in L5, but the shuttles were much better than this. The crew are nice, but I guess that will all change at midnight when we officially become part of the Army.

I don't know what's in store for me on the moon. We're heading for a place called Reinhold – I'd never heard of it until two hours ago – and from there it'll be what they call a 'short hop' over to the main training base at Mercator IV. As for military life, I guess if I was a volunteer I would have known more about it. But as I haven't really considered soldiering before

I've never paid it much attention. I'll soon find out, anyway.

Pa, Ma, even Triona. They all seem to be worried that the Army's going to change me somehow. That it won't be Jed Brindle who returns in three years' time. Hell, of course it'll change me. But people change anyway, it doesn't take the Army to do it. And sure as Hell, they're not going to make me someone I don't want to be.

Chapter Three

20 June 2084

If there's one thing you learn about soldiering, as opposed to training, it's that things can go wrong.

'*And if you'd like anything at any time during the flight*,' said the pilot, '*just ask a member of the cabin crew.*'

My first thought was that someone must have found the body back at Dallas airport. They'd worked out who was responsible and re-routed the flight as some kind of precaution. But that was too far-fetched – why re-route direct to Reno? I tried to shut it out of my mind. This mess was bad enough whatever its cause.

I looked down the aeroplane and saw Jacobi looking back at me. Ahead of him, Gil was still talking to the bemused old lady. I couldn't see Amagat over the back of her seat and my mind conjured up an image of her sat there with her head in her hands.

The sublieutenant's head appeared moments later and Comtac flickered in my belly. There's a limit to what you can say with a sequence of three-point codes and there wasn't a code invented for our present situation. You can't Comtac *Say, that was a piece of bad luck, wasn't it*? and then have a conversation about the various possibilities that were still open.

Comtac flickered again. *Stay put*, it said. *Stay put.* That must be Amagat – the leader has override on everyone else, when she wants to use it.

Stay put. I remained in my seat, that much was obvious. My first impression of Amagat had been that, like most inexperienced soldiers, she was inflexible, unadaptable. I had no idea how she would cope with a situation like this.

I didn't know how to interpret the order.

Did it mean 'Abort mission'? Stay in my seat until Reno, then try to make my way back to Grand Union?

Go ahead, came another burst of Comtac. Then: *Stay put. Go ahead.*

I cracked a smile as I realized what she meant. Clever Comtac. That must have been about the first time I had admired anything Amagat did. But I can't say I admired the actual course of action she had chosen.

I would have opted for one of the bail-outs. One plan was to suicide the plane, take over and crash it. Preferably on a military target. In tactical terms that was then the best option we had available. The other bail-out was simply to stay put and get together in Reno. In all other terms that was the best option. Unless someone had discovered the body.

But I should have known what Amagat would do. Go by the book. The plan would go ahead after ninety-five minutes regardless of where the plane happened to be.

I closed my eyes and accessed my chip's memory bank. A digital map of pure information scrolled past my mind's eye. I stopped it and zoomed in on Texas and the Midwest. I wiped the original route into limbo and traced on an approximate route to Reno via Santa Barbara. Then I called back the first route, superimposed on the new one, and it was as I had feared. The routes drew further and further apart, even with the westward swing the route to Cheyenne took to avoid Grand Union airspace.

After ninety-five minutes on the original route we would be fifty kay-ems east of Amarillo. After ninety-five minutes on the new route we would be over the New Mexico Desert. More than 300 kay-ems deeper into CalTex.

To carry out the plan, we should have moved it ahead and gone into action soon after the announcement of the diversion. But not Amagat. Too much change. She was sticking religiously to the plan and putting us even more at risk than Gil had with his drugs. Now we were going to have to take over the plane and somehow get it through 350 kays of CalTex airspace without getting shot down or forced to land.

Where were you when we needed you, Plato?

I looked up the plane and Amagat and Jacobi were still in their seats. Gil was singing a Mexican jazz-ballad to the old lady. She was smiling back at him and beating time on the top of the seat in front of her.

I could do nothing to change the situation so I settled back in my seat. At least Gil might have come down off his cloud by the time we had to move and, from my own viewpoint, I would be more ready for action after a rest. My leg was hurting and I would benefit from the extra time allowed for me to wipe the hypnotic influence, lose the limp.

I looked at my lop-sided reflection in the smoke mask hanging from the seat in front of me, ran my fingertips over the scar on my jaw, settled down for the wait. Chipped down on my juices. My fingers ran around to the base of my skull, the site of my suboccipital chip. I had the first surgery when I was seven and I still remember it clearly. Papa had wired himself into Lejeune only months before and I was gonna be like Papa. Not much like him, but that was how I saw it. We went over to the huge Merrywell medical torus in the main cluster of L5. A family outing, just like when Mia and Lacey had theirs done, the year before. They picked me up a week later. Time for the artificial nerves to be grown up into my thalamus, time for the pain to subside, time for me to be trained in the use of my new organ. That first chip was much more primitive than my Army one, only limited chip memory, a small range of biofeedback and the inevitable jack socket for shunts. But that first surgery was the most daunting. When the Army expanded my range in '83 I knew what to expect and I soon got the hang of the new set-up.

The man in the seat next to me was giving me a strange look, so I smiled and withdrew my hand from my concealed interface. Fear and anger are only instantaneous feelings with the military chip, they can be instantly cut out by control of the hypothalamus and one or two bodily substances such as adrenalin and the endorphins. The man next to me flushed and went back to his paper.

I looked up at the clock above the NO FURTHER ADMITTANCE sign.

16:34. One more minute. Amagat had sent the *Prepare* message a few minutes before. The man beside me gave a spluttering snore and moved in his seat. I looked back and saw Cohen laughing with his colossal bodyguard. I turned back to the front and the clock had clicked on a minute.

16:35. I paused and was paid with a worried look from Amagat.

I smiled and rose from my seat. Lifted my braced leg awkwardly into the aisle. I had to remember to make a conscious effort to limp my last few steps as an ordinary passenger.

'Can I help you, sir?'

I looked around with a start and there was the steward standing at my elbow. The one that had helped Gil.

'Uh, no,' I said. 'Thanks. I'm just going to the toilet.' I grinned an awkward grin at him. 'See to my leg. You know.'

'Of course, sir,' said the steward. 'There's one back there.' He waved his hand back to the rear end of the plane.

Shit. I looked towards the toilet at the front of the plane. Just by NO FURTHER ADMITTANCE. 'I think I'll go to the one up there, if it's all the same to you,' I said. 'It's closer.' I shrugged and indicated my leg. 'It needs seeing to.'

'I'm sorry, sir. That one's out of order.' My shoulders sagged and he must have noticed. Misinterpreted. 'But if you don't want to walk too far you could always use the galley, sir. You can draw the curtains and have complete privacy.'

I smiled my relief and he beamed back.

'This way, sir,' he said and led me up the aisle. I slung my bag from my shoulder and followed. Past Jacobi, past Lohmann, playing cards with his old lady – 'Snap!' she cried as I walked past. Past the worried face of Amagat, a smile for her. The steward looked back and paused; I had remembered to keep up the pantomime of my bad leg.

I caught up with the steward and he led me – more slowly, now – under the sign that told me NO FURTHER ADMITTANCE. What had been the aisle made a sharp left turn and then right again, so that it was running along the port side of the plane. There was a door at the end of the short corridor. Pilot's cabin. The galley was on my right, its curtains open.

Just like the 3D digital map we had seen back in Grand Union.

'This is it, sir,' said the steward. 'I'll draw the curtains and keep the stewardesses out until I see you're back in your seat. If you need me just yell.' He smiled and retreated, drawing the curtains after him.

I smiled to myself and looked around. Maybe three metres by four, shelves along three sides. Cupboards, fridge, a microwave browner that looked like they dug it off some refuse heap, a sink unit. I tossed my bag on to a shelf.

Squatting down, I began to unfasten the brace. A hopeless mishmash of wood and plastic, it only served to handicap my leg even further. I removed the brace completely and rolled up my trouser leg. Hand-sized zaps on either side of my calf, taped to the isothermal material of my body-suit. Four small, brown capsules stuck to my shin.

I ripped the zaps off my leg, flinching at the sound of the tearing adhesive. Then the capsules. Amagat had the other two zaps and some spare capsules as a precaution. I had mine in the brace because men just aren't equipped with the storage places women have. I lay the little laser guns on the counter before me, put the capsules in my jacket pocket. Looked nervously over my shoulder and deliberately avoided chipping down to calm my nerves. There are some times a soldier has to be on edge, ready for instant action. This was one of them.

Keeping my eyes on the curtain I assembled the zaps. Strapped to my leg they had been nothing more than plastic cylinders, six cee-ems by three. I popped the first one apart into its two halves. Clicked it together again at a different angle. A quick twist and turn of a tiny thumb-wheel. And it was ready. Lightweight plastic handle, moulded into my hand; stub snout protruding between first and middle finger by about two cee-ems;

shunt lead trailing off into mid-air. Made of plastics, poly-carbon fibres and various crystalline elements, it could only have been detected by a direct body-search. That was the reason we were using it on this mission. I would never have chosen it otherwise, it felt so weak and unreliable. It did also have the advantage that it lacked the power to burn through the plane's walls, so we could use it with assurance if it became necessary. But I hoped I wouldn't have to place my life in the hands of that little weapon.

When the second zap was assembled I rolled up the sleeve of my jacket and released a flap in my body-suit. There was a red mark on the inside of my forearm and I picked at it until the collagen-based glue released a tiny flap of skin to reveal a small fleshy hole, my median interface.

With everything ready, I strapped the brace loosely back on to my leg. I no longer needed it, but it might steal us a few seconds' more surprise. I shunted the lead of one gun into my median, palmed it, and slid the other into my jacket pocket. Suddenly I saw the room through a third eye, the snout of my zap. I blanked the extra image and chipped the gun into subliminal mode. Aiming and firing would be a subconscious, intuitive action.

A last check reassured me that I had done everything, then I whisked back the curtain and stepped into the narrow passageway. I walked around the corner and then resumed my limp as I appeared under NO FURTHER ADMITTANCE.

The steward looked up from near the back and smiled. I waved with my empty hand and nodded, as if to say *It's all fine, thanks for your help.* I edged up on the adrenalin, squeezed my fighting instinct.

Stopped next to Amagat. Dropped a zap in her lap.

Turned as if I had just remembered that I had left my bag in the galley.

And followed Amagat back through NO FURTHER ADMITTANCE, shielding her, I hoped, from casual observation.

We paused for a few seconds in the corridor, my heart echoing in my ears, zap held steady at my chest. Amagat Comtacked Lohmann and Jacobi to come, but that was unnecessary. I poked the snout of my zap around the corner and a flashed image from my subconscious told me that they were already on their way down the aisle.

This was a possible turning point in the plan. Someone might see Leo and Gil heading up here. Raise an alert. That would call for rapid action.

The two privates squeezed past me in the corridor and once more I poked my zap around the corner. Nobody had done anything. The CivAir blue uniforms were going about their business as if it was an ordinary flight. I withdrew my gun. We were coasting.

A glance around at the three soldiers. Silent acknowledgement. A grin from Jacobi, a wink from Lohmann, a flutter of Comtac from Amagat. *Wait*, she told us. But that was part of the plan, we didn't need to be told. Enter the corridor then pause for breath before Stage 2.

Gil seemed to have come down a little, his trip cut short. His eyes were still glazed, but at least he had control of his actions. We were back to a four-man squad again.

'Stick to the plan?' asked Jacobi in a hushed voice, nodding slightly in Gil's direction.

Yes, Comtacked Amagat, glaring at Jacobi for breaking silence. Hell, we *had* to know.

Jacobi reached into my jacket pocket and removed the capsules. I nodded at him. Amagat deshunted and handed her zap to Lohmann. She disappeared into the curtained room while we stood guard. Jacobi made as if to peek behind the curtain and I chipped down sharply to avoid a fit of nervous laughter.

I chipped back up to combat alertness as Amagat emerged a short time later with my bag over her shoulder. She handed a zap to Jacobi and as she turned away he wiped the gun on his trousers, as if it was wet. I grinned at him.

Amagat stood by the door to the cockpit. Me next, then Jacobi. Gil guarded the rear. The sub glanced over her shoulder.

And the door opened. A man in CivAir blue was framed by the door. Amagat stepped back in fright but the man was even more surprised and stumbled back into the cockpit. Amagat recovered her composure and burst in through the open door. I followed her in, covering the sprawled man. Jacobi was next. Then Lohmann, waiting by the door and scanning the corridor.

The pilot turned sharply in his seat and froze, a pair of bulbous data goggles wedged on his forehead. His mouth opened slightly, then closed. The other man looked up at me from the floor. Co-pilot, I decided.

The pilot finally managed to say something. 'What . . . ?'

'Quiet,' said Amagat, waving her zap in his direction.

The co-pilot began to get up from the floor, trying to stare me out. 'You're not threatening me with . . . with *that* thing,' he said.

A flash of subconscious imagery as I swung the gun downwards. Magnified view of his left hand. On the floor, taking his full weight for an instant.

I shunted an impulse from my median to the gun. A fine blue bolt etched itself across my retinas, too fast to see. A yell of surprise. The co-pilot was sprawled on the ground again, holding his hand and moaning. The tip of his little finger was burnt on to the floor, a small black lump.

'Not just threats,' I said.

The cockpit was a little bigger than the galley. It was barren and empty apart from the seats for the pilot and co-pilot, each with a small console on a swinging arm hovering before it. Despite my mental map of the plane I had still half-expected to see a huge bank of dials and digital readouts, monitors and meters, but there weren't even any windows to show us cutting through the clouds. I guess the primitive state of the rest of the Earth technology had influenced my imagination.

This was a high-tech plane. The controls wouldn't have seemed out of place in an old Lagrangian shuttle. The main difference was that extraterran pilots jack directly into their craft. Instant response, with computer-aided decision-making. This pilot just had a pair of data goggles over his head. More of a data *helmet*. It looked like an antique leather flying helmet with bulbous earpieces to feed the pilot aural information. Added on to the front were large blind goggles. Maybe false images in front of the eyes, maybe even direct retinal projection. Whatever system the goggles used, they replaced all the old dials and meters that had lasted surprisingly long into the century.

Amagat stepped further into the cockpit and dropped my bag on the floor. 'This is a hijack,' she said. I suppressed a grin at her unnecessary comment and chipped some more juice, aware that I was relaxing a little after the action.

'Aliens,' said the pilot and spat on the floor. Amagat waved her zap at him and pursed her lips. The pilot raised the palms of his hands in a gesture of resignation. 'What d'you want me to do?' he asked.

'First,' said Amagat, 'we're gonna get your buddy back in his seat.'

I felt a flicker of Comtac, but it wasn't directed at me. Jacobi responded and moved around me to help the co-pilot to his feet. But his help was refused and the co-pilot struggled up from the floor, walked over to his seat and collapsed into it, clutching his damaged hand tightly to his chest. Jacobi took a reel of packing tape from the bag and returned to the co-pilot, wrenched his hands from his chest and taped them methodically to the arms of the chair. Then he taped up the legs for an added precaution.

Jacobi taped the pilot up next, less securely as he still had to fly the plane when it wasn't on auto. Just the legs and body, leaving the hands free to play on the flight console. The co-pilot's groans became words every so often. I guess Leo didn't take very well to being called some of the things the co-pilot was calling him so he ran a strip of tape across the shit's mouth.

With the pilots secured Amagat relaxed a little. 'Right,' she said. 'Now I want you to get the cabin crew to come forward to the galley. Intercom it.'

The pilot pulled a lead from the side of his console and pressed the end against his jaw-bone. Bone-mike, I decided. He glanced at his partner and something passed between them.

I took a quick step forward, ripped the mike from the pilot's jaw and jerked his head sharply back by a handful of hair from the back of his skull. I brought my face slowly down until my hot breath was deflected back up at me off his cheek.

'You try anything funny,' I said in a low voice. 'I'm gonna burn your buddy's balls off.' I eased off and moved away. 'And I might not stop on him. You get me?'

I think he might even have challenged me. Maybe if it was only *his* balls at stake. But I guess he saw the look in my eyes. He knew I meant exactly what I had said.

He nodded almost imperceptibly. I backed off, my eyes fixed on the pilot's as he jawed his bone-mike.

Go easy, came a flutter in my abdomen wall. I looked angrily at Amagat. Why do they have to keep telling me to go easy? In his last few weeks with the squad, Plato had taken to Comtacking me with that one a lot. Hell, you've got to have a hard streak on these shits, else they just run you around on a piece of string.

I noticed Jacobi was giving me a funny look and I chipped down, knocked off some of the anger. Hell, it was a tense situation, I didn't need to be told how to handle my own head.

The pilot spoke into his mike and I turned my eyes back to him. The other guy had just caved in after his little tangle with my burner but the pilot had shown a bit of fight and I intended to watch him closely. 'This is your Civic Airlines pilot speaking,' he said. 'Staff announcement. Would the stewardesses please come forward to the galley.' He looked up at me and added, 'Union meeting.'

'OK,' said Amagat. She stepped forward and ripped the bone-mike from its socket on the flight console. 'You won't need that again,' she said. *Go ahead*, she Comtacked to us all.

We left the cockpit.

Jacobi slipped into the galley and I waited next to its entrance. Gil went a few paces forward and stood at the end of the corridor, zap at the ready.

Almost instantly Gil was pointing his gun and a startled-looking stewardess appeared around the corner. The young coloured girl must have been barely out of school. Her eyes, large to start with, grew even bigger when she saw me. I pushed her into the galley and turned to greet another woman as she appeared around the corner, prompted by Gil. This was the older one, mid-thirties and broad from her neck down to her ankles. That left two more.

They appeared together. I heard their chatter, flashed an *Alert* to Gil who was grinning up at me. He seemed to be coming out of his drugs by stages, clear for a time then back into a daze.

My Comtac snapped him back to reality and he turned just in time to cut off the chatter of the two stewardesses into strangled gasps. They came around the corner, their faces matching shades of white. Something was tapping away at my memory as I watched the four young buttocks move into the galley. I followed and helped Jacobi tape them up. We left them in a heap on the floor and returned to the cockpit.

The pilot had his data helmet back in place and was tapping out messages on his console. His partner was slumped in his seat, his weight pulling limply at his bindings. I looked at Amagat and raised my eyebrows. She grinned. 'After you guys left he got a bit temperamental,' she said. 'Sure, he couldn't *do* anything, but I didn't like the noise.'

'What did you do?' I asked.

'Just a little massage on his pressure points,' she said. 'Nothing lasting.'

Hell, she had been complaining at *me* about overreacting only minutes before. I nodded at the pilot and Comtacked a question mark to Amagat.

'I gave him the instructions,' she said.

'Where are we headed?' I asked, wondering if she had been flexible enough to change the plan to any degree in view of the diversion.

'Still to Wichita,' she said. The answer I had expected. 'No reason for any change.' That was Amagat, all right. 'Let's get out of this lot,' she said. 'Us two first, then Gil and Leo.' She deshunted her zap and started to remove her jumpsuit. Beneath it there was the standard tight-fitting body-suit. Isothermal, it would only let out or take in enough heat to keep the body at a comfortable 36.8. Any heat that it *did* let out was scattered by flecks of some sort of carbonate crystal in the material, so any infra-red scanner would receive a confused image. Under most circumstances that image would be unrecognizable as a human being. The suit was camouflaged with a sort of dusky grey-green pattern.

Amagat paused with her top layer rumpled up around her hips and gave me a questioning look. I looked at the floor and chipped down. The sight of Amagat removing her jump-suit had distracted me, God knows why. It wasn't as if I found her an attractive sight. Neat ass, but her legs were like concrete pillars and her face was too thick-boned. I slid my jacket off my shoulders, stretched out the waist of my trousers and let them drop. Then I pulled my shirt out of shape and whipped it over my head. That left me in a military body-suit just like Amagat's, except for a stripe and a star less on the left shoulder.

She smiled at me and nodded downwards. 'Pity about the footwear,' she said. I glanced down and it *was* a ridiculous sight. My military leggings looked completely out of place set against the smart businessman's wrap-around shoes. Amagat had a simple pair of plimsolls, much more comfortable, although hardly appropriate.

'You could do better, yourself,' I said.

'Have you two quite finished?' asked Jacobi. 'Maybe the two of *us* would like a chance to get out of these crappy clothes, huh?'

'OK, get to it,' said Amagat, reshunting her zap. 'Take the door, Brindle.'

I took Gil's place by the door. While the two of them were removing their civilian clothes the pilot slid his helmet back on his head. 'Swinging round for Wichita in a few seconds,' he said. With no windows, there was no way I could see if we were changing course or not. I was just wondering how we could check on the pilot when the floor tilted and I felt a slight tug at my stomach as we began the manoeuvre.

Gil returned to his place at the door.

I felt that jag of uncertainty in the back of my mind again and said. 'Check the corridor, Gil.' Amagat gave me her questioning look and I said, 'Just a check.' She shrugged and nodded at Gil, who had waited for her OK.

If Plato had been there Gil would have trusted my judgement immediately, but that had all changed since Amagat. Gil opened the door and I glanced at the slumped figure of the co-pilot. There was no colour in his face at all and I wondered just which points the sub had put her pressure on.

Gil was half out of the door when he shouted. I spun and instantly dropped into a stable firing position, images from the snout of my zap flashing across my consciousness.

A compound image from my zap and my eyes showed me Gil's back. Around him I could see a CivAir blue figure in the corridor. Bare calves, skirt. One of the stewardesses. An electric blue flash burnt my eyes and the stewardess dropped to her knees and slowly slumped to the ground.

Gil started to look back over his shoulder, a dumb grin on his face. Past his cheek I saw another blue movement in the corridor. '*Get the other fucker*,' I cried at Gil.

He turned towards me and looked blank. His mind was off somewhere on the remains of his trip. I leapt to my feet and pushed past him.

'Get the panhalothol,' I heard Amagat say as I left the cockpit. Orders for Jacobi.

I had to be quick or they would gas me. The blue uniform turned the corner. That had been the doubt that had been nagging at me. The steward. That bastard of a pilot had only asked for steward*esses* to come forward.

Bastard. And with the co-pilot out of action, there was nothing we could do to the pilot. Not yet.

I reached the end of the short corridor. Stopped myself on the wall and turned. Momentum gone, I stepped out under the NO FURTHER ADMITTANCE sign and stood underneath it.

The steward was only a few paces away. He had emerged into the normality of the passenger area and stopped. Maybe it was the sudden change, from a room full of bound and gagged colleagues to the bright babbling tube full of passengers. Maybe he couldn't quite believe what he had seen, once he had returned to this epitome of the normality of his working days.

Whatever it was that struck him as he left the staff-only area, it made him stop. Turn his head slowly.

The cheerful babble of the planeful of passengers was cut through by a sudden clap of silence. Faces turned to the front, to the scene of the oh-so-terribly-helpful steward transformed into a quivering wreck.

The scene of a man framed by the doorway, topped by a sign that read NO FURTHER ADMITTANCE. A man wearing a camouflaged body-suit and pointing what looked like a toy gun at the steward. One or two sharp gasps, a scream that cut off in mid-squawk.

An instant that seemed to last forever. Maybe it *did* last forever for that CivAir steward. Some people say it does. What scenes of personal history flashed across that little Earth shit's eyes?

Nothing interesting.

In that instant of eternity I took in the impressions of all the faces turned on the two of us. All those faces, and every one of them empty. Whatever had been filling them only a few moments before had been drained away by this scene that was being played out before them. Some of them thought *Alien*, maybe some thought *EP*. Most thought nothing.

It was all too fast.

The steward twisted when he saw me. It *had* all been real. All those taped-up stewardesses. Here was living proof.

His mouth opened. Closed. Formed the word *You*. Closed.

A thin line of sharp blue etched itself across the scene. A small black hole appeared between the man's eyes. His eyes were close together and it was a small target, but I rarely miss with my median shunt. Whatever the weapon.

There was no blood, the wound was neatly cauterized. Not even a puff of smoke emerging from the hole, like they show on the hee-vee cartoons.

The steward fell to the ground and the bubble burst. A scream broke the silence. It went unpunished and others followed, more confidently. People moved in their seats but didn't leave them.

I swept my zap in a wide arc and people cringed away. A mustardy smell reached my nose and I sprang back around the corner. Along the corridor and through the open door to the cockpit, screams following me all the way. Past Jacobi, wearing a smoke mask.

Amagat thrust a mask into my hands and I let the zap dangle by its lead. Already the gas was having a slight effect. I chipped maximum juices and pulled the mask over my head. The smell of sweet fresh oxygen kicked off the remaining effects of the gas and I slipped the small air cylinder into the chest pouch of my uniform.

I looked around. The same as before, except for the masks over everyone's heads and the loose panel dangling from the air system. I looked at Amagat.

'Not good out there?' she asked.

'Not good.'

Chapter Four

Transcript of 15th day counselling interview, 15 April 2083.

Subcolonel Gene Kettering sits at his plaz desk and rubs tiredly at his forehead. He is sixty-nine. From top to bottom: the sort of brown-going-grey hair that just looks dead, thin on top, short at the back and swept over the crown of his head; thick, free-standing eyebrows and a heavy, sagging face, folds of loose flesh obscuring his jaw line and chin; bulbous, glans-coloured nose; stiff military uniform, antithesis to his loose skin, struggling to contain his age-fattened body; size 39 military-issue black Gucci Permashine shoes.

A wide desk takes up a large area in this small office in the Mercator IV Personnel Complex. Kettering stops rubbing his head and selects a shunt-lead from a nearby panel. The desk is bare apart from the obligatory flat monitor (facing the colonel), a hologram projector panel (adjustable to be viewed either by the colonel alone, or from anywhere in the room) and a neat row of three CIBM data bubbles.

He plugs the lead into the central socket of his suboccipital interface. Thus linked to the Psychan Interview Prompt, he shunts a message into the PA.

Seconds later, the door buzzes and opens. Private J. B. Brindle walks in and stands to attention. 'Siddown, Jed,' says Kettering, waving in the vague direction of a lightly upholstered, ice-blue chair.

Brindle sits. He is eighteen. From top to bottom he is 183 cee-ems tall; black hair, wiry and kinked but not tightly coiled, short to above the collar; rounded pale chocolate face, large brown eyes; an unwiped scar runs six cee-ems along the line of his left jaw; his uniform covers a well-muscled body, size 45 military-issue black Slik combat boots.

Kettering speaks. 'Well, Jed, how are you settling in?' The tone is genial and meant to be relaxing.

Brindle replies. 'Very well, sir.'

Kettering: 'Oh you can cut the formality now, Jed, this is just a little chat.' Brindle moves in his chair and runs a finger along the course of his scar. Kettering continues: 'Tell me how you're finding it. This must all be very strange for you after Lejeune. How's the moon?'

Brindle: 'It does fine by me, sir. The low gravity takes some learning, but Lejeune's quite low itself and I've worked at different gees so I don't have the problems some are having. It's strange to be so closed in. There are ceilings overhead all the time and even if I was allowed out into the open I'd need a suit.'

Kettering: 'You feel claustrophobic.'

Brindle: 'Sometimes. But it's so big as well. You could get into a Rover and drive until the power dried up. That's . . . well, I guess that's *big*.'

Kettering pauses to nudge Psychan for data.

Kettering: 'Surgery on the 3rd. Comtac, median and suboccipital expansion. How did you take it, Jed?'

Brindle: 'It's weird, but I've done it before, sir. I can't say I like being unconscious for a day and a half. The Comtac felt strange and I don't know how I'm ever going to get the hang of my new suboxy. It seems to throw thoughts into my head at random – tactics, technical information, that sort of stuff. And I haven't gotten the hang of the biofeedback yet, the juices.'

Kettering: 'Control will come, Jed. You'll learn to cut out the data flow. And the juices – you'll wonder how you ever coped before. Do you think you can manage it, Jed?'

Brindle: 'Well yes, I always have been a learner. I pick things up, you know. I guess it's just a bit disorienting at first.'

The atmosphere in the room has changed over the course of the interview. Kettering, tired and perhaps a little depressed at first, has settled into his rôle of genial, friendly confidant. Brindle, tense and on guard at first, is now relaxed and comfortable, at ease in the older man's company.

Kettering shunts an instruction and one wall turns into a large viewscreen. Brindle is initially startled, but controls himself well, as if he *has* mastered his new chip to some degree; maybe he had good control of his reactions anyway. Kettering: 'We've just got one or two tests for you now, Jed. Logic and visual-spatial abilities. Things like that.'

A voice comes from a wall-speaker. 'Displayed are two-dee outlines of a four-dimensional object. Using the holo-wand paint two three-dimensional through-sections of the object. You have forty-five seconds.' Brindle at first seems stunned then rapidly produces broadly accurate holo-sketches. The test continues along the lines of a high-school Logico-Standards assessment. Kettering leans back in his chair and closes his eyes.

A high, sharp siren pierces the stillness. Rising and falling, the noise is added to by sounds of shouting, bells ringing, a masculine scream.

Brindle is guiding the wand through a three-dimensional maze. He drops the wand and stands. Kettering's eyes remain closed.

Wall-speaker: 'Incorrect move. Five second penalty. Resume manoeuvre.'

Brindle stares in disbelief at the motionless form of Kettering.

Wall-speaker: 'Resume manoeuvre.'

Brindle: 'Sir, wake up. *Colonel Kettering*.' He moves to the desk, leans over and hesitates slightly before shaking Kettering's right shoulder. Another scream breaks out over the din of sirens and shouting.

Wall-speaker: 'Hesitancy penalty, ten seconds. Resume manoeuvre.'

Brindle: 'But . . .' He looks momentarily at the screen as if to argue with it, then he looks at the door that he knows he cannot open by himself. More screams, closer now.

Brindle: 'Wake up, wake up,' as he shakes Kettering vigorously by both shoulders.

And Kettering springs out of his chair and throws Brindle away. Kettering, abruptly: 'Stand to attention.'

Brindle staggers back and is stopped by the grey office wall. Wall speaker: 'Resume manoeuvre.'

Kettering: 'Now get back to your duties, boy.'

Brindle: 'But, sir. There's—'

Kettering: '*Stand to attention*.' Brindle obeys. Shouting, screams and sirens come from outside. Kettering continues: 'Now pick up your holo-wand, pull yourself together and get back to your manoeuvres.'

Brindle snaps out a brief salute. Brindle: 'Yes, *sir*.'

Kettering sinks back into his chair, returning to his earlier state of quiescence. Noises of terror continue to bombard the small office in the depths of Personnel. Brindle carries out several more Logico-Standards tasks, shutting out the jabber of his own thoughts. Kettering, in an exaggerated theatrical manner, reaches for a black lever on the wall behind his desk. He pulls it downwards and the sounds of panic cut off sharply in mid-scream.

Brindle watches with peripheral vision as he carries out another L-S task. He doesn't falter in his work. Brindle carries out three more exercises. Kettering: 'All right, Jed. That'll do. The test's finished. Psychan should have enough to keep it occupied for a time. Next counselling in ten days. That will be all.'

Kettering deshunts the Psychan and calls up a report on his monitor.

Brindle stands. Brindle: 'Permission to leave, *sir*?'

Kettering: 'Oh, no need for all that, Jed. See you at the next session. 'Bye.'

Excerpt from Private Records of Training Sergeant Maxwell Abelson, 21 April 2083.

Right. I'd better get this all down, so as how I've got something to base my official reports on when the time comes. (I *do* wish they would rearrange the filing times so as I wouldn't have to report on things so far back in time.)

Right. Let's start with Brindle. And how I'd *love* to start with Brindle. But from all the signs I can read on him, he doesn't bend that way, not even for variety. Even if he did, I reckon as how he's so slow he just wouldn't get the message if I tripped him and landed first. Jeez, what a waste to mankind – women just don't appreciate that sort of a boy.

Private Jed Brindle. Mainly Negro, scar on his jaw, good physique (he'll cope well physically, as he's already showing). Neat ass. Psychan says he has a good solid personality and that shows in practice. He follows orders well, initiative could take some expansion. He accepts things, takes change easily. No, cut that: he adapts well to change, but I don't reckon as how it's *easy* for him, he just works at it. He's not lacking in intelligence, but he doesn't let it show on him; he learns slowly but thoroughly, once he has something he *has* it.

Another plus is that he has a kind of empathy. He's no extrovert, but people *like* him. They talk to him, share their problems. He's almost a big sister figure. Summing up? He fits well and I reckon as how he'll make a good soldier. Not a leader, but a good sub.

He wasn't densely wired when he arrived – most of the cons weren't – so he had to have the standard surgery: median, Comtac and suboccipital expansion. He's coping well, not the fastest to learn but he's not making the mistakes as how some of the others are.

Brindle is taking the weapons training well. He's one of my top trainees, he uses his median interface well. With a light-weight F27 shunted he's our top marksman. Other weapons he uses well, too. The rifle-thalamaic link is strong on him, he coordinates effectively and responds instantly. (Some are having problems with that, cerebral interference with their thalamaic functioning – I reckon as how they just can't let go.)

Training to date has revolved around coordinating the new interfaces and basic Comtac use. No combat training yet. Overall assessment: Brindle will do well. And what a good ass that boy has on him!

Extracts from the notes of Sal Buchner, reporter with Jensen's Agency, 6 May 2083.

Wow. Let me get my breath back and I'll update my notes.

OK.

This is data bubble G384, Mercator IV Military Training Camp. On the Moon. (Fuck. When's that boy on leave again? Check that.)

I made the hop from Reinhold yesterday and arrived here mid-morning. Met by a corporal – Carter was his name – who took me up to Captain Goldstein's office.

My first sight of the base was on the ferry's view-screen, domes and blocks greying into the lunar regolith. It was a small ferry with a bare interior. I was the only passenger. I'm sure they were trying to tell me something by sending me an empty transporter, but I'm fucked if I can work it out. The base grew bigger and the ferry landed on an adjacent field. A long caterpillar came out to meet the ferry and there was Carter. I stepped through the lock and the cat crawled us over to the Personnel Complex.

Carter is a standard military-issue, glans-oriented drone. All hump and no heart, as Jinny used to say. No comparison with Brindle, but *he* comes later.

Two minutes on the cat and Carter had told me his life story and made a pass at me. Why are soldiers such jerks? Still, you get to learn people in this trade and a first contact is always good to get. My producer would have me out on my ass if it turned out that Carter was my only positive contact and I'd blown it. I gently turned down his offer of a seafood sauna, made it seem like I was tempted but, *you* know, kind of shy in this big new setting. Flutter of the lashes, right breast pressed against his arm and he knew I was drooling for him. Yuk. He said he'd be playing cards that evening in the F Division crew room. I said, well, he knew how it was for busy little reporters and I don't know *how* I'll ever manage, but I might just drop by and watch him – I do so love to watch men doing manly things. Or some shit like that.

Fuck, it's spoiling the after effects of Brindle, thinking about a jerk like Carter.

The jerk peeled himself away from me after announcing my arrival to Goldstein's secretary. A short wait in a drab little cubby-hole of an office with a junior officer playing at a console. After I'd had time to realize my own insignificance in the grand scheme of things (and before Goldstein got bored waiting in his office for my wait to come to an end) the junior looked at me, said, 'Go in now,' and returned to his console. *Thank* you *for your decency and politeness, you little ass-licker*, I wanted to say, but that would have blown it and it wasn't the little runt's fault anyway. I walked into the office.

Goldstein is mid-thirties, military in his looks and in everything he does. Precise uniform, precise hair (chestnut brown, short), precise manner. A slight-looking body but his movements betray his precise body tone and control. Functional.

A sharp movement of his head and he was surveying me; not the usual soldierly glance at the face (passable), swift pass down the body (slim but unbalanced) and then the slow pass back up again, lingering briefly on the pubis (ginger, if they could see through the layers of clothing) and longer on the bust (oversized, a useful tool, expecially at low gees), before returning to my cold (by now) grey eyes. No, Goldstein just looked up from his desk, fixed my eyes for a second and then moved his gaze to a vacant chair. 'You must be Buchner,' he said to the chair. 'Take a seat.'

Change of gears. Tits and simpering would get me nowhere with this one. *Precise* had to be the approach. Businesslike. 'That is correct, Captain Goldstein,' I said. 'I'll try not to take up too much of your time, sir.'

'No need to worry about that,' he said. When he had finished the sentence he shaped a smile on his face, held it for a second and then dropped it. Success, I had pierced his armour. Or knocked it a little, at least. 'I'll have someone show you your quarters, show you around a little. Then leave you to your business.' He stood, so I followed suit. 'If you need to see me, just tell someone and they'll pass on the message. Good day.' He reached over his desk and shook me by the hand. His skin was cool and had the feel of chitin.

I left the office and there was a young private waiting for me in the cubby-hole office. With her soft brown face and something absent in her expression she barely looked old enough to have joined up. Maybe she was a cadet. (Check that.) Name was Johnston.

'Hi,' she said. 'I'm gunna show you to y'room.' Weird accent. After spending the afternoon with her I'd put it at Asteroid Belt. That's always a safe one, they're such compact and isolated communities that all sorts of social changes occur. Anything weird and 'Oh, it's a miner' explains it.

She led me along a series of nondescript corridors – they must have worked out the route just to confuse me, impress me with the bigness of it all – and then stopped and buzzed open a door. 'Officers' quarters,' she said. She seemed awed by being in such a place. 'It's juz like a hotel: y'can voice actuvvate the door at the board.' She indicated a console and leads jammed into the corner of the room.

The room was small. We stood in the narrow gap between one wall and the hard-looking bunk that occupied the length of the other wall. At the end of this aisle there was a curtained doorway hiding a shower and a crapper. 'I'm gonna have a shit,' I said and curtained myself in.

Johnston took me to a canteen for lunch and I instantly lost my bearings. 'How will I find my room again?'

I asked her over a forkful of stewed moondust.

'Aw, juz ask someone for corridor C38, Personnel.'

My guided tour took the whole afternoon. An endless flow of 'This is the . . .' Canteens, a library, offices, dormitories, gyms, training areas. And in the end yawns. I did get some use out of the tour though. I was shown around a medical unit where they do the surgery on new soldiers. They let me look in on a suboxy implantation. Gruesome, but worth a story.

At the end of one particularly nondescript corridor that awed look returned to Johnston's small round face. 'We've gotten one of the generals here,' she said. 'A general.'

It took a moment to sink in. Then: 'You mean an AI?' I asked.

'Yeah,' she said, drawing it out into a sigh. 'It's not one of the big ones, but it's a general.'

Shit, I hate being a war-time journalist. That was one of those 'Ah!' moments, when you know it's worth some digging. But I knew I would be wasting my time. The AIs – I don't know how many there are – are behind military strategy. There are people higher than them who make policy, but when it comes to tactics a well-informed AI general can outstrip any fleshy one. And I can't report things like this – strategic information. Jee, woman, just cool it. I don't want to give away anything important, any more than Captain Goldstein would, but there's a bug somewhere deep inside me that just wants to tell the story. Any story, so long as it's a good one.

I've been feeding that bug with good personal interest stuff. That's safe and I know it'll get through Goldstein to the agency. Shit, I'm lucky at the amount of freedom they've given me, I shouldn't complain. I'll be getting some good stories out of these few weeks.

After the tour Johnston deposited me back at the

canteen. I ate alone and then asked the way back to Corridor C38, Personnel. It was surprisingly easy to find. Then I saw that there were over twenty rooms to choose from. There were numbers on the doors but of course I hadn't had time to notice that sort of thing when I was trailing away after Johnston. I decided that my room was roughly halfway down. Standing outside the door of an officer's room and speaking your name into a small panel on the wall can earn you some strange looks when the door doesn't open. Five of them didn't open before I found the right one. Before the door whisked shut I made a mental note of the room number.

Before setting out for the evening I tried to have a shower. *Just like a hotel*, my guide had said. Fuck. Moon hotels have jetstream showers, to make up for what the place lacks in gravity. Warm air ionising body driers, too. The water from the shower in my room is so weak that you have to wait half a day before it reaches you. It just seems to hang in the air, like you're in a zero-gee aquadrome without the nose-filter. And to make it worse I was all lathered up before I noticed how ineffective the weak spray was at rinsing away the suds. In the end I'd had enough so I rubbed the rest of it away with a coarse towel and dressed myself in a green all-in-one.

I had passed the crew room at least twice on my tour of the base but of course I couldn't remember the route. The first set of directions lost me – soldiers have a sick sense of humour – but I found a girl who said she was heading there so I followed her.

A big, low-ceilinged room. Smells of booze and smoke (No-Cee, I hope). Interested to note a whiff of marijuana on the air – the Army have made that illegal, blaming it for the hard drug problem (weird reasoning). Huddles of small tables crowded with soldiers in their light blue off-duty jump-suits. The nearest soldiers were giving me the usual once-over. Auto bar at one end of the room.

'Heyah, baby!' A loud, coarse shout from somewhere in the crowded room. 'We're over here! Come and put your pretty little ass on me.'

Chiselling a smile on to my face, I waved and wound my way through the soldiers to a crowded table at the back. I ignored Carter's proffered lap, drew up my own chair, and squeezed it into a non-existent space at the table. There were four others and they had to shuffle around to make room for me. They were all young, slightly drunk or high and studying the parts of my body that were available. Typical military drones: great believers in their own masculinity but, as I have found before, these beliefs are usually completely misfounded.

I find it interesting that in an army that is almost thirty per cent female, these men – the ones I always find myself thinking of as typical soldiers – they hide themselves away in all male groups. Like they're scared.

I leaned forward and, predictably, they leaned forward in impression, taken unawares by a glimpse of my cleavage. It was like they were holo-puppets and I was guiding their wands. Yes, I had a tight grip on their wands.

And then I saw Brindle. A black guy with one hell of a body, just sat on the floor, leaning against the wall. He was jacked into something, a bubble in his suboxy, his eyes unseeing. The quiet ones are often good contacts if you can penetrate their shell. At least that was my excuse for keeping that horn under close observation.

The drones went back to their card game once their hormones had settled and I watched for a few minutes. 'It looks so . . . so *complicated*,' I said in my best little girl's voice. Carter had just missed a pick-up for a diamond slam.

'Aw, it's OK when you get the hang, I reckon,' said one of the troops.

Carter flushed angrily, his territory intruded upon. I used this. 'Well,' I said, leaning my cleavage in Carter's direction. 'Do you think I could have a go? I've played something like it before but I never did get the hang.'

'Hell, yeah,' said Carter, staring at my chest and talking through his penis. 'But don't go betting too much, we don't want you to go home broke now, do we?' Sucker. There followed an over-simplified, patronizing explanation of the rules of Multiple Stud, leaving out all the subtleties that make the difference between scraping even and raking it in.

'Why . . . I *think* I follow it,' I said, fluttering my lashes.

I let them win the first two hands, keeping my losses to a minimum and folding early. Then I found myself with a good starting hand and I couldn't resist coming on them. The stakes increased slowly and then, instead of folding and flashing my eyes, I put down a twenty.

'Heyah, did you mean that?' asked Carter.

'Huh?' said I. 'Oh fuck, that was a twenty wasn't it?' I retrieved it and put down a hundred. To cut a long story short, I ended that round with a Trader's High, Jills over Jacks. Two more rounds and they were making excuses. I found myself alone at the table, laughing at the sight of Carter's retreating butt as I imagined him fending off the complaints of his pals.

The horn was still by the wall. I went over and passed a hand in front of his blank eyes. 'Hi there ma'am, can I help you?' he said. I was taken aback, not many people can be shunted *and* keep a track of the real world at the same time.

'Um, I was just wondering if I could have a chat with you,' I said.

'Sure,' he said and deshunted his bubble. 'Pull up a floor.'

I sat down beside him. 'I didn't mean to interrupt.'

'Hell, no ma'am, I was just updating my diary.' He grinned. 'I noticed how you saw off old Crap-ass. It was a pleasure to watch.'

'You mean Carter? Good name for him.' Brindle is a real cutie, not at all the usual soldier. We talked and in the end we went back to my room. He had a thirty-six hour leave so he didn't have to go back to his dorm. *Is this OK?* he kept asking, and I kept assuring him that he could tell me anything, that Goldstein would be vetting all my copy before broadcast.

We had a drink and he told me about his surgery, how he was coping with his new implants. His new suboxy has a chip in it that gives him all sorts of control. It gives him autohypnosis for learning, anti-tension, sleep and so on. Override of the adrenal medulla: a kick of adrenalin to keep him alert, keep him on a fighting edge, or a slowdown to relax, stay cool. Control of other juices, too.

Now this isn't the place to go into what went on that night, how many times, how many positions – it makes it somehow impersonal. But, boy, he was good! I'm sure he was using his chip to good effect, chipping some adrenalin, slowing down and staying on the edge. He lasted hours. This morning too. He was so tender and careful, he really cared how I felt. Even today there aren't many men like that around. And he's so cute. 'How come you weren't called up?' he said early this morning. From any other man I would have taken that as smooth talk, the sort of crap they think women like, but Brindle couldn't do that if he tried. Hell, I could almost be his mother, the young whippersnapper. 'I've been fucking longer than you've been born,' I said. 'They reckon you're past it when you get to my age.' 'Oh yeah?' he said, and went on to prove just how wrong they can be sometimes.

This is just how it should be: business and pleasure. Yes, I got some business out of him, too. Lots of information. He gave me a good angle on the training. Fighting away from the Earth is either long-range and technical (thankfully little of that) or guerrilla (like the Fight for Independence). The troops are trained mainly for the latter so the Peacekeeping force has ideal preparation for the Grand Union. I'll have to follow that up.

I'm gonna have to get out of this bunk soon. Get some copy. But I can still smell him on the sheets, smell him on my body. I think I'll just lie here a little longer, plan my notes or something. Hmmm.

Chapter Five

20 June 2084

Jacobi closed the cockpit door and the screams and shouts became muffled. As the noise died the few remaining cries increased their intensity, but soon the only sounds were those in the cockpit.

'Shall I put some more pan-H in the system?' asked Jacobi.

'No,' said Amagat. 'We don't want to kill them. Four capsules should keep them out for the next few hours. We'd better check them in a few minutes, just to make sure they've all gone under.' She turned to me and said, 'What went down back there, Jed?'

'It was the steward,' I said. 'This fucker over here—' I indicated the pilot with a nod of my head and he looked away, scared '—this fucker didn't order the whole crew to come forward. The steward came along and stumbled on the pile of shit in the galley. He's dead.'

'The screams?'

'He reached the passengers first,' I said. 'Nothing I could do.'

'Was it necessary?'

The same old question. Of *course* it was necessary, the bastard was raising the alarm. He needed stopping.

I suppressed my anger. 'Yes, it was necessary,' I said and shrugged. 'He needed stopping.'

'OK,' said Amagat. 'Let's just wait for Grand Union.'

She glanced at the watch on her left wrist; that was one part of her civilian outfit she hadn't let go of. 'Hundred minutes to Wichita,' she said. 'Leo, cover the cockpit. I'll cover the corridor. Just in case. Forty-five minutes duty, then we swap.' She turned to me. 'You and Gil chip down, conserve yourselves. Take over in forty-five. *Ciao*.'

Amagat stepped out into the corridor, left the door open. I watched her retreating figure then closed my eyes. Maybe I *was* a bit on edge, chipping down might do me some good. There wasn't a lot for us to do from that point. The hijack had gone down as well as we could have hoped. We were on course for Wichita. All that remained was to get out of the plane at the airport.

Yeah. Chip down. Take things easy. Slow my whole world and let things just *drift*. Hmmm.

The military chip has great advantages sometimes. Chipping down is only one of them. Ma had been scared of what the surgery might do to me, but it was nothing. One of the first things they did to us at the Merc was to wheel us into the operating cylinder. You could imagine the view, your world being rapidly cut off as your body slips down the big surgical tube. You always imagine it to be all shiny and brightly lit, but I guess it's plastic or fibre and probably not lit at all. Scalpels and grips and whirring drills coming out at you on robot arms. Cutting into your skull, your arm, your abdomen. Planting chips and interfaces. But all the time you're well under, none of it gets through to you.

You wake up thirty-six hours later, weird feelings chasing each other through your body. The operation only takes a few minutes, the cybernetic surgical tube working in a blur of action. What takes the time is the growing. New nerves grow out from the implants, following pre-programmed paths. If this happened when you were awake, the agony would drive you insane, as they found in the earlier trials.

As it is, you just wake up with these weird feelings. Tingling sensations down the spinal column. Headaches. Headaches that split your head into a million tiny pieces and trample on them one by one. Even after several months you get pre-migraine twinges. Thankfully, one of the applications of the Army chip is pain suppression – just chip a few encephalins and a pre- never turns into the real thing.

Lots of the guys had problems adapting to their new chipping abilities, but I didn't understand what was wrong. After the initial feelings of strangeness, I just fell into the use of my new organs. Extra control of the body; extension of the body through the interfaces, shunting into tools like the zap and feeling through them. It was a whole new world.

No, I didn't see what was the problem.

And chipping control of adrenalin, sweat glands, sex hormones. Well, that just brought a whole new angle on living. You chip up some testosterone for hair growth, maybe. Chip down on sweat, when you want to conserve water, avoid obvious smell signatures.

Chip down on the adrenalin. Relax. Keep your eyes closed and your pulse way, way *down.* Stay cool.

Tugging on my shoulder, head rolling against a hard wall. Funny things, dreams. Especially when you're chipped right down.

I grunted and moved a little.

Alert. A stab of Comtac and I was scrambling to my feet. Amagat grinned at me.

'Very funny,' I said, arching my back in a bone-cracking stretch. That was one Comtac command that had a direct route to my suboccipital. Chips up sharply, puts you on instant alert.

'Only way to wake you, dope-head,' said the sub-lieutenant. 'Your turn for duty. Tell Leo, will you? He's back with the sleepers. I'll just settle down here.' She sat down, back to the wall. 'Wake me in forty-five,' she said, already closing her eyes and settling into her break.

'Yeah,' I said. '*Ciao*.'

Nothing had changed in the cockpit. The co-pilot was unconscious and I wondered if he was still under the influence of Amagat's assault or was now being kept under by the panhalothol. Gil was slumped against the back of the co-pilot's chair, his lax young face looking almost angelic despite his smoke mask. People had often questioned whether he was old enough to be a soldier, but I had no doubts. You might be able to misinform the Army of your age if you volunteer, but Gil was a draftee. You can't lie to the computers before you know they're going to select you. Not deliberately, anyway.

The pilot was turned in his chair, a half-smile on his face. The tape stopped him from turning any further. For some reason I couldn't quite read his expression. I remembered his treachery of before.

I walked over to him and his smile broadened. It was an unsteady smile, but he couldn't let it slip once it had found its way on to his face. That would mean losing credibility.

I pointed my zap at his crotch and the smile vanished. 'Maybe I'd better plug this in, if I'm going to use it,' I said in a pleasant voice. I jacked the zap's lead into my median. 'That's better.' I sat on the taped-up arm of the co-pilot, on the arm of his chair, and a glint of anger showed on the pilot's face. 'Now what was the idea of your little trick earlier?' I said. I kept the zap aimed in the approximate direction of his crotch.

The pilot didn't say anything.

'Not going to answer?' I asked. I squeezed my first finger, snapped my hand up as if I'd just fired a manual gun, like they use on Earth. The pilot flinched against his tape, his free hands leaping to protect himself.

I laughed at him. 'That's not how we shoot these things,' I said. 'These are *real* guns.' I flicked my hand and released a lightning bolt of blue. It burned a small black hole in the chair. Just by the pilot's ear. You can be very accurate without even trying, when you have a gun shunted. I laughed again. 'You'd better watch it, boy.'

That look on his face again. He leaned forward as far as he could and spat at me, missing by a good metre.

I stood and walked away. *Bastard.* I chipped down wildly. Calmed myself. We needed that pilot to get us where we wanted to go. And the bastard knew it.

I kicked Lohmann's feet. 'Wake up, dreamer,' I said. Calmer now. 'Time for work.'

I walked out through the open cockpit door and headed down the short corridor. Jacobi was leaning against the door of the out-of-order toilet. 'Your turn for break,' I said.

Jacobi looked up casually. His Advance Warning must have told him I was coming. 'Hey you look ill,' he said. 'Maybe you should take my break. Hey, change that.' He grinned. 'Take the sub's. I don't want Gil telling people I slept with *Amagat*.' He pulled a face and I grinned in return.

'Seen any action?' I nodded along the aisle. It looked spooky, all those passengers sprawled in their seats. Like a plague had struck.

'Sure,' said Jacobi. 'I been dancing with 'em, but I tired 'em all out. They're dead beat now.' He chuckled at himself and headed down towards the cockpit.

'Hey,' I shouted after him. 'Send Gil out here. All these bodies give me the creeps.'

'Hah!' he said. Then: 'Sure thing.'

A couple of minutes later, Gil came down the corridor and said a sheepish, 'Hi.'

'How are you feeling?' I asked.

He scratched at his head. 'OK I guess.'

'I'll see you in forty-five,' I said and then grinned. 'Don't make too much noise. There's people trying to get some sleep out here.' Gil smiled and I headed back for the cockpit. I wanted to keep an eye on that pilot and I couldn't trust Gil not to just drift off into some dreamworld. I stepped through the door and closed it. On consideration I stepped back and re-opened it. You never can tell what might happen.

Leo was keeping an eye on the pilot, waiting for my return. I squatted and leaned back against a side wall. 'Sweet dreams,' I said as Jacobi settled down on the floor. He blew me a kiss.

The pilot was looking at me. Not challenging, but not scared. His attitude still puzzled me. After maybe half a minute I stood and strolled over. I picked up the roll of tape Jacobi had discarded and gave it a few more turns around the pilot's legs and body. His unwavering look made me uncomfortable and I returned to my position leaning against the side wall. I found myself wishing I could access the GPS grid, check on our course, but the metal skin of the plane cut out most of the signals. All I ever got was a confused buzz, an occasional fragment that seemed to put us in about the right place. Amagat would have a clearer picture of things but she was asleep on the floor.

I let my zap dangle from its lead and looked down at the two still figures. Amagat was facing me, head on one side, one knee raised, the other leg stretched out.

Almost touching me. I followed the lines of her tight body-suit. The hardness seemed to vanish from her features with the relaxation of sleep. Especially the chipped-down sleep you get from a military chip. I noticed she had undone the tail at the back of her head and her lank mousy hair was strung loosely down to the shoulders, one lock curling over her left cheek. Made her look almost child-like. Her shoulders and chest were well-muscled. Solid-looking stomach, narrow hips and those pillar-like legs. I had to admit to a perverse attraction to her, and somehow I had to find an explanation for it. It made me uncomfortable.

She was not beautiful in any traditional sense of the word, but she was not *un*beautiful. I guess it was a sort of beauty through power, something that reached me on a baser level. A Dionysian thing. And that power was vaguely underlaid by a streak of weakness, vulnerability.

Hell, I don't know. All I know is that sitting there, looking at her lying before me, gave me one Hell of a hard-on.

I shifted and saw that the pilot was still looking at me. I gathered up my dangling zap and he looked away hurriedly. I guess he didn't trust me to any great degree. At least I hoped he didn't.

I looked back at the still bodies in front of me, my desire rudely shattered by the little exchange of posturing with the pilot. Jacobi's hand had stretched up above his head and rested comically on Amagat's right thigh. Her mouth sleep-twitched and smiled for an instant.

Yeah. They made a much better couple. Much better suited. Jacobi snored and his hand slid back down to the floor. My mind conjured up an image of the two of them moving together in something resembling passion and I grinned. Yeah, they made a *much* better couple.

The pilot had his headset on when I looked away from

the two dreamers. 'What you doing?' I demanded, standing quickly.

He looked round and slid the set up on to the top of his head, a resigned look on his face. 'In-flight checks,' he said tiredly. 'Standard procedure. Every fifteen minutes or at any sign of a problem.'

'What—?' I started to say, but the pilot cut me off.

'No problem,' he said. 'Just a fifteen check. Calms the nerves, you know?'

I looked more closely at him. Yeah, his nerves needed some calming. He'd been keeping a straight face, but the cracks were showing through his smooth exterior. Sweat glistened on his forehead, his right eyelid gave the occasional tic.

I had the sudden urge to tell him to chip down, he'd get through it all. I guess that was an honest impulse. He had more fight in him than any of the Earthshit I'd dealt with up until then. One whole Hell of a lot more than those kid revolutionaries back in Grand Union. Yeah, I wanted to tell him some of this, show that he had earned some respect by his actions. But I didn't.

'Maybe I'd just better check on that,' I said, stepping towards him.

'Oh yeah?' he said, a genuine smile reaching his face. 'How you gonna do that? Alien.'

I couldn't fight the smile that came to my face at that. None of the fight had left him yet, and the blood claat certainly had a point. My smile confused him and he flinched as if I had hit him. Maybe he thought I was just a little bit crazy, huh?

I stepped back and leaned on the wall. Glanced at the wall clock. 17:34. Click to 17:35. Forty minutes until I had to wake the other two. Fifty to Wichita and a long stiff drink. I looked back at the pilot, his unmoving partner.

An explosion ripped through my head. Gunfire. Single shot. From down the plane. The pilot looked around, scared. The first look of genuine 100 per cent fear I had seen on his features.

'Stay there,' I said unnecessarily. His tape would fix him for a while. And his fear. I felt an odd sense of satisfaction at his fear as I sprang to my feet and moved to the side of the door. There was no sign of anything in the corridor.

I swung into the doorway and took two big steps to the galley. Landed on my right foot, pushed off the wall with my hand and was into its relative safety.

I stepped clear of the stray hand that I had landed on, noted that its fingers were now dreadfully broken. Glanced at the heap of CivAir blue bodies.

A quick thought activated the Advance Warning program in my chip. Sensitive, now, to danger signals at the periphery of my senses. Signals that might not otherwise get through to my consciousness until too late. Then I sent a quick burst of Comtac back to the two sleepers, hoping the aircraft walls wouldn't block the signal. *AlertAlertAlertAlert.* Another one for luck: *Alert.*

I moved the zap to my finger tips, poked it around the corner. A subconscious image of the corridor flashed through my mind. Empty. No warnings flashed into my brain by the AW.

I stepped out, slid the zap back into a more comfortable grip and advanced, more slowly now, the last three paces.

To the corner. The first few seats crept into my field of view. Still, corpse-like figures. I stood by the doorframe, poked my zap around the corner. Nothing.

Then I looked down. Saw a pair of grey sneakers, camouflaged legs.

Gil.

My view from the zap revealed no movement. No warning from the AW. I stepped out. Nobody shot me, there were no sudden bursts of sound, of light, no explosion in my chest. I knelt quickly and grabbed Gil's feet, keeping my eyes fixed on the rows of still people. I backed into the relative safety of the corridor, Gil a limp weight following me around. My AW told me someone was coming from the cabin. A glance told me it was Jacobi and I dragged Gil right into the corridor.

'Jesus fucking Christ,' said Jacobi.

I looked down at Gil, the dark red mess of his chest. In death his face had taken on much the same relaxed angelic look he had shown in sleep. His pale blue eyes stared up at us and there was a dreadfully vacant smile on his lips. Like he was stoked up on the purest, cleanest synthetic he had ever taken. One huge trip. I looked away. Exchanged a glance with Leo. His face was devoid of emotion, that in itself signalling the intensity of the feelings that burnt beneath his skin.

? I Comtacked to him, indicating the single stripe of rank on my shoulder. Where's Amagat?

Jacobi nodded back at the cockpit. Guarding the pilot. I was glad she had taken that on, that I was with Leo. We both had something personal in it. For Gil.

Advanced Warning, I Comtacked. Then: *Go ahead.*

Jacobi slipped past me. Paused. Scuttled down to hide by the first row of seats. A scan with the zap then I was out and crouching by the first row on the left, opposite Jacobi. I glanced across at him. Nodded.

My Advance Warning was jabbing at my brain. There was something not right, further down the plane. *What in Hell's name had Amagat been playing at?* She was on guard down here, first of all. And it was Amagat who had stressed that the passengers should be checked early on. To make sure none of them had somehow resisted the pan-H. I almost wanted to go back and burn a hole in *her*.

I poked the tip of my zap around the seat. No subconscious images flashed warnings at me.

Go ahead, I Comtacked.

Jacobi stepped out into the aisle, crouching low. Two short steps, then he ducked into the next row of seats. I withdrew my zap and there was a short pause while Jacobi took over surveillance. Then: *Go ahead.* I went.

Out into the aisle. Stopped myself against the seat opposite and sprang back into the next row on my side. Squeezed into the gap left by an overweight businessman. His head was leaning forward, chin sunk into a cushion of fleshy neck. His eyes were closed, spectacles dangling from one ear. A shining ribbon of saliva reflected the plane's lights on its journey from the corner of his mouth to oblivion in one of the deep folds in the junction between face and neck.

I tore my eyes away and glanced across at Jacobi. He didn't seem to have noticed my digression.

I put my zap out again. No warning images, although my AW was dancing an excited jig in my brain cells. *Go ahead.* Jacobi went.

We advanced several rows in this leapfrogging manner. First Leo, then me. I found myself back in my old seat, the journey eased for a moment by not having to squeeze into a seat with an unconscious passenger. My AW had been flickering on and off for quite a time. Our target was moving about back there, a little over halfway down, I guessed.

I poked the zap out once more, the target hadn't registered an image in it yet. Then there was a flutter of AW and for an instant I received a subconscious image of movement amongst the seats. About ten rows further down the plane.

Stay put, I Comtacked. Jacobi paused and looked over at me. No more signs of movement. *Go ahead.*

Jacobi slipped forward another row. This was the sort of situation they're never very clear about in training. Should you chip down and stay calm and collected, or should you chip up to a fine cutting edge, ready for action? *Use your judgement*, they say. Crouching in the foot-space of my empty seat, I was chipping the juices furiously. The cutting edge was for me, it seemed to take the action out of my own hands, put me into overdrive.

Go ahead, Jacobi Comtacked. Out into the aisle again, paused but didn't see anything in the area I guessed our target to be hiding in. Each jump along that aisle seemed to last longer and longer. The first trip, from the door to the first row was just a flash of activity, then the cool sanctity of the seats. They seemed to tower over me, sheltering me and protecting me from the outside world. This moment drew out into an eternity.

And then I was back into the cramped confines of the seats. Staring up at the blank face of a middle-aged woman. I looked over at Jacobi. Poked out the zap, noted that the AW was silent. No activity at all. *Go ahead.*

Jacobi stepped out into the aisle, moved forwards rapidly. Funny how the move from row to row seemed to speed up for Jacobi. Slow down for myself, speed up when I'm watching Jacobi. The analysts would have fun sorting out *that* little conundrum.

Gunshot. My skull wanted to burst, like the explosion happened in my own head. The sound alone stunned me for an instant. The burst of AW came a moment after the shot, the subconscious image of movement came soon after. It was all so quick and in the wrong order. Whoever fired the shot had moved too fast.

The explosion, the burst of warning from my sensors. The swing of my head and the sight of Jacobi stretched out on the floor. My zap was flashing images at me and I sent a quick burst of three shots up the plane. There was nothing to aim at but I had to buy time. For Jacobi.

Just in case.

Then he moved, groaned. Dragged himself slowly into the protection of a seat. There was a trail of blood on the floor, following Jacobi to his hiding place. I looked across at him, fearful of what I might see.

It wasn't as bad as I had feared. He was clutching at his left leg, below the knee. Blood was seeping between his pale, white fingers. He looked at me, a weak grin lining his lips. Then he looked back down at his hand, his leg. He lifted his hand slightly, winced and put it back.

Chip down, I Comtacked. *Chip down.*

He looked at me, shook his head. Crossed his fingers for me. Then he twisted slightly, the pain of movement creasing his face. He poked his zap around the corner of the seat. Standing sentinel for me. *Go ahead*, he Comtacked.

I stepped out, ducked back in. Somehow my sense of time had speeded up again. It was a blur of action.

I found myself staring up into the face of a stupidly grinning young man. I moved, shoved his knee out of my rib-cage. Glanced back at Jacobi's pale face, poked my zap around the seat.

And then there was another explosion, ripping through the silence. Ringing in my head. Followed an instant later by a flutter of AW, a wild cascade of images from my zap, a stabbing Comtac of *Alert.* It all came in the wrong order, my target was too fast. But I had her in my sights for an instant. Not long enough to let off a shot, but I got her range. About eight metres.

That brief subconscious image was enough for me to recognize Cohen's bodyguard. The huge black piece with a moustache and muscles that rippled through her leather jacket. I poked my zap around the seat again, but there was nothing.

I paused, wondering who would make the first move. She seemed pretty keen to get the fight over with.

Then my AW started feeding me warnings. A stab of *Alert* from Jacobi. She was moving about back there. I went into action without even enough time for my plan to reach my consciousness for approval.

I slid over the young man and into the vacant window seat.

Paused.

My AW was still flickering with the movements of Cohen's bodyguard. Maybe she was moving around for a better angle on me, now that she knew my location. I chipped a spurt of adrenalin, took a deep breath. Then I heaved the young man forward in his seat, free of the arm-rest.

Paused again.

And pushed, with every gram of strength at my disposal. I had to get this right first time, there could be no halfway.

The young man's limp body tumbled into the aisle and I followed it through and paused for an instant in his vacant seat. Another loud explosion, ripping the air. A scream, this time, of a nearby bullet.

Then I tumbled out after the man, even as his body jerked with the impact of the bullet. Even as a jet of blood leapt out of his back and then died back. I held my zap clear as I fell. A series of images. The bodyguard coming into my sights. I sent a nerve impulse to the zap, releasing a laser-bolt at the target.

Crashed into the limp body. Kept my zap clear and found the target in my sights again. Released another shot.

Gathered myself and released another shot into the falling figure. Collapsing in an untidy heap. Even in the heat of the moment I found myself wondering at the distance she had to fall. Tall woman.

Then there was silence. I scrambled off the body of the passenger and back into his seat. Realized what I had done and looked back at him. He was dead. His face was still grinning but there was a large red patch on the back of his honey-coloured jacket.

My AW was telling me that there was still somebody alive near the dead bodyguard and I turned in my seat, the sight of the young man vanished from my mind. My zap revealed nothing when I used it to take a look.

Then I heard the voice of Cohen. 'I don't have any weapons,' he said. 'Don't shoot.'

'Come out into the open,' I said. 'We have you covered. Hands over your head.' I moved so that I could just see around the seat. I wanted a full conscious view of this, not just zap images.

First came the head, sticking out above the seats. It moved across and his legs poked out into the aisle. He pushed himself to his feet and then raised his hands above his head. He turned in the aisle to face us, a clumsy large smoke mask pulled over his face, the large black body at his feet. The steward's warning must have given them time to pull out the masks before the panhalothol hit.

Cohen kept his eyes levelled down the aeroplane, avoided looking at the motionless figure of his bodyguard.

Happy that there was nobody else back there, I stepped out with my zap trained on Cohen's chest. His gaze flicked slightly downwards to me. I stepped slowly forward. It took several steps before recognition dawned on Cohen's face. A smoke mask and a uniform can make a lot of difference. Then his jaw sagged and he glanced down at my leg, without its brace. His eyes turned to flint. I stopped two metres short, the length of the dead bodyguard.

Keeping my zap trained on Cohen, I looked down and kicked at the bodyguard's limp feet. Dead. A zap image and a flash of AW made me look back up at Cohen. I kicked the body again and this time he had more restraint. The surge of anger only showed in his eyes this time, not the reflex jerk of his body.

I kicked the body again, for effect.

The bodyguard looked even bigger on the floor than she had on her feet. She was lying twisted, half on her right side, and the highest point of her body – her left shoulder – reached halfway up my thighs. I felt glad that it had been a gunfight, not hand to hand. I knew that she had been hit three times but I could see only one burn hole. It had gone through her smoke mask, then through her left cheek. I wondered if perhaps it had been a lucky first shot, the gas helping my later shots. But panhalothol doesn't act that fast. I had outshot her, fair and square.

I stepped to one side and waved my zap. 'Come on,' I said to Cohen. 'We're gonna give you a guided tour.'

He half-lowered his hands, then stretched them up again and stepped awkwardly around the huge body. I followed him down the aisle, still uncomfortable about turning my back on the bodyguard. I shuddered and chipped down a little. The action was over.

Cohen glanced down at Jacobi as he passed. 'OK, wait,' I said as I drew level with Leo's resting place. His zap was still poking around the seat but his eyes were closed. His mask was slightly askew and I repositioned it to make sure he had clean air to breathe. A surge of uneasiness, then I saw that he *was* still breathing. Good.

I turned to Cohen. 'On you go,' I said, and prompted him with the zap.

Under NO FURTHER ADMITTANCE, around the corner. Cohen hesitated, then stepped around the sad figure of Gil. I followed with a brief glance down at the dead face. At least he looked happy. Maybe it was a good trip. Cohen paused again at the open door to the pilot's cabin, then stepped in past Amagat. I followed.

'Gil's dead. Leo's hurt,' I said. Amagat went pale. I looked at the pilot, he'd been eating at me for quite a time. 'I'm gonna check on that blood claat.'

It was the pilot's turn to lose his colour. No *How you gonna do that?* this time. The situation had taken on a whole new shade and the pilot knew it. I walked forward and stood by the unmoving co-pilot. Grabbed the set from his skull and pulled it on to mine. It was a tight fit. I slid the eye-pieces down and slid them up again quickly. I had to sit down for this.

The co-pilot was taped to his seat so I sat in his lap. Then I pulled the head-set forward again.

The cabin vanished from my experience and I was in a surreal world of retinal scan-projection. My AW set up an instant clamour and I cut it off with a quick impulse. I chipped down, cooled my thoughts. Then I focused on the world that was imposing itself on me.

It was like a weird, harshly coloured, holo-cartoon sequence, but it was more than that. It was like I was *inside* the hee-vee arena, part of the action. I was in a three-dimensional grid, figures locating me in space. There were numbers that kept changing, image-fragments that flashed into existence and then disappeared into some electronic limbo. Figures that looked like coordinates. 1024:0367. Wrong way round if they *were* coordinates. There was a menu down to the left. I glanced at the first entry and the view suddenly changed to a high clarity two-dee view from the outside of the plane. Clouds receding, must be from the tail. It made me feel sick and I drew the headset up to rest on the top of my head.

There was that look on the pilot's face again and suddenly I recognized it. It was a superior look. He was pulling wool over our eyes and he knew we couldn't tell.

Angrily I pulled the set down again and re-entered the surreal world of the Boeing pilot system. It was the first view again, the harsh colours of the grid burning into my retinas. I tried the second item on the menu. A screen dense with data sprang up before me. I saw with horror that it was multi-layered, a glance at a cue-block flipped the view down another layer. Deeper into the data.

I back-pedalled. And then stopped. Something had caught my eye. I looked closer. This layer was written in a sort of pidgin programmer code and I could make out some of the words.

Rev Route Plan. Wide swing. Initial tangent: Wichita. Destination—

That bastard.

Destination: *Denver.*

That would put us safely into CalTex territory. I tried again to check with the Global Positioning Satellites but there was only a jazz of interference and nonsense-codes. Furious, I ripped the set from my head and swung round on the pilot.

'Reprogram this fucker!' I said, shaking the head-set at him. Then I swung to Amagat. Why hadn't she known? It was her job. 'We're on course for Denver. He's been fucking us all the way.' Back to the pilot. 'Your buddy gets it, you hear?'

The pilot moved his hands slowly to his console. Then he looked at me and his fingers started to type instructions. The tension had gone from his face and it hung slackly, like he was one of the passengers. Or like Gil's face had gone when he had been shot.

He glanced at the console, then said in a quiet voice, 'Go to Hell, Alien.'

He made his last contact with the console with a flourish and suddenly the floor tilted away from under us. Amagat and Cohen tumbled and I felt myself lifted in a momentary loss of gees. Then I hit the floor and landed in a tangled heap with the two others.

I looked around in a panic. The plane was in a dive. A steep, steep dive. The pilot was still in his seat, dangling by his safety belts and Jacobi's tape. He looked down at me, a sad smile of victory on his lips.

There was only one person who could fly the plane and it was that person who had set it in a steep nose-dive. I closed my eyes and realized that I had wet myself.

The pilot had won. Amagat screamed.

Chapter Six

Selective transcript of Lejeune News holovision documentary, Freedom Fighters of Lejeune. (*Recorded 2 to 8 August 2083 and broadcast to coincide with Independence Day on the 29th.*)

Opening Credits, over: The tiny sphere of Lejeune hanging in space, dwarfed by its sixteen companion Grow-Coils. Main viewpoint pans away, impression of shooting through space. Cut to full projection Moon, seventy-five per cent lighting, Earth in background. Cut to notice: Mercator IV, Extraterran Armed Forces, Training Camp. Background music: Roblein's *Fighting Anthem.*

Scene: Soldiers on firing range. Fade *Anthem.*

Commentary: 'To some of us, the Fight for Independence may seem a long time ago. To others it may seem like only yesterday. National wounds take a long time to heal, even in such a loose grouping as the Extraterran Peoples.

'Twenty years of struggle led us to the Declaration of Independence. Since that day we have grown. Wealth from the Belt, from new technologies, from the vitality of the people. Yes, we have grown. And when we received a plea for help from our brothers and sisters on Earth, well of *course* we heeded their cry. Yes, we have our wounds but also we have our pride.

'The need for our help increased, the situation on Earth

deteriorated. Attacks on our satellites. Threats to our very homes. The Grand Union has powerful enemies. So we needed more troops. And on March the sixth this year our little farming colony of Lejeune heard the Army's cry for help. Notices sent to each of our young people between the ages of seventeen and twenty-five produced an overwhelming response. Our acknowledgement rate ran at ninety per cent; only a few Lunar colonies, with strong military traditions, could beat that.

'We are proud of our sons and daughters.

'Here at Mercator IV is the initial training camp. Soon our soldiers will be headed for what is known as The Disc, a vast training base at L4, but now they are polishing up their skills here on the moon.'

The view had been moving around the range, picking out fresh young faces. Faces that will be recognized in the homes of Lejeune. The view lingers for a moment on a young brown face, then angles down his shattergun barrel to see a neon target flash into view and then flicker out. The gun fires blanks, but its laser sights register a hit. View returns to the soldier's face, a scar on his left jaw, and then pans to a girl who takes more care and misses.

Scene: Soldiers running over fitness course. This section is a series of steep inclines; the soldier runs up, drops two or three metres and then runs up the next one. A training officer shouts timing and harangues stragglers.

Commentary: 'Four and a half months our boys and girls have been in training here. In that time they have seen more changes than at any other time in their lives. Surgery to expand their human-machine interface capacities and to give them conscious override of many bodily functions. Drilling in weapons, navigation, communication, leadership, initiative. The most comprehensive military training that has ever been available to humankind.'

During the commentary the view has cut to the F Division crew room. Neat rows of tables, genteel laughter, no smoke hanging in the air like a death pall.

Commentary: 'But if you just take a look-in at the crew room you'll see that these kids are the same young people that left Lejeune. They play games, they joke, they make friends. *They have a good time.* Of course, some of their games may involve gambling, they may drink a little, but they're *soldiers.* They've got to have a bit of fun, huh?'

View closes in on one group. On the table there is a small glass of froth and beer, several glasses of soft drink and a cigarette. Seated around the table, smiling and laughing amongst themselves, are five young recruits. Sitting slightly apart is an older man, obviously the reporter. He puffs out a smoke ring and reaches for the beer. A quiet young soldier sits in the background against a wall, staring into space. The viewpoint pans slightly, excluding background details.

'Vincent O'Connor, Sheilagh LaBrunne, Barbie Gill—' the viewpoint pans, emphasizing each of the five faces in turn '—Pam Rumford, Chan Wicksinghe. All are young recruits from Lejeune.' The viewpoint settles on a group shot, with generous emphasis on the reporter. 'How's the military treating you?'

'Why, just swell,' says LaBrunne, a small girl with a delicate oriental face.

'Hey, like it's the atmosphere, you know how I'm putting it?' says Wicksinghe. 'Well, like, they get at you pretty brutal sometimes but, you know, you've got your friends around you. It's like we're all in this thing together and we can pull it better as a group, you know how it's put?'

'You mean,' says the reporter, pausing for a breath, 'it's a hard life. Tough. Disciplined. Yet with your wealth of local ties back on Lejeune, the presence of old friends and acquaintances here at Mercator IV, you pull together as a group and give this military life the best that you can give, proud of your background on our small but loyal colony.'

'Like yeah,' says Wicksinghe. 'You know how it's put?'

'Do you all find it easy to keep up your Lejeune connections?' asks the reporter. 'Do you keep up with old friends?'

'Just swell,' says LaBrunne. 'I'm in a dorm with Sheilagh and although Wicky is in a different Division I fucked with him only last week. It was swell.'

'You see, folks?' says the reporter, smiling in a helpless-but-amused manner as the viewpoint closes on him. 'Soldiers will be soldiers . . .'

Scene: Door with a red cross on it.

The door whisks open to reveal a young man in a lay-back chair being talked to by a soldier wearing a red cross armband. Viewpoint moves in and around to settle on a general shot of the room, from seventy-five per cent behind the patient.

Commentary: 'Of course, war has its casualties, even at this early stage.

'This young man is Austin Whitney. By the time this is broadcast he will be back at home on Lejeune. His family has acknowledged our right to broadcast this next sequence.'

A printed update floats up and settles at the front of the frozen scene. It reads: *Austin Whitney made a rapid recovery and is now back on Lejeune. His case demonstrates the resilience of the human spirit and this sequence in no way reflects on his courage and loyalty. 29 August 2083.*

The reporter is smiling down at Whitney in a fatherly manner. View pans round to take in Whitney's face. 'How are you feeling now, Austin?' says the reporter.

Whitney stares at the reporter, eyes big and wet: His lip twitches. The medic nudges him. 'How are you feeling?' he says gruffly.

'Huh,' says Whitney.

'Not so good, hey?' says the reporter.

'Huh,' says Whitney. The medic nudges him and he says 'Huh' again.

'You'll be going home soon, Austin,' says the reporter in a hushed voice.

'Huh,' says Whitney. He picks at his left nostril and studies his finger intently. 'Huh.'

Scene: Whitney's medic sitting in an office, the reporter sitting facing him.

'Jeez, man, army training *has* to be tough,' says the medic. 'We get a few like Whitney in every batch. They can't take the pace. But they're just the shit, you can't blame the system: it turns out the best trained fighting force that humankind has ever seen.'

'Could you explain to our viewers what exactly happened to young Austin?'

'It's what we call *bugging out,*' says the medic. ''Cept he hasn't even fought yet. You get a lot of it in combat, it gets too much for them and they go chickenshit. Just freeze up. Like, it's sometimes called *battle fatigue.*'

'But can you tell the viewers at home exactly how Whitney got the fatigue without the battle?' says the reporter.

'Well, like I put it to you before,' says the medic. 'Training is *tough.* It has to be. In their first few months the jellies – that's new recruits – go through their training and assessment. They're tested under all kinds of stress situations – mock emergencies and the like – and that gives us a good idea of their strengths and weaknesses. Then we can tailor their training programmes individually, get the best out of them.'

'It sounds like a tough way of life,' says the reporter in reverent tones.

'It works,' says the medic.

'It can come as no surprise that some of our young people find it too much,' says the reporter.

'Yeah,' says the medic philosophically. 'I guess there's some chickenshit in every barrel of eggs.'

'How many of the Lejeune recruits have taken it the way young Austin has?' says the reporter.

'Oh, Whitney's the only one.'

Scene: Back to the firing range; following the reporter as he strolls.

'Yes, there are the sad cases,' says the reporter, glancing back at the camera. 'But there are also the successes. Some of our young people have gone on to greater and greater things since joining the Extraterran Army. Take Alvin Coleridge, for example . . .

'. . . Yes, these young people have done us proud.' The reporter stops by the prone figure of a young troop, firing at neon targets with his shattergun. 'But surely the champion of them all must be young Jedburgh Brindle. Born and bred on Lejeune, he is the only son of Louis Brindle, our colony's coordinator.'

Brindle scores another hit.

'Jed, my boy,' says the reporter. 'You have an outstanding record. In a period of four and a half months you have risen to be one of the finest new recruits in the Army. How do you account for that?'

'Hell, I don't know who said all that,' says Jed, rolling on to his side and leaning on an elbow. 'I just go about things like I always have: I learn things and then I *do* them.'

'You've been scoring high on all the training tests, Jed. Winning the prizes at shooting and fitness. You can't say that's not a good record, Jed.'

'Yeah, but Hell, other guys win the prizes for leadership, initiative, tactics. Jee, I don't win it all,' says Jed. 'Not by a long way.' He rolls over and in a split second shoots another target. 'But I can sure shoot shit out of anyone else.' He grins. 'I don't hold out much hope for those Frags when I get down Earthside.' He shoots another target.

'You're looking forward to the conflict, Jed?' says the reporter.

'Hell, I wouldn't say *looking forward* exactly,' says Jed, the grin vanished from his face. 'But I'm ready to do whatever the Peacekeeping force wants of me. Yes, I'm ready for it.'

Viewpoint pans up and away giving an aerial view of the shooting range. Little figures lie firing little guns at little targets. It looks almost like a game.

Scene: External view of Mercator IV Training Camp, domes and blocks picked out harshly against the black, star-spangled sky.

Commentary: 'It's the spirit of the Extraterran People. The spirit that took us to new lands on the Earth, the spirit that took us to new lands at Lagrangia and on the moon, the spirit that gave us our freedom from the Terran colonial powers. The spirit that will one day give us the stars.

'That spirit is alive and thriving in our young people. Called away from their homes and families, they do their duty. Fighting for the freedom we have won up here to be granted to those who want some of it down on Earth.

'When they return they will be changed people: they will have grown into their adulthood with the assurance of people who know they have done what is the good and proper thing.

'*Freedom—*' emotion-filled pause '*—is the prize.*'

Fade up Roblein's *Fighting Anthem.* Cut to receding view of the Moon. Pan to the black sky and then cut to black sky with Lejeune and its Grow-Coils at bottom left of view. Roll credits.

Extract from the diary of Jed Brindle.

9 AUGUST 2083

Time for an update. Jee, it's been a strange week. They've been recording a hee-vee documentary for the Lejeune News Group, so we've had to fit in around it all.

I haven't seen so many familiar faces in four months, now. I guess they had to move all the Lejeune recruits temporarily into F Division to make it easier for the hee-vee crew. The military must see it as good public relations, a bit of propaganda.

When I first arrived at the Merc I thought I'd never fit in, but I soon found my way around, got to know the system. Laid me down some roots. I've seen people change over the four months, or maybe it's just that they're finding their feet like I did. Lots of the guys have developed from a quiet start into the loud, mouthy, confident type that Sal called 'the typical glans-oriented soldier'. Hell, I always thought she was a bit hard on the guys, a bit hard on everybody. She thinks the whole world is out to get at her in any way it can.

I get on quite well with the other recruits. I'm not the loud social type and I guess they've come to respect that in me. Some of the guys lean on me – they're having a rough time and they think I can help. Hell, I don't do anything – how can I? – but they stay friends when they're through it.

Like I said: it's been one weird week. I've been seeing people I didn't even know were drafted. Like Alvie Coleridge and that dumb fucker Chan Wicksinghe (*Like, uh, you know how I'm putting it?*)

All these familiar faces. Jee, in my time here I've only glimpsed a few of the people I know from Lejeune. Yeah, there was Soriya. She was in F Division, she was even moved to my training squad when she started to do well. Then she bugged out. I guess she was just bottling up all the stress, or something like.

They really do put the pressure on in this place. I guess they're testing us and, at the same time, drilling us to cope with it all. Mock attacks on the Base, waking us up for fitness sessions and L-S testing in the middle of the night, giving us thirty-six-hour leave and then interrogating us for thirty-five of them. They treat us like shit sometimes. Yeah, I guess all that just got to Soriya and she flipped.

I checked it out shortly afterwards and the med-tech told me that it happens sometimes, but Soriya was the only one in months. It's not a permanent condition, they say, she'll come out of it.

Soriya makes me think of Stin. His is one face I haven't seen over the last week. I wonder how he's getting on. He'll make one Hell of a soldier. He's strong, he's bright, he's got the sort of confidence that seems to get people past the psyche tests and up the ranks like it's a game and they're holding the wild card. Yeah, if one of us is going to do well, I'd put my money on good old Stin.

I was sitting in the crew a few days ago, listening to the guy interviewing Chan and some of the others. I tried not to puke. The whole place had been cleaned up and there were MPs in the background, you know, just to make sure things went along nicely. The guys had been fed some ludicrous lines by the hee-vee people, *what a good life it is* and all that trash. Hell, don't get me wrong, I'm not saying it's *not* a good life. Just that it has its rough edges, it's not how they paint it on the hee-vee: all medals and videotech blood.

The reporter had a go at me later. Painted me as some kind of war hero. Bullshit. OK, I've won a few of the prizes for shooting and fitness, but I'm not how he painted me.

I had heard him feeding lines to the other guys he'd interviewed and I was determined not to let him do the same to me. But these journalists are slippery (sorry, Sal!). Somehow this guy managed to drag words out of me I didn't know were there. Like how I'm looking forward to fighting on Earth, how I'm ready for anything. Gonna shoot the ass of any Frag who crosses my path, and several that don't come anywhere near.

When the reporter had gone I felt somehow . . . Hell, I don't know. *Dirty* is the nearest word I can think of. Violated. Like this guy just came along and buggered my speech centres.

I don't know what they're going to think back home. Jed Brindle turned into some sort of maniac. Hell, he must have made me look like some kind of killer.

Well, I'm not.

*

Reshunting on that, I guess I might have been a little hard on the guy. Those words *did* come from me. He didn't feed me the lines. I guess there must be something in what I said. I'm no maniac and I don't want to fight (Hell, none of us do). But I'm ready. If I'm called on I'm going to do my duty. Fight the good fight, as some jerk said.

I just don't want the folks back on Lejeune to get the wrong idea of it all. Jed isn't a killing machine. They haven't drilled me *that* far.

Chapter Seven

20 June 2084

Amagat's scream tore right through me. It seemed to last for ever. Eventually I managed to find some sort of balance, lodged between the wall and the floor, both at forty-five degrees, and the struggling bodies of Cohen and Amagat. I couldn't seem to focus on anything, so I just closed my eyes and clung tightly to the two of them. After a time, Amagat stopped screaming and the three of us just lay there, awaiting death.

A long interval when all I heard was the pounding of my heart, the rough rasp of my breath. Then I heard the light patter of fingers on a console.

I opened my eyes and looked at the co-pilot, thinking he must have come around, fought off the gas somehow. I was wrong. He still hung limply from his harness of safety-belts and packing tape.

My mind. Playing savage tricks with my senses in my last few minutes – seconds? – of life. But the trick persisted, the tap-tap-tapping seemed to fill my head as if no other sound could possibly matter. I looked with disbelief at the pilot.

The sound was no trick, the pilot was feverishly working at his console. His face had changed, come to life again. The slackness had vanished and there was a fierce intensity to his actions. He had the headset down over his eyes, pressing against his mask. Off in the abstract world of retinal projection.

Then the floor began to level. Almost imperceptibly at first, then faster and faster. The pilot hit the last key and leaned back. He slid the set up over his head and threw it away over his shoulder, glanced down at me and looked away immediately. His lips moved and I decided that he was counting. I saw that the colour and life had drained from his face again, his job done.

He closed his eyes, still counting.

I closed mine again, as if we were responding to the same instruction. The floor had stopped levelling at only a few degrees from horizontal and I began to feel the tug of gees pulling me forward, increasing my weight on the bodies of Cohen and Amagat.

The plane was slowing, landing us somewhere.

Then there was a tremendous roaring, ripping sound. A jolt. A great upheaval in the laws of physics as my body seemed to be tugged and pulled in every possible direction.

Pain. Sharp, stabbing pain.

And a constant background of sound. Like an old nuke had gone off in the cockpit. A flash. Then I blacked out.

Came round with a cold tingling on my cheeks. A general, dull pain. Opened my eyes and the cockpit was a grey blur. Closed them again.

Opened them more slowly. The blur resolved itself into an image of the cockpit. The tingling on my cheeks. I lifted my hand to my face and realized the smoke mask had come away. The gas must have cleared.

The lights had gone but the door was open and I saw that there was daylight flooding in from beyond. A hole, somewhere in the corridor. I must have been out long enough for the gas to have escaped through the hole. A shallow blanket of smoke clung to the cockpit floor and there was a fine mizzle of water floating down.

Gradually, the layer of smoke dispersed, smothered by the water and drawn out by the hole in the corridor.

My senses began to find their way back into my body. The pain resolved itself into sharp focus in my lower back, my forearm. I noticed the metal taste of blood in my mouth, ran my tongue gingerly over a raw gap on my gum. Spat out a premolar in a spray of dark spittle. The senses of hearing and smell returned in a sudden crescendo of ringing and burnt-out electrics, but beyond the ringing was the most terrifying silence I have ever known.

I moved my arm and the pain didn't get any worse. Tugged at my leg, but it was trapped under the weight of bodies and my back twinged.

Then I heard a groan. Amagat. With her sound the whole scene seemed to come to life. Cohen grunted and moved, freeing my leg. Amagat groaned louder and tried to move, but she was trapped against the front wall and all she managed was to increase her own pain, judging by the yelp that her movement produced.

My leg free, I rolled over once. On to my side, completely free from the entanglement of Cohen and Amagat. The movement produced a loud click in my spine and the pain vanished with one final flare.

I raised myself to my knees, stood up slowly. Looked around again. The air had cleared and the desmoker mist cut out, but still the cabin was bathed in an eerie half-light. The floor was cold and damp, but the cockpit itself was full of a horribly tight heat. The floor was beginning to steam. The co-pilot was still slumped in his seat, as if he had somehow slept through the crash. Next to him, the pilot was also limp, but still conscious. His eyes stared ahead of him and I noticed the streak of a tear on the one cheek I could see.

There was movement down on the floor, to one

side of the co-pilot's seat. The space I had just rolled out of.

A figure stretched out its arms and almost in slow motion dragged itself towards me, settled on its knees, looked at me. Cohen, his mask still on his head but knocked askew in the crash. 'You OK?' I said. 'Can you move all right?'

The set of his head changed slightly, maybe some new expression came on to his face, but I couldn't tell in the half-light of the cockpit. He paused before answering. 'No breaks,' he said. 'Haven't found any bleeding. Aches and pains is all.' He stretched and rose to his feet.

I glanced down at Amagat. Her first try at movement had been enough for her and she was still. I stepped past Cohen, crouched. It took a couple of minutes to check her for any obvious breakages, the dampness of blood. She groaned while I examined her. Her face felt sticky and hot, but there was no other damage. I looked over my shoulder at Cohen. 'Will you help me with Amagat?' I said. 'I wanna get her outside, she's hurt.' I cast around for my mask and put it on. There might still be gas back there. Then I hitched my hands into the sub's armpits and pulled gently. Cohen waited until I was past him, put his mask straight on his face. Then, without a word, he lifted the sub's feet.

I backed out into the corridor and Cohen followed.

It was bright out there. After the dusky cockpit it felt like my eyes were being slowly burnt out. I had to squint and hope I would get used to the glare.

Amagat's face was a terrible sight. Her left cheek was a deep, angry red, her nose was charred and the nostril on that side was burnt away completely. Her left eye was swollen and closed, the lid blackened, like much of the rest of her face. The hair on the left side of her head was partly burned away, the scalp a violent red, darkening to the black stub of her ear. Clumsily, she raised a hand to her face. 'Dark,' she said, her voice little more than a whisper.

I exchanged a worried glance with Cohen. 'She's flash-blind,' he said. Then, to Amagat: 'It'll get better. Just needs some time.'

After several shuffling, backward steps, I came to the opening in the wall. Not a hole, as I had thought, but an emergency exit, as the notice above it told us. Of course. My mind-plan of the aeroplane flashed in my memory. I had completely forgotten about it.

I hesitated in mid-stride. Realized that there was much that had been an automatic part of my memory that I now had to struggle to recall.

I decided it was the shock.

I moved back a few more paces and stopped, put Amagat gently down on the floor. As we moved her she had stopped groaning and lost consciousness altogether. I stepped around her, glanced back at Gil's body, still in the corridor, and then looked out of the exit.

As I stood in the opening I was hit simultaneously by an intense, dry heat and a view of a wide, bright landscape. I slid the mask to the top of my head and the hot air stung my nose; I tried to control my breathing to limit the discomfort. The landscape was wide. That's the only word to describe it. Wide. Surface, horizon, sky; that was all there was.

The surface was a dry, cracked, stony soil. It seemed to extend for thousands of kay-ems into the distance, its flatness only broken by the occasional cowboy-film cactus, standing ghostly and alone. The wide, flat horizon was broken only by a shimmering heat haze. And the deep-blue sky hung over it all, the sun picking out any deviation in the uniformity of the scene and cutting a sharp black shadow around it. Underlining any flaws in the flatness of it all.

In all my months on Earth, I had never seen anything so *big.* Its openness scared me more than a little.

Cohen misinterpreted my hesitation. 'It's OK,' he said. 'She won't get hurt going down the tube.'

I looked at him, confused. Then I looked more closely at the exit. The plane had dug itself into the ground on impact but we were still about four metres from the ground. A flimsy-looking flattened tube of some gauzy material trailed from the bottom of the exit to the ground. I looked back at Cohen, still confused.

'Never seen one of these things before?' he asked.

I shook my head, tried to hide my unease.

'OK,' he said. 'I'll go first. With the girl. You'll see how it's done and follow.'

Dumbly I accepted the course of action. Hell, I guess I would have gone along with anything right then. I just needed the decisions taken out of my hands while I gathered myself together.

Cohen thew his mask out of the door as if he was glad to be rid of it. Then he dragged Amagat over to the exit and positioned her with her legs dangling into the flimsy tube. He lowered her slowly and then slid down and held her in an intimate embrace, keeping a firm grip on the edge of the exit. When he was satisfied with the position, he nodded and let go. Slowly they began to slide downwards, the tube stretching open for them, limiting the speed of their descent. Cohen was using his embrace on Amagat to keep the gauze from rubbing at her damaged face. He spread his legs in the tube and slowed their descent at the bottom.

When Cohen had wriggled himself and Amagat free of the tube I followed them down. It was a painfully nostalgic experience for its few seconds of existence. It was as if I had suddenly defied gravity, the slowing tug of the material at my feet giving the impression of a very low gee. Like I was back in the colonies. And the soft, delicate material flowing past my face was just the downy softness childhood memories are stored in. No pain, no tears, just happy memories and that beautiful softness of infancy.

Then I hit the ground. I hadn't slowed myself as I had seen Cohen do, but the landing was still quite soft. I drew myself free of the tube and looked around. I was crouching on the hard, hot ground, just clear of the great furrow of debris the plane had thrown up in its dive into the ground. The sun was burning down on to my head. It had to be a CalTex sun, assaulting me so furiously.

Cohen sat nearby, Amagat's head on his lap. 'We'll have to get her into the shade,' he said. 'Then see to her face.'

I stood silently, lifted Amagat from the ground and walked the twenty metres or so to the shade cast by the plane's mighty wing. I lowered her gently and slid the mask free of my head, stood stupidly with it dangling from my hand. Another memory of my distant military existence sprang into my mind: Don't stop for the wounded. Army statistics dictate that it is more beneficial to save your own skin than to risk it with the injured; saves on med-tech fees, too. It's far more efficient to save your own ass.

That was one piece of Army philosophy I was happy to put aside. In Army terms I was the only surviving soldier from the crash; I should get out with Cohen, find my way to Grand Union.

My head still felt muddled and for a moment I couldn't call up the GPS to check our position. If we were in Grand Union we were OK, but deep inside me I knew it could never be that easy; a vague GPS reading seemed to confirm that feeling. I chipped up, tried to clear my head. If we were in CalTex territory we had to move out, try somehow to escape. That might not be much of a hope but if we waited to be found I didn't much fancy our prospects, either.

To leave Amagat or Leo would be a death sentence. To take them with us would be a military crime, but I now recognized it as a human necessity.

'I'm going back,' I said to Cohen and marched back to the tube.

Sure, it was easy to get out of the plane, but how to get back in? I stopped and thought about the problem. I pulled my smoke mask back on to my head while I wondered what to do. Flattened out, the tube was about a metre across. I gathered it up in my arms and found a good grip. Leaned back against it.

And fell right over. The tube had just stretched with my weight and allowed me to fall gently to the ground. I stood again, brushed myself off. Then I gathered the tube up and pulled at it. Moved my hands up and pulled again. Eventually I met with some resistance. The next time I pulled, my feet lifted momentarily. I pulled again, then I bounced and climbed my way up and swung into the exit.

I sat facing the wideness of the world for a moment, then I stood and turned, walked down the corridor, past Gil, to the passenger area. There were bodies everywhere and the sight shook me right through to the marrow. Before I even reached the corner, the doorway, I saw the first signs. There was a hand trailing into the corridor. A slim mid-brown hand, maybe Asian. Painted red nails, a single plain ring. I approached and through the doorway saw a heap of bodies. Passengers from the first few rows had been thrown out of their seats by the crash.

They hadn't been able to put their safety-belts on.

I stepped over the young Asian and stood in a small gap, under NO FURTHER ADMITTANCE. Many of the passengers were heaped in the space just forward of the front row. The angles of the limbs and the bodies revealed death and injury more clearly than any statistics. Splashes of blood were daubed on to the scene for emphasis. I looked down the plane.

Passengers further back had been stopped in their flight by the seats. Some lay bent over the seat-backs, ass-high and hopeless. Others were just the occasional arm or leg, sticking out at improbable angles. The remaining bodies were scattered in heaps along the aisle. Neon EMERGENCY EXIT signs blinked over hatches that had failed to open, but the passengers didn't seem to notice.

I looked down at the face of the Asian girl at my feet. Only eighteen or nineteen. Why did the gas have to give them all such contented expressions? I felt for the scar-line on my jaw. Followed its course.

'Aren't you going to get me out of here?'

I looked up sharply. 'Huh?'

Then I looked along the rows of seats, found Jacobi. The shock of the bodies had taken him right out of my head. He had been unconscious in an empty seat before the crash. Somehow he must have come round, realized what was happening. Belted himself in.

And here he was, still belted into his seat. As I climbed over the bodies to get to him I saw that he was trapped under the limp form of an ageing businessman. Only his head was clear.

'How's the leg?' I asked, not quite sure what to say. Back with Leo, the soldier in me wanted to take over again. I decided I was still in shock.

' "How's the leg?" he asks!' Jacobi looked to the heavens. 'The plane crashes, I get bombarded with flying bodies, I'm sitting here with one of them half-crushing me to death, and that's all you can ask.' He took a calming breath. 'It was only a flesh-wound, nothing to 'Gram home about. Right now, all I can feel from my neck down is this great fucking weight of a boonie spread all over me. Will you get him off? And this fucking safety-belt, too.'

I pulled at the body, then put a bit more back into it and the man came clear. I noticed that he was only unconscious, no obvious damage from the crash. Maybe that was the case with most of the bodies that filled the aeroplane.

'Jesus,' said Jacobi, tugging at his safety-belt, 'I can feel things below my neck. Mostly pins and needles and pure agony, but at least I can *feel* it.' He looked up at me and grinned. 'What's been happening, Jed? Must have been one wild party.'

'Wild,' I said, looking round at the heaps of bodies spread over the seats and floor. One woman's spine was broken at right angles over the back of a seat. She still had that dumb panhalothol smile on her face. 'Crash-landed in the desert,' I said. 'Nearly nose first, but the pilot changed his mind at the last minute. Cohen's alive. So's Amagat, but she might regret it. We're getting out. You OK to travel?'

A look of horror passed over Jacobi's face. 'Hey, *sure* I'm OK to travel,' he said. 'I'm no battle injury. I've been chipping since I was hit, the leg's healing fine.'

'Hey, cool it,' I said. 'No question of leaving you, none of that shit stands out here. We're just gonna get the Hell out. You get me?' He got me, but I don't think he believed me about not planning on dumping him there if he was wounded. I guess the training must go pretty deep.

I leaned forward to help him to his feet but he did it

by himself. Had to prove his fitness. Even with his chip, he wouldn't be able to heal as quickly as he claimed and he limped badly as we climbed back over the bodies to the corridor. He *had* stemmed the bleeding though.

Leo stopped by the emergency exit and looked out. The seriousness of our situation swept over his face and he stood quietly. *Sure, we're gonna walk outta here*, he had thought; but the sight of all that distance made it clear that we were taking the least bad option, not the best.

'Gonna be one long walk,' he said, staring past me at the dead form of Gil. 'Jeez. You gotta plan?'

'No plan,' I said. 'Just get Cohen out to Grand Union, somehow. The first thing is to get away from this plane. We're dead if we're found here.' I crouched down by the escape tube and pulled it open. 'Down through here,' I said. 'And watch your leg, you're going to be walking on that.'

Jacobi stepped over and wriggled halfway into the tube. 'The leg's fine,' he muttered. Then he gave himself to the tube. Seconds later, there was a pained yell as he hit the ground. I grinned sadly as I headed for the cockpit.

The door was half-open and I pushed it as I entered. The pilot and his partner were still in their chairs, the light still a sad half-light. At the front, where the three of us had been sprawled during the crash, I saw a blackened panel in the wall. Burnt-out electrics. Amagat's head had been right over that black panel. That was where her burns had come from.

I squatted and scanned the floor, saw what I was looking for.

I stepped forward and picked up my zap. It had been ripped from its socket during the crash-landing. I winced as I jacked it back into my median; there must have been some damage there. I hoped it still worked. I left it shunted, despite the pain. I guess it made me feel more comfortable.

'Come back to finish us off?'

I looked across at the pilot, still wearing his smoke mask. Beneath it his face looked a deathly grey in the light of the cockpit, his eyes shone despair from the depths of his being. 'No,' I said simply.

I found my shoulder bag. Yes, there were still some pan-H capsules in there. 'Why did you pull out of the dive?' I asked.

Life burst into his face. 'I didn't do it for you alien shit,' he said and spat on the floor. Then he subsided again. 'I went into the dive to beat you,' he said. 'I wasn't going to end up in a stinking Union jail. But then . . . then I remembered that I wasn't alone. There was Rob—' he nodded at his co-pilot '—and there were the passengers. So I pulled up, landed here. I couldn't kill the passengers.'

I saw the image of over a hundred passengers in tangled heaps, limbs at strange angles. It still hadn't dawned on the pilot that none of them could have belted themselves in for the landing. Maybe he hadn't been clear about the gas, but no, they still hadn't been given any warning. Maybe his mind was blocking out some of the dreadful truth.

'Are the passengers all right?' he asked.

'Yeah, they're fine,' I said, the vision of one of them snapped backwards over the back of a seat. 'You did the best thing.'

'What are you going to do to us?'

'Nothing,' I said. 'Just going to leave you be.' Our eyes met and there was a flash of understanding between us. We had been sparring since the hijack, but there had been no outright winner. *Scores level*, that flash told me. End of contest.

'Where have you put us?' I asked.

'Oh-three-seventy: ten-twenty-four,' he said, the truce still in his eyes. That look told me he was telling the truth, but also it rang true with the figures I had seen in the headset and the confused messages from the Global Positioning Satellites. 'Middle of the Dust Bowl,' he said. 'You'll never walk out of here.'

'No choice,' I said. 'I don't want to end up in some stinking CalTex jail.' I grinned and there was a momentary response on the pilot's lips.

I had been fidgeting with the panhalothol capsule in my hand. I stepped forward. 'Just one thing I've got to do,' I said and put my hand out to the pilot's jacket.

He looked up at me. 'You gonna kill me now?' he said.

I shook my head and slipped the capsule into his breast pocket. Eased the mask from his head. 'Just have to make sure nobody knows about us until we're clear,' I said.

He nodded slightly and I crushed the shell of the capsule. Panhalothol reached his nose a few seconds later, his brain a few seconds after that. His head slumped to one side. I picked up my bag and left the cockpit.

I paused at the galley and looked out through the emergency exit in the opposite wall. I could just see Jacobi and Cohen in the shade of the wing. Amagat was out of sight on the ground.

I turned to the galley.

The heap of stewardesses had been shifted from one side of the room to the front, thrown forward by the crash. There was a splash of blood on the front wall. Trying to ignore the bodies, I looked around. Yes, it was how I remembered. Under one of the shelves there was a large trolley, used for wheeling refreshments around in the plane.

I pulled it out, dumped my bag on it. Then I went through the cupboards, found some plastic bags, two more shoulder bags. Other cupboards held large plastic containers of fruit juice; these fitted well into the shoulder bags. I ignored food in favour of as much drink as I could fit in. Seven days at most, I had decided, so starvation would be no problem. The only non-drink item I put in was a small medical kit that I found in a drawer.

With the filled bags sitting on the trolley, I looked around again. I picked out packets of food that were low in protein – I didn't want to go increasing our water needs unnecessarily. Finally I topped up the trolley with a second medical kit and as many more cartons of drink as would fit.

When I got the trolley to the exit I had to work out how to get everything to the ground. I decided to just drop a bag into the tube and see what happened. It seemed OK, then the problem was solved when Jacobi limped over to catch things as they fell.

I pulled my mask off and sat there, my legs dangling, for a moment or two more. Watched Jacobi take the supplies over to Cohen and Amagat. I closed my eyes and called up a digital map of the Northern American continent. Zoomed up the Mid-West. 0370:1024. Near the point where the old states of Oklahoma, Kansas and Colorado joined their borders.

In the middle of the Dust Bowl Desert.

I zoomed up some more, fixed a few details and then opened my eyes again. Somehow the artificial colours and multi-dimensional projections of the mind-map didn't ring true against the real thing. All that open space. But the heat of the sun, burning down on my head, rang with the truth of the Desert. The flaky dryness of the air, too.

My isothermal suit was keeping my body cool. Storing

the heat in its fibres, radiating the rest in a random pattern. I came to a difficult but necessary decision. Climbed to my feet.

I stepped over and crouched by Gil. Loosened the fasteners at the neck of his suit. Tugged at the material and eventually it stretched and lost Gil's shape at the top. I peeled it away from him and rolled it down over his shoulders, clear of his arms. Over that terrible hole in his chest; so small, yet he had lost such a lot of blood through it.

Down over his hips and legs and clear of his sneakered feet. The body-suit felt comically light in my hands. It was hard to believe that this flimsy piece of cloth could be such a vital part of a soldier's equipment.

I looked down at Gil's nearly naked body. Such a waste. I went into the galley and fetched a blanket from a cupboard. Went back out and covered Gil. Back in the galley, I put the body-suit in a basin of water – I didn't want the blood showing for the entire journey. I wrung it out and most of the crimson stain had gone. The light material would dry quickly under the desert sun.

On impulse I headed back to the passenger area, before leaving the plane. I picked up a wide-brimmed straw hat, found a floppy cap nearby. Then I spotted two cowboy hats on a young couple and took them.

I left the plane for what I expected to be the last time. Outside again, the signal from the GPS grid rang clear through my head, confirming our location. Everything seemed clearer by then.

We sat for a while in the shade of the plane's wing, fighting off the time when we would have to set out. Gil's uniform was drying quickly in the heat of the sun. Amagat lay still, the damage to her face making it impossible to tell if she was conscious or not.

'Eat all you can now,' I said. 'We're only taking drinks with us.'

'Where are you going to take us?' asked Cohen.

I put down my biscuit. 'We're in the Dust Bowl Desert,' I said. Cohen's face dropped. 'Officially CalTex. Unofficially a no man's land that nobody wants. Nearest Union base is at Askar Rock, one-twenty kay-ems due north. That-a-way,' I said, pointing slightly to the right of the line the plane had been following. I didn't mention that there was a Cal base close to the Union camp at Askar; Jacobi and Amagat could read their own maps if they wanted. Only one kay-em apart, the two bases would make the last part of the journey the most risky.

Cohen was still looking at me, maybe in disbelief. 'We walk,' I said.

His face snapped into acceptance and he drank greedily from a carton of pineapple juice. Cohen's response to adversity had impressed me ever since the crash. He had seen his bodyguard shot, found himself the target of kidnapping, been through a crash-landing on the floor of the pilot's cabin. Yet he responded to it all with tremendous practicality. *Right, this is gonna happen*, he seemed to think. *Now how am I gonna make the best of it?* I'd like to think some of this attitude rubbed off on me over the next few days, helped me get through it.

When we had eaten our fill Cohen took Gil's isothermals around the plane and reappeared a few minutes later, wearing them. He would need them in the desert. Then we turned to Amagat.

I put my hand on her shoulder. 'How are you feeling, sir?' I said. She moved but didn't answer. 'We're just going to clean up your injuries. OK?'

She rolled over on to her side, her back to us, and said something I couldn't make out.

'What was that?' I asked, moving around so I could see her more clearly.

'Go,' she said. The left side of her mouth was burnt and it made speech difficult. 'Leave me.'

'Why should we leave you?' I said. But I knew why: the rule. Let the injured look after themselves; don't put yourself or the mission at risk.

All she managed to say was another muffled 'Go'.

'Amagat,' I said, angry at her and angry at the Army that had made her what she was. 'I'm going to tidy up your burns and then I'm going to carry you if you're not going to walk. You get that? You're dead meat if the Callies get you.'

I moved over to her and she made as if to roll away again, but she didn't have much fight left in her and she stayed where she was.

It was then that I looked at the medical kit and realized that I didn't know how to use it. There were no creams or sealing gels, no dermal pastes or infusers. I looked helplessly at Cohen. He took the box and I watched as he conjured up a dressing that looked primitive but proper in our present surroundings.

He looked at me, said, 'The dressing's non-stick. It'll promote the healing.'

'Right,' I said to Amagat. 'You hear that? Now are you going to walk or am I going to drag you?'

She said nothing and I chipped down on a burst of anger. *Go,* she Comtacked.

'Come *on*, Amagat. You're putting us all at risk out here.'

'Then go!' she croaked. 'That's an order. I'm no good. I'm gonna . . . gonna *die* out here. Just go.'

'Face burns,' I said, in a tightly controlled voice, 'are not terminal. The only way you are going to die is if you sit here and wait to be shot. You hear? Sure, it's going to hurt, but you can chip it better. Leo was shot only an hour ago, yet he's chipped away the bleeding and he can walk now.' Chip-induced healing was one of the basic techniques. 'You're coming with us,' I told her.

She tilted her bandaged face up at me. 'No,' she said.

I stood and went back to the exit tube. I shinned up it easily this time. The drinks trolley was in the corridor where I had left it. It fitted comfortably into the tube, slid down and landed with a light crunch on the ground. I shook it free before following it down.

Amagat was still lying on her side. I checked her legs again, then the rest of her body to be sure. She should be perfectly capable of walking. She just needed the will to do it. I picked my shoulder bag up off the ground and put it on one end of the trolley.

'Right,' I said. 'I'm going to carry you.'

Before she could protest, I bent down and picked her up. Half a turn and I put her down again on the trolley, her head roughly cushioned by my bag. The trolley was too short and her legs hung over the front, but I didn't expect to need it for long. I stepped behind and pushed.

It didn't want to move so I pushed again, harder. It went with a judder, stuck on a stone then moved a bit more. The trolley's tiny wheels weren't designed for outdoor use, even on this baked-hard soil. Every tiny flaw in the surface sent a violent tremor through the trolley to Amagat. The roughness of the ride got worse the faster the trolley went.

'Come on,' I yelled to the bemused figures of Cohen and Jacobi. 'And grab the bags.' I gave a wild yell and pushed the trolley as fast as it would go over the rough surface.

Chapter Eight

Transcript of 20th Day Report, Sublieutenant Thom Sorakin, 28 September 2083.

Report format: 1) Training, 2) Socio-functioning, 3) Personal Assessment, 4) Conclusions.

1) Training. Shaping up well, perhaps the finest squad I've worked with. I expect a high Achievement Ratio over the coming months.

First, the mundane aspects. Weapons, tactics, basic fitness, communications, first aid. All acceptable, if not first class (have to watch Lohmann on the fitness). They're adapting well to the gravity, although Lohmann needs pushing. We're quartered on the Ground level of the Disc – one gee is higher than any of them have lived at before. Brindle is the strongest and it seems almost as if he's been at Earth-gee all his life. We're all finding it tough on the high-gee manoeuvres, but even as early as this I can see it starting to pull together.

As usual, it has been the manoeuvres that have pinpointed the various aspects of group functioning.

Our first real action was the first TV-Ret (Target eValuation and RETrieval). The Training General pulled a nasty on us and set the TV-Ret down below Ground level. I'd guess it was near two gees. It was a standard fifty square kay-em manoeuvre patch, twenty-five competing four-troop squads set to track and retrieve ten targets. It was dark and misty. Jacobi, being the experienced trooper, took point with the task-map shunted into his suboxy.

The squad clicked from the start. We'd been through a lot of the basics in our three days together, before this first TV-Ret, but when it comes to manoeuvres a new squad usually makes lots of mistakes. These boys didn't need any reminding about the usuals like noise discipline, coordinated surveillance, formations. Towards the end Lohmann started to have trouble with the gees we were pulling but Brindle helped him through it. Brindle is a good man to have as corporal (see *Personal Assessment*).

Contact with other squads occurred on three occasions; we went to ground and none of them detected us, even as they blundered noisily through the undergrowth. We found our targets, avoided the booby traps and registered our presence at every target in a total of less than two hours. Twenty-seven and a half minutes ahead of the nearest opposition.

There have been six major manoeuvres since then, three of them combat. I won't say much about them (except for the following report on Combat 3, as specified in Report Instruction 38/D20). The only relevant point, I think, is that we have consistently gained Top Three places in the major tactical and combat manoeuvres, winning on four occasions.

Combat 3, 26 and 27 of September 2083. With no prior warning we were roused from the squad dorm by three bursts of the squealer, the signal for something big. Barely into our clothes, we were called over to the prep block for drilling.

The prep for this one was thorough, bigger than any the squad has been through before. In retrospect, with the post-hypnotic instructions wiped, I can look back on what went on, but during the ensuing thirty hours we thought it was the real thing. They shunted the hypno-programmers into our suboccipitals and downloaded enough prompts, suggestions and commands to make the simulation real for us.

Dumped in stupors in a drone personnel cart, we were taken down a level or two by elevator and dropped in our starting positions. About fifteen per cent over a gee, I'd put it at.

We woke up in the biggest training patch I've seen (we never found the edges and I don't remember seeing the ceiling) and we *knew* that we were on Earth, routing guerilla units somewhere in the Grand Union. It was dark and cold and there was a feeling of dampness in the air. Strange sounds of birds and animals appeared to come from all around us. Even now, I'm not clear on how much of it was genuine (or at least outside of my head) and how much was a hypnotic construct, framed by my chip.

We took up loose formation, intimate enough for Comtac. Brindle took point and we moved out. In retrospect it was a fairly standard TV-Ret, with other squads as the targets. But it was given a new dimension by the clarity of the simulation. (Note: This *must* be the direction for training in the future.)

Hearing sounds (bad noise discipline), we fanned out for a near-surround assault, using Comtac for co-ordination. Closing in, I heard the enemy discussing tactics, of all things – it's too late for that, when you're out there fighting, for Chrissake.

Night-shades in place, I found a good route and crawled closer. A slight clearing, ten metres by twenty, trees on three sides and a thick tangle of some vicious-looking thorn bush on the far side. Two of the guerrillas were on look-out and the two seniors stood at the centre of the clearing debating what they should do. Four targets; my chip picked mine and highlighted him in my night-shades.

It couldn't have been a better set-up: the one angle we weren't approaching from was cut off by the undergrowth. *Move to viewpoint*, I Comtacked my squad. A few slow breaths and the acknowledgements came in. No sign of detection. We were ready.

Then I Comtacked the command, *Fire*, waited a split second so that I wouldn't be ahead of the others' reactions. And fired at what I guessed was the second-in-command of the guerrillas.

The fire was silent – PT11 laser rifles, for night work – and the enemy squad dropped like they'd been gassed or bioed.

Of course, now I know what really happened. The PT11s were training weapons, low power. Just enough burn to register on sensors painted on to our uniforms. The hit was then relayed to a sublink of the Training General, which commanded the victim – via his or her suboccipital – to lapse into a hypnotic semi-coma. Sleep-a-byes until end of manoeuvre.

Four comatose soldiers, looking to us like four very dead CalTex guerrillas, lay in the clearing.

We moved on.

We knocked out six 'enemy' squads over the thirty hours of the manoeuvre. I'm not going to detail each hit.

I will, however, have a quick look at one or two aspects that I find important, things that I've noticed as a result of Combat 3.

The first point is how the squad reacted to the long hours and stressful nature of the manoeuvre. Towards the end we were all suffering from fatigue and overstimulation. (I was pleased to note that Lohmann coped as well as any of us on this exercise; I think the group spirit is pulling him along.)

Our last hit was an assault on two fighting groups. We heard the commotion, acted on the situation and went in hard, wiping out what was left of both squads. We all went on overdrive, so tired that we weren't really conscious of what was happening, we carried on like machines. It didn't appear to affect our performance at all, we just went through the motions and knocked out the enemy troops. I guess that's what happens anyway, to exhausted troops, but the fact that our performance remained so high must be down to the chip, feeding us with the moves, keeping us going.

After all, the present version of the chip is new to other than specialist use, so we keep learning new uses for it all the time. I know interfaces have been around for most of this century, but the actual chip itself – the availability of *built-in* cybernetic control – is an entirely modern military development.

The expansion of C-cubed is a great advantage of the system: Command, Communications and Control. And the improved man-machine interface coordination. But there are other uses that I find just as worthwhile.

I guess it's the simple things that appeal to me. Like the mechanization of hypnosis, the manipulation of Comtac (that has sure paid off in the manoeuvres), the control of the juices.

The Advance Warning system is one little gadget that I was initially sceptical about, but I was rapidly converted in practice. My understanding of it is that the body can detect danger before it is consciously recognized. I suppose the delay is to avoid false alarms. The stomach contracts, muscles tense, adrenalin is pumped. With our chips spotting these changes we found that our detection of the enemy was exceptional. Faint sounds, sounds muffled by wind, movement in the periphery of vision. There were very few false alarms.

Another major use is endocrinal and nervous control. *Chipping Juice*, as the soldiers have taken to calling it, is the conscious pumping of adrenalin. A troop on the edge is often better than an over-relaxed one. And there's that dangerous moment, perhaps the most dangerous of all, when you've just had some action. You get a few seconds of almost religious calm, like you've just fucked the Virgin Mary, as Jacobi put it. Even when you know there's more danger, if you've just removed one source of risk you get this high. And then you might be shot. A kick of adrenalin keeps you on the edge right through a piece of action, takes away some of the danger.

Sometimes excitement can be a problem. Say an ambush, where you might find yourself sitting in the same position in some desolate jungle for hours on end. *Chipping down*, as they call it, cuts the juice, slows the heart, stills the mind.

Yeah, the new interface approach is a very productive one.

2) Socio-functioning. Right from the start, only twenty days ago, we clicked as a squad. I waited for them at Transport Bay 6, at the narrow end of the Disc. The troops were sorted into squads as they left the ship and eventually I picked out my little threesome. Even though they'd all come from Mercator IV, they'd never met before. Considering the numbers, I suppose that must be how it usually works out.

Lohmann was full of himself. 'Gonna have a wild time,' I heard him say before he laid eyes on me and stopped his jaw. Brindle was looking around, like he was sizing up his new situation, seeing what was there. Jacobi hung slightly apart, sizing up his companions. ''Bout as wild as we can make it,' he said. 'And I've been making it for years.'

Like I said, something sprang up between us right from the start. We drew sparks off each other. Of course it's standard procedure to promote the bond with your squad, but we didn't need any of that.

I took them on a buggy along to our dorm and then we went to the crew room. We dropped a few drinks and worked our jaws. I told Jacobi I was from New London and he said, 'What sort of a place is that? Some mining rig?' I told him it was near Plato on the Moon and from that moment the squad took to calling me 'Plato'. 'Plato, *sir*,' in Jacobi's case.

As the squad has settled in they've made new friends, but that's secondary. Their primary social group is still the squad. We do most things together when we're off duty. I'd say that's the main reason for our early successes as a squad.

There *have* been differences, of course. Jacobi has rubbed up Lohmann the wrong way once or twice, particularly in the early days. Jacobi can be a little abrasive at times, sometimes he seems to enjoy kicking at people's soft spots. (Of course, we've mostly gotten that out of him, by now.)

And Lohmann's young and easily stirred.

Nothing ever came of it. Brindle has a calming influence – that boy is so *laid back*, it's unbelievable.

Then I found them one time, moments away from each other's throats. This was only the fifth day. 'OK, guys,' I said. 'We're going to have this thing out in the open. *What the fuck is eating at you?*'

They didn't know. When they sat down and thought they just couldn't put a label on it. And there's been no trouble since then. I guess if they ever come near to blows they just remember that they can't think of any reason and it all calms down.

Competition with the other squads pulls us together

too. Especially as how we usually win. With the Army's carrot and stick idea of training we're getting a whole lot more carrot than stick, right now.

And in my objective evaluation, that is sure how it's going to stay.

The boys are recognized wherever they go. *Hey, that's Plato's squad*, people say. *Don't cross 'em.*

We tend to work to a system, wherever it fits the circumstances. Like when we're on a TV-Ret we have an ultimate goal, but we break the task down. With a series of smaller goals we get more instant feedback on how things are going.

Like writing this report. Shunting the report-formatted data bubble, I didn't know how I'd get through it all. Then I decided to break it down into sections by the subjects I have to report on and somehow three short reports and a conclusion seem a much less formidable task.

It's not just military situations, either. We're one of the top slap teams this side of the Disc. Whenever we go to the zero-gee slap chamber we go in there with a system.

Goal: gain possession. *Goal*: gain territory, control as much volume as possible. *Goal*: get the ball to the man and hit the highest target possible. Of course the system isn't everything, but it gives us an edge.

Jacobi has a tendency to mould the rules to his own belief system. Others call it cheating. Like he makes less than momentary contact with the ball and maybe he likes to get a little physical. But he's a good man to have on the team, good for the high targets and the big defences. Lohmann is excitable but agile and very experienced in zero-gee. I tend to plug the holes, smooth things over. And who but solid-as-a-rock Brindle could make all the plays, squeeze up the pressure?

We're a good squad.

And we're going to get a whole lot better. I think this training period is going to be too long for us, we'll be ready long before any of the other squads.

I'd like to think that if we weren't thrown together by circumstance we would still be good friends, and I think that's true.

3) Personal Assessment. I'll start from the bottom and work my way up.

Private Gilbert Lohmann. Gil's the youngest member of the squad and I suppose that might account for some of his excitability. I'm working with him on his chipping technique and we seem to be getting somewhere. If he can just chip down on some of his excitement we could iron out that source of weakness.

Physically, Gil had problems at first. He's got himself a good, strong-looking body and the only explanation for his problems could have been a mental one. Now that he's settled into the squad, he has adjusted well.

Gil is a good prompt to the squad. Whenever there's a lack of enthusiasm it's Gil that makes up for it and fires the others up. He's a real optimist, just wants to get on with every day that happens to him.

Problems that may develop? He has a girl back on Seneca and she's just had a baby. But he was aware of the situation when he acknowledged. That would have been a legitimate reason for missing the draft but he has too much of the soldier in him to duck out. He'll see his child at the end of next year, after his spell on Earth. The girl will understand.

Sometimes there seems to be something vacant in his eyes, like he's not really here. I think he might be doing some drugs, but it can only be light. We're with him too much of the time for us not to notice the effects of anything harder.

I'm turning a blind eye at the moment; it might make being away from his girl a little easier on him. We'll see how it goes.

Private Leotan Jacobi. One hundred per cent soldier. The oldest and longest-serving squad member. He saw some action back in the early seventies when we snuffed the Manila-backed infiltration at L4. But despite his experience, he's not cut out to climb the ranks. He's an excellent private and he seems quite happy to stay that way.

Sometimes he reminds me of a hyena on one of those old nature films they show. The lion sits guarding its meal and then suddenly a hyena dashes in and runs off with a mouthful. Jacobi hangs back from the action and then when he sees an opportunity he darts in and makes a grab for something. He's always the guy who makes the most cutting remark, twists the knife just that little bit further. But you have to admire the style that he does it with. A sharper wit there has never been; he always has the right phrase for a situation.

He has a cruel humour and he likes to goad people, lead them out into the open on some things that maybe they'd rather leave unsaid. But his wit has a diffusing effect. Put him in a tense situation and he'll say something that breaks the moment, gives you a new perspective. He's sharp.

Very popular. A hardened soldier, he has no problems with the military side of things, physical or psychological.

Corporal Jedburgh Brindle. There's hardly much that needs saying about Jed. The star pupil from Mercator IV and I can easily see why. Physically there are no problems at all.

Technically, he has the greatest command over his chip that I have seen in a new recruit. Tremendous self-control.

Socially, he is the ideal foil for Lohmann and Jacobi. Any friction that remains between those two is greased by the influence of Brindle. He gives the impression of slowness, but that's just how he appears. He is thorough, learns things and then never forgets them. He can be summed up in one word: *solid.*

People seem to be drawn to him, like he has a sort of magnetism. He could win anyone over if he wanted to try. He's a solid source of support for anyone who needs him, he just seems to soak up everybody else's problems and leave them clean and fresh. Anyone else would break under all that pressure, but Jed just sops it up.

Ironically, it's his attitude that I think might be his number one weakness. He's just so *nice.* Easy-going. When we're on exercises he does begin to show something of a cutting edge. But it needs sharpening. When it comes to action he's going to have to *kill* people, not listen to their problems. We need to give him something more of a killing edge, put some fire on his breath.

4) Conclusions. Early success isn't always a sign of things to come, but if that is the case with my new squad, I can only think that the reason is that things are going to get *better.* No major weakness, several major strengths. Just wait and see which squad is way ahead of the opposition at the end of the three months on the Disc. We're going to wipe the floor with them.

Chapter Nine

20 June to 3 July 2084

'Stop! Stop it!' Amagat's screams pierced the still heat of the afternoon. 'Will you just stop it?'

I slowed to a halt. The trolley gave a final lurch and then stopped. 'You walk or you ride,' I said. 'Which is it to be?'

No words, but Amagat stepped away from the trolley and walked a few paces; that was a good enough answer for me. She stopped and turned around, a surreal sight in these surroundings. From the neck down she was the epitome of the sublieutenant that she was. But the lower half of her head was black and red and swollen and the top half was wrapped in a crisp white bandage. It just didn't fit with the baked desert around her.

'Leo,' I said. 'Will you look after the sub?'

Jacobi caught up with us and stopped by Amagat. 'Sure,' he said. 'You forgot this.' He threw me one of the cowboy hats. He was wearing the straw hat and he placed the big floppy cap on Amagat's bandaged head.

Cohen joined us wearing the other cowboy hat. The hole in his body-suit gave me another surge of the creeps. I added one of the other shoulder bags to my own and picked up two plastic bags of drinks. Leo couldn't carry so much while he was Amagat's eyes and Cohen and the sub wouldn't be able to manage much.

'We can stop in an hour, then we keep on,' I said. 'We've got to get away from the plane before they send search parties.' I re-checked the direction against my mind-map and started to march. In the short time we had taken to organize at the plane, the sun had burnt out to a golden memory of its former self. It was still hot, but it was with the dry heat of the air, not the beating rays of the sun. The going was a lot easier than I had imagined it would be and I found a ray of optimism creeping into my mind. Fool that I was.

I took point, walking four or five metres ahead of Cohen, who was a few paces ahead of Leo and Amagat. I set a stiff pace. We had to get clear.

After an hour we paused, drinks of fruit juice welcome in the dying heat of the day. It was strange how the sun died out while its heat lingered on. As the sun sank and seemed to swell into a fiery orange ball I noticed that the heat was coming from the ground; the day's warmth escaping into the evening. I wondered how long it would last.

The land that had looked so flat from the aeroplane was really a series of gentle slopes, broken by the occasional winding gully. The ground was hard and dry. I guess there must have been rains in the Dust Bowl at some time or other – that would be why the ground was set so solid – but judging by the lack of plant life there had been none for a long time.

At first I had wondered at the naming of the desert, maybe it harked back to the previous century when there had been great dust storms. Back when people had lived out there. But we had been climbing a gentle slope. As we started our descent, I found my feet stirring up little clouds of dust. I saw that there were cracks in the hard ground and that they were filled with a fine grey powder. When we reached the bottom of the first downward slope we came to a gully. Maybe a century ago there had been water winding its way along the bottom of that gully but we found only dust piled in ankle-deep drifts so fluid in their dryness that we had to paddle through them. We all needed drinks after that, just to clear the desert from our throats.

We walked on.

After a time that seemed like forever the last sliver of sun vanished beneath the horizon. The first hour of walking had already taken its toll on Amagat and Jacobi. Amagat grew tired very quickly. I couldn't find any physical reason, so I guess it must have been psychological. Hell, she had already decided once that day that she was going to die; the crash must have really screwed her mind. Too much deviation from the plan and she was overloading.

Leo's leg was slowing him down. The first time we stopped, he was so tired he even let me examine it. I guess he believed I wasn't going to leave him behind by then. It was only a flesh wound, but it was one big lump of flesh that was wounded. I was amazed he was even walking. At least he had been able to stop the bleeding.

My respect for Cohen was still growing. His response to the situation seemed to be that his only way out was to walk. So he walked. I thought I detected a slight limp at times, but decided it was just an effect of the ground he was walking over. His wiry old body seemed almost to have been built for the conditions, but it was his attitude that made me think that if any one of us was going to get out of this desert it would be Cohen.

I was coping well. My only injury was where my zap had been yanked from the median interface. Over the hour of walking I had chipped away the pinpoint of pain in my forearm, but I was left with the tingling sensation of healing. The low currents in the nerves surrounding my median had miraculous curing powers, but they set up one mighty powerful itch. The heat that was left in the desert air was enough to show the limitations of my isothermal suit. It may be isothermal in normal conditions, but its fibres were not enough to shield me from the heat of the desert. My head and hands were not protected at all and the heat seemed to focus in these areas. It seemed to create a haze through my head so that all I could think of was left foot, right foot. Left foot. Right foot.

And this was only the first hour of walking. We had days ahead of us, if we could avoid the Callies.

The break breathed some life back into me and I started to walk feeling much better. Jacobi was guiding Amagat again. I hoped she would recover her sight soon and be able to walk on her own, but I guess even chip-aided healing doesn't provide instant remedies.

I walked a dozen metres ahead, an eerie chirruping sound teasing me from the growing shadows.

After a few minutes my AW told me someone was catching up with me. Cohen, I guessed, walking alone. 'Elf owl,' he said, finally drawing level. 'Anywhere there's saguaro, there's an elf owl chipping away at the dusk. Fundamental rule of the universe.'

We walked on in silence.

A few minutes later I said, 'What's saguaro?'

'Big cactus,' said Cohen. 'Looks like it has arms coming out from all over. The owls nest in them.'

Silence again, surrounding us as we walked.

In that second session of walking, the cold crept in around us, held us tightly in its clutches. The night closed in rapidly and soon all we had to guide us was the light of a few dim stars. My body-suit was feeding me with its warmth but, again, the extremes of reality were proving too much for it. And again it was the extremities of my body that suffered the most. I started to shiver as I walked.

'It'll get colder, boy,' said Cohen. 'It's the clear sky – there are no clouds to keep the heat in.' He hugged himself. 'We won't get far in the dark.'

'Tonight we will,' I said. 'Even a few more metres could make the difference between being found and getting away. We walk all night. All day if we have to.'

'We might be able to stumble our way through the cold and the dark,' said Cohen. 'But we won't get more than a hundred yards under that sun.'

'Maybe,' I said and waited for silence to descend once more.

'Where are you from, boy?' asked Cohen. 'The moon? My cousin's daughter emigrated there after the revolution.' He shook his head. 'Didn't like it, though. She came back after three months. Probably still paying off the debts.

'Are you from the moon?' he repeated, remembering his question.

'L5,' I said. 'Place called Lejeune. Started my training on the moon.'

Over the next few days I found that most of our talking was broken up by spells of silent walking. The rhythm of the desert, I guess. 'What sort of a place is this Lejeune?' asked Cohen, after a time. He was usually the one to break the silence of the march.

'It's a Bernal-type sphere,' I said. 'A small one. A lot of it's a farming museum. That's what I used to do before the draft. We've got grow-coils, too. My pa runs them. He had an accident – severe neurone damage. Now he's wired into the whole system. He says he grows half of L5's food, but I've seen the records and it's nowhere near.'

'So you're a country boy, then.' Cohen laughed. 'A country boy from the colonies.'

The cold silence fell again. I wished I hadn't placed so much confidence in the body-suits. Should have grabbed some warm clothes from the plane before we set out. But I hadn't and I grew colder and colder. Thankfully the temperature was as low as it was going to get. Any lower and I think my blood would have frozen.

Cohen broke the silence again. 'I was born on a farm,' he said. 'Near a town called Prescott, Arizona. Father ran twenty-two acres of high-intensity glasshouse. That was real farming. Man and machine against the environment, not man-machine against man-made environment.'

'More sporting, huh?'

He looked at me, the ever-growing darkness obscuring whatever expression lay on his face. 'No, not sporting,' he said. 'More *natural*.'

A period of quiet took over for a time.

There was something I had been wondering for quite a time and for once it was me that spoke first. 'Why did you talk to me at the airport?' I asked.

'Fate. Who knows?' said Cohen. 'Why did you have your leg braced up?'

'Makes people less keen to search you,' I said. 'They don't like to touch a cripple.'

'I used to wear a brace,' said Cohen. 'Bone disease when I was a baby. There's a lot of that sort of thing about these days. It's the environment. Grew out of it by the time I'd finished at college. I suppose you must have reminded me how it used to be.

'And I suppose it showed how much I've changed since my days at college. It was only when you got angry at me that I remembered the humiliation of being handicapped. People holding doors open, giving you their seat on the subway. You got angry very convincingly, I'll give that to you.'

'I chipped it,' I said. 'Used my implants.'

Cohen looked away. 'Might have guessed it wasn't real. Makes me wonder just how much of a person they leave when they fill your head with hardware.'

'Didn't your brace make you a cyborg as much as any EP?' I said.

'That's different,' said Cohen. 'I needed it. You don't need to make yourself into a machine, but you do it.' The ensuing silence lasted a long time. I walked on in the cold and dark and Cohen dropped back, exchanged a joke with Jacobi that I didn't quite catch. Pretty soon Jacobi came forward and took over point duty.

'What about Amagat?' I asked.

'Cohen's got her,' said Jacobi. 'I think he wants to ease his rocks on her.'

I dropped back and walked alone for the rest of the night.

The first rays of sun the following morning were just about the most precious things I had ever seen. Jewels of pure energy sent to bring life back to my body. We had not stopped often in the night, hardly drank at all. The signal from the GPS beacons told me we had covered around fifteen kay-ems. Not bad going for a group that included a blind woman, a guy with a leg wound and a fifty-year-old CalTex State Rep. Even if that Rep. was Luke Cohen, who was turning out to be as fit as any of us, and perhaps a little more determined.

There was a beautiful period of an hour or so when the sun gave off just enough heat to take the chill out of our bones. Somehow it seemed to inspire a feeling of energy in me, as if I had chlorophyll in my skin. Then

I began to realize that, nice as the warmth was, I was grateful for the shade of my cowboy hat. Soon even the hat couldn't prevent the stifling heat from penetrating my good feelings. I began to realize that Cohen had known what he was saying. We would have to take shelter from the day's heat.

Looking around at the others, I could see that the enforced rest might not be such a bad thing. I had been chipping away through the night, calling on my body's reserves. So had Jacobi. But I guess Amagat was in no state for that, she looked like she would collapse at any moment. And of course Cohen had only his natural well-being to carry him through. I began to look for somewhere to rest up for the day.

Along with the sun, there was some good luck shining down on us that morning. The next gully we came to was a deep one with a good overhang on one side. At least we would have some shade to rest in.

After that first long walk we fell into a kind of pattern. Walk for three or four hours at dawn, then shelter from the day's heat. Walk again for maybe five hours at dusk and into the cold night. Then we would spend the coldest hours in a huddle of bodies, hoping we weren't going to freeze.

Cohen didn't want to share body heat at first. Old body-contact taboos made him uncomfortable, maybe a touch of revulsion at our artificial implants. That was the first crack I had seen in the older man's armour. 'Don't tell anyone,' he had said in my ear as the four of us lay shivering in each other's arms. There was a good chance he might freeze to death and he was worried about what people would think! I felt a touch sorry for him and was reminded again of the differences between our two cultures. I guess homosexuality is more acceptable in the colonies, most of us try it for size – Max Abelson can vouch for me on that one. But it's no big deal. It seems most people have some of it in them, yet Cohen was almost prepared to die rather than lie hugging two men and a woman.

After the first night, Cohen forgot his worries. I think he remembered how cold it had been even with our shared warmth. I don't think he fancied going it alone.

Physically things just got worse and worse. The tiredness, the strain of constantly chipping to keep alert. The thirst was bad even with the drink we had brought along. Thankfully the heat and exhaustion made hunger less of a problem. Sure, there were the early complaints from my stomach, but they didn't last long and soon settled into a distant throb that I could forget if I set my mind to it. I guess my body had enough to cope with. The damage to my median was slow to heal and an infection found its way in. My feet hurt. My body was just a general cacophony of pain and discomfort. But I chipped an element of control over it all. Kept a level head.

The others didn't fare so well. The combined slowness of Amagat and Jacobi kept us down to only a short distance each session. I helped Amagat some of the time, a hand on her arm and a verbal warning of any big obstacles. Cohen did his share, too, but mostly it was Leo who limped along with Amagat.

Over the days of the march it was curious to see Amagat steadily improving while Leo deteriorated. The sub's strength remained almost constant throughout the ordeal – even *I* lost my strength over those days, but she just kept on at her slow pace. Towards the end she began to say she could see light through her bandages. She began to complain about the pain of her face and the tingling of regeneration as her chip speeded her repairs.

I found myself thinking of that moment in the plane when I had admitted to myself that I found her attractive in a strange sort of way. Could I still find her appealing? No way, I thought, but that thought wasn't me. I remembered Triona, thought a bit more. Yes, I could still want Amagat, but I had to admit that I would have to work at it. It shouldn't matter how someone looks, I tried to tell myself.

Leo began to find that his injury was more serious than he had first thought. Maybe more than he could handle. After the first two or three days it was Leo who set the pace. And that pace became slower and slower. My early estimate of six or seven days increased and eventually doubled. The ordeal dragged itself out.

Walking point became something of a ritual. We had no real need of a man up front: if we were going to be found then there was not a lot we could do about it. But I guess it had a sort of reassuring effect, lent a hint of normality to the situation.

Cohen used to bounce about between the three of us, helping Amagat, taking point with me or Jacobi, sometimes walking alone. But he spent more time with me as the other two made it clear that they didn't want to talk. Leo didn't have time for anything but survival and Amagat seemed confused about things. I began to wonder if the only damage she had received was to her face.

One dawn, maybe on the third or fourth day, Cohen said to me, 'Why do you think they want *me*?'

'You're the State Rep. for Northern California,' I said. 'Politics,' I shrugged. 'Not my line.'

'It's *everybody's* line, boy. Has to be.' After a moment or two of silent walking – we were going very slowly, Leo and Amagat vying for last place – Cohen continued. 'Things have been in one big mess down here for an awfully long time. That's why your leaders took their opportunity to grab some action in the Union. It's all down to the greenhouse disaster.'

He paused as we came to a small gully and padded through its dust drifts. On the other side he said, 'The greenhouse disaster. Melting ice, expanding water, crustal stress. I was born when it really got going, I lived through all the big changes. The US split into a huddle of small squabbling nations. In the Alignment we've been trying to re-establish some of the old order, get ourselves sorted out.

'It's been one whole lot of confusion in every branch of government. My job is sorting out the military, finding out what our capabilities are. Listen, boy, if you aliens had come down just five years ago you could have had the entire continent. We didn't even know where our military bases *were*.' He shrugged. 'We're still finding some, even today.'

'Seems like a good reason for wanting you,' I said.

'That's not entirely it,' said Cohen. 'The reason they want me is because *your* side is just as confused as *we* were. They don't know what we're capable of doing to them.'

'You're fooling yourself if you think we're worried about how well equipped you are,' I said.

'Just because we don't have holograms and computers in our heads doesn't mean we're as primitive as you might think, boy. No *you're* not worried, it's your leaders we scare. They keep that away from the boys on the ground.'

Silence for a while, then: 'They tell us about the satellites you hit,' I said.

'That's a surprise,' said Cohen. 'It must suit their purposes. Do they tell you what happens?'

'Lasers, or something,' I said, trying to remember the

news reports from just before I left Lejeune. 'They blind them.'

'Hah!' said Cohen. 'That's more like it. The truth hurts them. Your spy satellites use huge arrays of scanners. Mosaics. Each one scans a particular area constantly. The old ones could be blinded but, to blind a mosaic, we'd need a laser shooting from just about everywhere in the Alignment. Don't you think that's a little impractical?'

'Maybe,' I said, losing him somewhere on the way.

'They're protected by special filters, too,' said Cohen. 'Selective screening. You just can't blind these things.' He paused, then after a few more steps said, 'So we knock them out completely. We use pulse weapons that can destroy entire space stations. We've got them scared, Jed, they don't know how we're doing it.' He shook his head. 'So they send you in on the slight chance you might pull off this crazy mission.'

Somehow the old man's rantings had disturbed me, found their way through my shell. Hell, I couldn't still blame it on shock. That crash seemed to have shaken something loose inside of my head and every so often it rattled.

'All this technology,' I said, more to myself than to Cohen. 'Sometimes I think they're just using us like in a lab, testing out their latest ideas on us, seeing what the results are.'

'*C'est la vie*,' said Cohen.

The heat in the middle of the day was a terrible thing, but we were lucky and always managed to find shade to spend the worst hours in. Once or twice I ventured out. Curiosity, I guess. You can't see much in the half-light of dusk and dawn, particularly as we tended to travel at the darker times, avoiding the heat. One day

I stood above our gully and looked around, my tattered cowboy hat protecting my head and eyes from the light, if not the heat. There was flatness in every direction; I almost expected to see the aeroplane on the horizon, a few kay-ems back on our trail. But there was only more horizon. Reading the GPS grid I estimated that we had travelled maybe eighty kay-ems. The vegetation had grown thicker as we moved northwards, Cohen kept saying it would thin out again but it didn't. The cacti were more abundant, a shorter variety adding to the saguaro. The commonest plant was a sort of low scrubby bush that seemed to creep its way outwards across the desert.

Standing there, atop the gully, I was surprised and delighted to see the sameness of the landscape broken by a tall figure. It was a sunflower standing brave and alone. For some crazy reason I walked the short distance to it and saluted.

I walked back and sat on the edge of the gully, chipping down the pains in my body. Let my mind just mellow out. Floated. I hadn't slept much in the desert, the nights were too cold, the days too hot. Somebody had to keep guard anyway. I did doze occasionally, but not for long, my AW snapping me alert every so often to the sound of the wind, or maybe Amagat moving slightly.

My mind mellow, I began to think about recent events. At first it was the shock of the crash that had blunted my killing edge, made me question some of my military training. But it had lasted and I couldn't still be in shock. Could I? As I felt then, I could never raise a gun against anyone again. Something in me had snapped and I couldn't go through with soldiering any more.

If this was a new me then what should I do? Go on and deliver Cohen? He would be interrogated, his life not worth the experience; I would be forced back into the military mould. Something in me that felt very tight at that moment might break. But that was my only choice. I couldn't hand Cohen back to his own people, I'd end up shot or in jail. If the rumours about the Callies were true, then shooting would be the best option. I'd heard that they have an interrogator chip that could force you to tell them anything they want; they just shunt you into a recorder. Only bad design means that a lot of what's taken out never finds its way back in. It scrambles the brain. No, we had to get to Grand Union, whatever future I chose.

I stopped thinking about it. At least consciously. The thought of some of the things I had been responsible for as a soldier threatened to break me apart at times. I could never think about it for long. I continued to chip down, but somehow didn't get the same mellow feeling I had experienced a few moments before.

Cohen joined me with Amagat when we set out. We took it nice and easy, so we didn't catch up with Leo on point. Amagat had learnt to use a stick and she was managing to walk on her own until we reached any tricky bits.

For some reason Gil had lodged himself in my mind. Seeing Cohen in the uniform with the hole in its chest was getting on my nerves. 'Why did your minder have to start a shooting match, back on the plane?' I asked him.

The older man's face dropped. He seemed to be watching the little puffs of dust that his feet kicked up. 'We were going to hide out the journey,' he said. 'Mosander pushed the mask over my head after you shot the steward. She always was quick.' He paused for a long, steadying breath. 'I don't know what we were going to do, we were just hiding.

'Then I sneezed. There was nothing that could be done. He was going to come for us so Lyn shot him. Then you shot her.' He looked away again, walked in silence. Losing valuable moisture.

'It was only a bodyguard,' said Amagat. I revised my opinion of her: it wasn't just that she didn't understand how the Army worked, it was the whole human race she couldn't follow. Cohen moved away and after a moment or two so did I.

In the dusk session on the second of July we only covered about two kay-ems. We were all operating on overdrive, exhaustion weighing us down. Amagat and Cohen shared the few remaining drops of juice out of our last big container before we set out. We had been hiding the empties in little caches as we went but I just dropped this one with my shoulder bag, the effort of hiding it too much for me.

We had about fourteen kilometres to go. With nothing to drink.

We came across an old road late in that session. That fixed our position on my map. I was alone on point and I waited for the others to catch up. A light gust of wind drew great swirls of dust along the road. Probably the only traffic for decades.

'A road!' said Cohen, his voice little more than a faint croak. 'A goddamned *road*!'

'Gonna hitch a lift, Rep?' Jacobi's voice was about the only strong thing he had left. I guess that was because he hadn't used it much over the previous days.

'A road,' repeated Cohen. 'Which way do we go?'

'Straight on,' I said, nodding across the road at the continuing desert. The horizon was still a straight edge to our world.

'What?' said Cohen. He seemed hypnotized by the

sight of this old dust-covered road. 'It's a *road*,' he said, as if that explained everything. 'It'll take us somewhere . . . They always do.' He stopped lamely and watched an eddy of dust racing a broken-up bit of tumbleweed down the centre of the road.

I looked to where the wind was coming from, worried by Cohen's tales of dust storms, but there was no great black cloud closing in on us. Back to Cohen, I consulted my mind-map to be sure of our location. 'That way—' I nodded to my left '—there's nothing but deserted ruins until the Rockies. That's one-fifty kilometres.' I nodded the other way. 'Other way, we might find what's left of Garden City in a hundred or so. Now I don't want any of your Earthshit complaints, we're going on. Maybe ten kays, that's all.' I walked ahead, annoyed at myself for losing my cool. I'd just about decided that I'd been able to overcome the soldier in me, but my burst of temper was the fighter taking over again. I guess he'd never really gone, was just waiting until the going got better. It was like there was a killer hitching a lift in my body, running whatever programs he found convenient or amusing. I began to wonder if I was going mad, cracking under the strain of it all.

I didn't come to any conclusion on that one.

We came to a halt when I decided that we were well clear of the road. Hell, we were all losing our senses to some extent and I didn't want Cohen getting any ideas about heading off along that road on his own.

We settled down amongst a cluster of large boulders. I didn't sleep at all that night. It wasn't because of the cold, in fact it was quite a mild night. We started off in the usual heap of bodies, but then we realized that we could stay apart without too much discomfort. I rolled away and sat, hunched against a rock. I had been lying mostly on Amagat and became aware of stirrings for her again. Jeez, I hadn't felt like that since we had been on the plane. Exhaustion, I guess.

After a time, I heard the repeated sharp yap of a coyote, a sound I had heard a few nights before; it was closer this time. The sound stopped and I settled back again. A short time later my Advance Warning set up a flutter in my head. I stood and looked around but I couldn't see anything in the dim starlight. Then I heard a mournful howl and relaxed. The coyotes were close.

I thought of a rumour I had heard in one of the Grand Union cities. St Louis, perhaps. It was said that the Callics had packs of trained animals guarding their borders. They sniffed out invaders and sent signals to troops by radio transmitters built into their brains. Scare-mongering, I had laughed.

Until that desert night.

I shot a burst of blue laser into the darkness, aiming at the spot where I guessed the yelp to have come from. Nothing happened.

I went back to my sitting place and sat. The ground was still warm.

Later in the night a coyote howled in the distance and I decided that it was a good sign. *Any* life was a good sign after the emptiness the desert had offered us up until then.

The night seemed to last a long time and I set off feeling worse than when we had stopped. I wanted a drink and my head was threatening to ache too much even for my chip to handle. Hell, my chip was overloaded with the other pains of my body. I was wondering just how much it could take. What would I do if it gave out?

My head just got worse and worse. There seemed to be no stopping it. The wind was flicking at my head, sending my hair flapping about, thudding on my skull.

I began to feel dizzy. I began to wonder if this was really how it was going to end. Only a few kay-ems to go and my body gives out. I concentrated on lifting and placing my feet, keeping a straight line.

Just walking.

I guess the feeling probably only lasted a minute or two, but it seemed to drag out into hours inside my head. And each second of those hours hurt like hurting was the latest trend.

The whole world was a haze. Thundering in my temples, my neck. Hurting. I felt sick and realized that it was at least partly due to a jabbering of Comtac in my abdomen. Normally I can read Comtac without thinking but not this time. A few seconds and I realized it was because it said nothing, it was just a wild stabbing of impulses. My head hurt even more.

I stumbled, fell to the floor, hit my jaw on a rock. The surge of pain and adrenalin cleared my head of everything for an instant and I grabbed that clear moment, chipped up frantically. That was all I needed and despite a wild haze of confusion in my senses I managed to hang on to that moment of clarity, stay chipped as high as I could go.

I looked around. Amagat was walking on with her stick tapping on the ground as if everything was fine. Cohen had stopped, his attention divided between me and Jacobi, who was weaving about all over the place. He fell over a few seconds later.

I heard a strange whining roar in the distance, getting louder, and I realized what was happening. 'Get down!' I shouted. 'We're being attacked. *Get down!*'

Chapter Ten

Selective extracts from transcript of Elpress News Feature, The Stuff of Heroes. (*Recorded 17 to 18 November 2083, broadcast on holovision, 22 November 2083.*)

. . . Scene cuts to: colourized satellite picture of the continent of North America.

Commentary: 'The struggle for liberty in Northern America has lasted almost since the terran defeat in the Fight for Freedom.' Pause, then: 'The United States, wrecked by the climatic upheavals of the global warming:'

The colouring changes, turning the satellite view into a map of the old US of A. Horizontal red and white stripes cover the forty-eight states, Alaska is daubed a star-spangled blue, Canada is a neutral, peachy tinge and Mexico a forgotten grey. The pattern dissolves, the sea crawls up the shores, all the forces of nature appear to be venting their fury on the geography of the old industrial nation. The Great Lakes merge into the Great Lake, landslides and unpredicted earthquakes producing an inland sea connected to the Atlantic by the St Lawrence Inlet; the San Joaquin sea, created by a combination of the 8.7 quake (with the old San Andreas foolishly oiled and shored up, its energies were diverted into the new Xiao Ping fault) and Hurricane Ronnie which came along three days later; the Independency of Florida is cut off from the mainland by New Tampa Bay. The colours of the map are reforming into the current political situation, Grand Union occupying a delicate lilac band from New England to the Great Plains, the CalTex Alignment a violent red growth over the south-western quarter. The rest of the map is a mosaic of variously coloured Free States, People's Democracies and The Lord's States on Earth. Northern Vermont still proclaims itself to be the United States of America.

Commentary: 'And now it is a loose scattering of peoples sharing little more than a common heritage and a continental land-mass. The one great upholder of the principles of liberty – the principles all extraterrans must hold dear to their very hearts – is the Grand Union.

'But their struggle has not been easy. They face opposition from beyond their borders, they even face opposition from *within* their borders. Such is the course of democracy.'

Scene cuts to smiling, laughing faces, pulls back to show that these happy faces are welcoming the Extra-terran Peace-keeping Force, lines of troops marching off a vast transporter.

Commentary: 'Peacekeepers from off-planet, invited in by Acting President Dolly Rubenstein to preserve the rule of democracy against the totalitarian threat. But the opponents of liberty had a stronger hold than anyone ever imagined. Once committed, we had to send more troops down to support our greatest ally on Earth.

'Then, in March this year, events became even more ominous. Gathering their primitive technological capabilities, CalTex launched an attack on our reconnaissance satellites, blinding two AC3s. Their methods were primitive and repair was easy, but they continue to launch unprovoked attacks on our equipment.

'We can, however, pinpoint where the attacks are coming from. A ground-based laser attack can blind no more than one or two scanning cells. With the multiple redundancy of the focal plane arrays used in most of our reconn satellites these attacks are no more than niggles. But by identification of the particular cells damaged, and comparison with other damaged satellites, we can extrapolate down to the point on the Earth's surface where these attacks are coming from.

'Look out, Frags, we're coming to get you!'

The scene has been cutting in and out in a complex manner. Synth shots of lasers firing from the Earth, satellites being hit, cut-aways of a multi-spectral scanner to indicate the precise nature of the problem. The commentary pauses and the scene cuts to a caricatured synth of a beam leaving a small tin shack on the Earth's surface. Ricky Robo-Mouse, a popular cartoon character in Lagrangia, dances up the beam to his theme tune, wearing a comical military helmet and carrying a 20th-century rifle with a bayonet. The viewpoint follows Ricky up the beam and he lands on a shiny network receiver array and gets tangled up in some fibre optic cables. He gives his winning *oh-bum-don't-I-just-always-do-things-wrong*? smile and the viewpoint draws sharply away and cuts to a military communications room. Soldiers sit at screens or shunted into retinal scan helmets. Sounds of busy activity have been dubbed on for verisimilitude.

Commentary: 'Here at the Mercator III intelligence centre, on the moon, we can report on perhaps the Callies' most comical attempt to bring the struggle into space.'

Viewpoint cuts to a simple flat shot of an oscilloscope, displaying a horizontal green line.

A voice with a strange accent cuts in and the line dances and changes colour in a flickering chromatic dance of its own. 'People of the colonies. Lend us your ear and we'll tell you what's here.' A weird jangle of music is in the background, apparently having little to do with the voice. 'The soldiers that you send to the American war, well you don't know a no-no what they're fighting for; they're fighting for a system that is thick with sin, they're being used by old Grand Union cos they'd never win; they keep their poor and hungry people in the damp and cold, so they can live their sugar lives so they can keep their hold. I say now, Keep On Back, I say now, Keep On Back; EP man a-fighting for the whole wrong pack. I say now Keep On Back, I say now . . .'

The voice and music fade, the oscilloscope trace stabilizes and returns to its neutral green. Viewpoint cuts back to the communications unit.

Commentary: 'That's an extract from one of seven propaganda transmissions, beamed to us over the last two weeks. Presumably the musical treatment of the message is supposed to give it some popular appeal. Well, of course, I'm sure it *has*, but . . . ?

'There is farce on several levels with this new approach. The most basic comic element must be the belief that the Extraterran Peoples could ever be even slightly influenced by such a crude attempt at propaganda. They're had too much experience of the Ad Agencies for *that*.

'And the cultural *naïveté* that it takes to assume that a – well, I suppose we'll have to call it a *music* form – the assumption that a music form that is presumably popular in CalTex is the best approach for an "alien" culture.' (A holo-inset shows Ricky Robo-Mouse trying to talk to some green bubble-eyed aliens.) 'Well, if we use this as an indicator of intelligence we could easily fall into the trap of assuming that the Callies are a push-over.' (The inset shows Ricky being cooked by the aliens in a giant cellular grill. Inset fades.)

'But the whole thing descends to the level of true farce when you consider the technical means they use to transmit these presentations. The context of the messages suggests that they were meant to interrupt entertainment shows. So they used radio. *Radio.*' (Holo-inset returns with Ricky pulling uncomfortably at the earphones of an antique Walkperson. He throws it away in disgust and the inset fades.) 'It wasn't even tuned to any comms frequencies we use. Surely they must know that no civilized peoples still use radio for anything other than bare necessity?'

Viewpoint cuts to a smoking house in a smoking terran city. EPs stand wary guard as anti-contamination-suited techs emerge from the building. It is raining a light misty drizzle on the grey scene.

Commentary: 'Our satellites have defensive capabilities way beyond the strike power of CalTex technology. Comic broadcasts serve only to provide amusing escapism of little substance.

'But there is a more serious threat.

'High in our superorbital homes, we can be assured of our safety. But we have young men and women striving to preserve what freedom and dignity remains in our terran spawning ground.

'Originally a policing force, the EPs have been drawn deeper and deeper into the domestic struggles of the land we were invited to protect. The leaders of CalTex have brought those struggles away from their own backyard. They have brought the fight to us. Now those domestic struggles have become our very own.'

Viewpoint closes in on the masked face of a tech passing the cordon of troops. Tears line his face.

Commentary: 'Guerrilla tactics have escalated. Terrorist cells have been located throughout the Grand Union and her allies. There have been bombings, attacks on EP leisure facilities, large underground recruitment campaigns. Routing this blight on the face of democracy is a slow and painful experience.' (The tech removes his mask and aims a big wet look out of the holovision arena.) 'This house was one of the main terrorist centres in Kalamazoo, on the southern shore of the Great Lake. Arrests have been made and the house has been bioed and smoked with piaphilic gas. These weapons only last a few tens of minutes in the terran atmosphere. After the safe period, Rayo—' the tech offers a weak smile and then blows his nose '—and his fellow techs were sent into the house to investigate.

'What they found displays close correspondence with similar investigations and street-level rumour.'

Viewpoint pans slightly to place Rayo front left and thereby displays a background of a small body being stretchered out of the dead building.

Commentary: 'The mind of the terrorist can be but a small step removed from that of the lowliest animals. Rumour on the streets has it that the terrorists capture pre-pubescent children and keep them at their head-quarters. They are rewards for the successes of the killers that call themselves freedom fighters.

'That is the rumour. And sadly it can be confirmed that chained bodies *have* been found at these houses. It is a great thing that our troops are striving to bring enlightenment to these primitive lands.'

Viewpoint cuts to a series of shots of EPs dug into defensive positions, large army units in transport trucks, patrolling squads displaying a feast of military hardware.

'In addition to the escalating guerrilla war our reconnaissance satellites have detected large build-ups of CalTex troops behind their border with the Grand Union. Our response has been to increase our own presence in this sensitive area from a handful of mobile units to a vast human presence.'

Viewpoint cuts to a small town, seemingly overrun with troops . . .

. . . And viewpoint cuts to aerial view of several hundred extraterran soldiers marching drill in a large open area surrounded by plaz walls.

Commentary: 'No, we cannot ignore this escalation of hostilities. It is a challenge to our integrity as human beings.

'And we are almost ready to unleash our response: the largest EP delivery in history, more even than the very first force. The new Acting President, Felix Concetti, after consultation with the Extraterran consul, has invited this unprecedented peacekeeping force into the Grand Union.'

Flat inset appears, bottom left. President is talking to a press conference. '. . . to make it a better place for the people of tomorrow.'

Inset fades.

Commentary: 'The extraterran army is now in the final stages of preparation for movement to the Grand Union. The soldiers have been split into groups according to the regions to which they will initially be allocated. The circadian patterns of these troops have now been altered to local conditions, to avoid environmental shock when they get to Earth. The amount of daylight and the timing of day and night now correspond to the various time zones of the Grand Union.'

Viewpoint cuts to a soldier in combat gear standing in the middle of a road, surrounded by frost-encrusted vegetation and buildings. A shattergun is strung loosely from his shoulder and he looks cold.

Commentary: 'Not only has this soldier's day changed; his whole environment has changed to prepare him for existence on the surface of our mother planet. No more comfortable bunk, no more beers in the crew room, no more low-gee sports.

'This soldier, and thousands like him, are living a simulation of terran conditions until the very moment they set foot on Earth.

'The Disc is a vast military complex. In it troops can be prepared for any previously encountered environment. Even in a stay of several months a soldier will not see more than a tiny fraction of the available space here. Some of this area has now been opened up for this exercise in simulation at an incredible scale. It has never been done before and hopefully we will never need to do it again.

'The project involves complete simulation over an area totalling more than five thousand square kilometres: day length, temperature, humidity, general weather conditions. And then there is the topography itself: there are samples of all the major habitats that are to be encountered in Northern America. Large urban tracts, agricultural plains—' the viewpoint cuts to shots of the habitats, keeping step with the commentary '—mountain, forest, desert, swamp. It's all there. And of course the gees are kept at one point oh-oh-oh.'

Viewpoint cuts to a medical surgery with a soldier being given a dermal infusion by a pretty young medtech wearing a badge that says *John.*

Commentary: 'The soldiers are being given medical help to prepare them for terran action. Here a young troop from Reinhold is being given his fourth in a series of calcium boosters to make up for his low-gee lifestyle before joining up. Some electrical stimulation, initiated by a suboccipital med-bubble, is all it takes for his bones to grow thick and strong.

'They're being protected against other hazards, too.

Boosts against the various environmental diseases that are now prevalent on Earth, boosts against the old killers that we've eliminated out here, a catalogue of horrors that includes measles, genital warts, some of the HIVs.

'But our young people are prepared. The risks have been minimized.'

Viewpoint cuts back to the wintry urban scene . . .

. . . And viewpoint cuts to a group of four soldiers smiling and laughing; they are sitting on a cut-down tree. Conifers are on drill behind them and watery sunlight appears to shine down through the dark green canopy. You can almost smell the pine needles.

Commentary: 'Another of the top squads here on the Disc is an independent action squad, under the command of Sublieutenant Thom Sorakin. Sub, will you tell us about the squad's record to date?'

Sorakin grins out of the holovision arena and spits to one side. 'We've been together two and a half months,' he says, 'all of that time on the Disc. And right from the start we pissed on the opposition.'

Commentary: 'Could you elucidate?'

'Wrong time of month for *that*,' says Jacobi. Lohmann pushes him off the log.

Sorakin grins and says, 'On exercise ratings we've never been lower than eighty-seven per cent, never ranked lower than fourth. That's usually in competition with no less than fifteen squads. We've come top in exercises eleven times, that's a win rate of forty-eight per cent.'

'We're top of the slap ratings, too,' says Lohmann as Jacobi settles back on the log. 'We're pissing on 'em.' Jacobi pushes him off.

Commentary: 'Um, Brindle. What do you have to say on all of this? Your colleagues seem quite convinced.'

Brindle gazes steadily out of the arena and into

people's homes. 'I guess,' he says, 'well, I guess we're pissing on 'em.'

Commentary: 'Sub, how are these simulations working? Do you feel ready for Earth?'

'Simulations?' grins Sorakin. He looks around him and, almost on cue, a chickadee trills out of a nearby tree. 'Shit, ain't we in New England, then?'

Commentary: 'How do you boys feel about being out in the open? Under the weather?'

'Why, the sky gonna fall in and ain't *none* of us gonna get to Heaven!' says Jacobi in sham excitement.

The viewpoint shifts slightly to give emphasis to Brindle. 'Open spaces and unplanned weather don't bother us none. We're just going to get down there and blow ass off the Callies.' Viewpoint shifts back.

Commentary: 'Are you looking forward to seeing Earth? Are you going to find out what the women are like? The men?'

'Does the moon go around the Earth?' says Sorakin. 'The Frags are in for a whole new experience when we get down there.'

Commentary: 'And finally, I know you've been on Null Communications for the past two weeks. Once you get to Earth, messages can take some time to get through. Do you have anything to say to your loved ones?'

Viewpoint swings for strong emphasis on Jacobi. 'I reckon I've loved the whole solar system before now, so I'll just say: I'll be back, mother. Keep my dinner warm.'

Viewpoint swings to Lohmann. His eyes glaze and he momentarily loses the effervescence that he has displayed throughout the interview. 'Marie,' he says. 'Tell Marietta I'll be back to see her some day.' He looks down and then away into the woods.

Viewpoint swings to Brindle. 'I guess I'd just like to

say—' he pauses and grins quietly at the camera '—"Hi" to everyone and I hope the wedding went just fine. I'll be back when I've shot me some ass.'

Viewpoint swings back to Sorakin. 'No, I don't have any messages. I've always been a soldier. I don't want any ties, it just hurts people in the end.'

Viewpoint pulls away to show the squad in its woodland setting. The chickadee repeats its trill.

Viewpoint cuts to . . .

. . . And viewpoint cuts to aerial view of troops being drilled on a large parade ground. The parade ground is dirty and potholed so it must be on Earth. Fade up *The Stuff of Heroes* theme tune. Roll closing credits.

Extract from Triona Brindle's memo file, next to index entry for a bubble-record of The Stuff of Heroes, *22 November 2083.*

THAT WAS NOT JED.

Chapter Eleven

3 July 2084

'Get down and cover your heads!' I shouted. There was a tense gap as the roar slowly grew louder. I looked around, my arms tangled about my head. If they used any heat-seekers the isothermals would disguise us, but our heads weren't shielded. They *should* have been too small as sources of infra-red, but I wasn't prepared to chance it. I just hoped another of the rumours wasn't true and that they didn't use smell sensors – we had no way of hiding from the sniffers.

I chipped down frantically, striving for that elusive element of calm.

The roar of what I had decided was an approaching jet was curiously difficult to locate. Somewhere in the north-west, I guessed. I looked but couldn't see anything out of the ordinary; the light was still bad, the morning sun not yet risen.

But there was still the distant roar and that terrible feeling of illness that had overcome me moments earlier. Somehow the Callies were interfering with my circuity. Trying – and nearly succeeding – to jam the system. Maybe they thought they could leave us standing in the open, switched off and out of action like comic-strip robots.

It had nearly worked.

I still had the curious buzzing ache in my head, the dizziness, the nausea. Comtac was still stuttering foreign messages in my abdomen and my AW was sending wild warnings through my brain. I couldn't decide if the AW was malfunctioning or simply reporting a multitude of danger signals. Probably both.

I cautiously removed an arm from my head and felt for my median interface. I found it and fingered the swollen flap of skin, still raw from injury and infection. Slid the lead from the socket and pushed the zap into the chest pouch of my body-suit. I didn't want to risk their interference sending the wrong signal down my median.

I looked away from the noise. A slice of deep red sun hung on the horizon, shading the desert a sad crimson. The moment drew itself out, that instant before something terrible happens, the instant that seems to last forever.

I spotted a shallow dip in the ground nearby, a man-sized trench. Wriggled over to it on my belly. Its scant protection would be better than none at all.

As I moved I had a brief view of the scene around me.

Jacobi had mastered the interference in his system and lay quietly on the ground, a few metres to my right. His arms were shielding his head and his suit gave him good camouflage against the murky background.

Cohen lay nearby, hands on his head. 'Use your *arms*,' I said in a hoarse whisper. 'Not your hands.' He glanced over at me and nodded. Moved his arms.

Amagat was lying several metres away from the three of us. Her arms were wrapped around her head in the recommended manner, white bandage showing through at the side. Even at this distance, I could see that she was shaking uncontrollably. The interference had only seemed to affect Jacobi and me. The image I had in my memory of that instant when I realized what was happening to us had Amagat walking along normally. Yet again I found myself wondering exactly how much damage had been done to her in the crash. Burned and blinded, and now I knew that her circuits, too, had been affected. Maybe her damaged chipping system was responsible for the suicidal depression she had fallen into immediately after the crash.

The instant was drawing itself out far too long. I raised my head again. The sound hadn't grown any louder. Maybe I was wrong. Or maybe they didn't know where we were.

About twenty metres ahead of us there was a large cluster of boulders. They would provide good cover from any attack.

I moved slightly, raised myself on my hands.

And then the tone of the noise changed, a Doppler shift as the aircraft's direction changed. A shift upwards: it was coming towards us. I lowered myself, waiting for that inevitable moment.

A few instants and the sound changed from a distant roar to a terrible approaching thunder. The ground shook as if cowboys still stampeded cattle across that dead landscape. Stones and sand rolled down into my shallow trench and I smelled dust in the air. I kept my eyes closed, didn't see the approaching jet at all. Pressed my head into the ground, tasted dirt, grit between my clenched teeth. EPs were just not designed for battle in the open. I longed for the safety of a Bernal.

Then the sound was overhead. Another Doppler shift, the roar hanging for an instant in that no man's land between high and low. My whole body quaked to the sound. Maybe they tuned it for resonance with human tissues.

Doppler to a low roar, the jet's voice breaking to a masculine *basso.* Nothing had happened. There was almost time for a manic grin to tweak the corners of my mouth.

Then the outside world was ripped away from me in a monstrous explosion. The brightness of the flash reached my eyes even through clenched eyelids and the hard dry mud that my face was pressed against. The sound reached me an instant later, crashing into my eardrums with horrendous rage. A pulse of pressure. Hot, hot air. Sudden weight on the small of my back.

And then a moment of heady silence, a burnt-earth smell permeating the air. A beautiful moment because I realized that I was still alive, hadn't been ripped from my body, torn from the world. I didn't even feel any pain.

I just had time to chip down before the next explosion burst into my world. This one was further away, the attack on my senses less violent than before. More diffuse.

I opened my eyes to narrow slits and the third and fourth explosions went off. My chip somehow left me more able to cope with the experience, a stoic acceptance that if this was my end then so be it. The flashes of the two explosions dazzled me and I closed my eyes again. The world was an impressionist mass of unlinked colours, a terrible image of destruction. This was my Apocalypse, my Armageddon. The empty greys of the desert were smothered by clouds of smoke; flashes of the brightest yellow-white attacked my eyes through the haze; the smoke was lit from behind by a huge orange half-sphere, tinting the whole scene in a delicate warm glow.

Another flash through my closed eyes. A series of flashes, explosions, bursts of pressure and sound that left me feeling numb and senseless. The roaring jet had left the scene, its bombs detonating at intervals after its passage.

They were still exploding when I detected the jet's return for a second sweep. The Callies were being thorough.

The second attack was a repeat of the first. The terrible roar of the jet for a moment drowning out the explosions from its earlier strike. The shift from the high warning note to the low roar of retreat. The momentary pause between Doppler shift and first explosion. Longer, this time; I thought that perhaps they might be using some intelligence, trying a different tactic.

But no, the explosions came. The flashes, the thuds of pressure, the shaking of the ground. There were fewer bombs the second time and none was as close to me as that first one.

The roar of the jet retreated through the bursts of its bombs. I waited for it to come around for a third attack but the sound continued to fade. Soon it was lost to my ears. A final blast from nearby and then there was a silence that was almost painful.

I lay in my trench, eyes closed. Chipped control of my senses. Moved and felt the weight on my lower back again. I reached around with a free hand and found that I was half-buried beneath a mass of soil and stone. I moved again and felt the weight shift, leaned on my elbows and heaved my body forwards. The weight shifted again and much of it moved. I levered myself out and squatted by my trench.

I had opened my eyes while I worked myself free. Saw the gritty texture of the ground, cee-ems from my eyes as I pulled against the weight of rubble on my back. Opened to a wider view as my head rose above the surface and settled a metre up as I squatted and looked around.

There was still a feeling of confusion in my chip, but I decided I was just getting used to being unjammed again. It took me a few seconds to orientate myself in the dizzy swirl of my circuitry.

The sun had lifted itself clear of the horizon and was burning a golden path through the clearing smoke. Its heat was beginning to penetrate and I felt for my hat but it had come off in the attack. I spotted it nearby and moved over to pick it up. Pulled it down firmly on to my head.

As the smoke began to disperse I saw the still bodies of my companions lying where they had gone to ground before the attack.

Jacobi moved. Groaned.

Looking closer I saw that Cohen was moving too, rising to his knees and looking around in apparent confusion. Further away, Amagat was still lying down, but I saw the shaking, heard her sobs. Incredibly we had all lived through the attack.

The jet had certainly not used any of the rumoured sniffers on us and I doubted that they had even used heat-seekers. They seemed to have dropped just two batches of small bombs on us, probably hoping to saturate the area with shrapnel. The randomness of shrapnel bombs had kept them in use for centuries, but somehow that randomness had spared us out there in the Dust Bowl Desert. I silently offered my thanks to any god that would appreciate them.

Most of the smoke hung about twenty metres ahead of me. As it lifted I saw what had become of the cluster of boulders that would have been my refuge had the attack come only a few seconds later.

It wasn't there.

The image in my memory was of rocks some two or three metres high, the gaps filled by their smaller cousins. The image before my eyes was of rocks no greater than half a metre in the longest dimension, bomb holes several metres deep, the ground black and still smoking.

I rose to my feet and stretched, my vertebrae popping loudly. Cohen was standing and I went over to him. There was blood in a long streak across his forehead. I looked around for the small medical kit the old man had been carrying. It was on the ground nearby. Cohen was silent as I checked his wound – shallow, nothing embedded – and tied a length of bandage around his head. Hell, I didn't know how to work those things but at least it kept the blood out of his eyes. What I needed was some Johnson Healant-Sealant gel, but they don't pack useful things like that in CivAir medical kits. I could have played witch-doctor with as much skill as I tied that bandage.

'Closer than a fucking depilatory,' said Jacobi from behind me.

I looked around and there was an awful dead look in his eyes. Like the funeral was already booked. 'Look after the prisoner,' I said. 'I'll check on Amagat.' I left the two of them. Private and prisoner. Why had I called him that? *The prisoner?* I hadn't even thought of him in those terms when we set out from the plane crash.

We were just a small group trying to get away.

I realized that the soldier had quit hitching and taken over the driving seat. All it had taken was the sound of a CalTex jet and he had leapt out and taken control. Maybe he had kept my head, saved my ass, but now I wanted to know just who was in charge up there. As I approached Amagat, I tried to keep the soldier from gaining the upper hand.

I shook in an uncontrollable shudder as I stopped by the sub. Trying to shake the soldier loose, but I knew it was impossible. There was no way I could just lose fifteen months of my life, no way I could shed my burden. Amagat was curled into a tight ball, facing away from me. I crouched and put a hand softly on her shaking back.

She made a strangled choking noise as she tried to shut off her tears, but she continued to sob. 'Hey,' I said – the only dumb thing I could think of to say. 'Hey. It's over, they've gone.' A pause. 'We're all still alive. It's OK.'

I gave up trying to calm her and sat, waiting for her to stop in her own time. The soldier in me had subsided.

Soon Amagat's sobs eased into ragged gasps and then a more even breathing. She uncurled herself from the foetal ball and I removed my hand from her back. I spotted blood on her left forearm. 'Let me have a look at that arm,' I said. I took her hand and rolled up her sleeve. The wound was a mess. Deeper than Cohen's and in the growing daylight I saw that there was something embedded in the flesh. A tiny sliver of shrapnel, too small for me to hope to remove with my clumsy hands. There was too much blood, anyway, for me to see what I was doing, and no water to wash it clean. I had to stop the bleeding, somehow.

I looked around and found a hand-sized stone. Yelled for the medical kit. I shunted my zap and wrapped my left hand in several layers of bandage. Cohen and Jacobi stood watching. I fired the zap at the rock, fired again until the charge suddenly died. 'This'll hurt some,' I said. Then I picked it up with my bandaged hand and pressed it against Amagat's wound, ignoring the burning of my own hand.

She screamed. After a pause for a quick breath she screamed again, the sound tailing off into another bout of sobbing. I dropped the stone by my de-shunted zap.

At least the bleeding had stopped.

Another few moments passed and the sub's breathing steadied itself. 'Will somebody *please* tell me,' she said. '*What happened?*'

Jeez, it just never occurred to me. All she knew was what she could hear and feel. Shouts to get down, take cover. Nothing for a time. Then the terrible roar of the jet, the explosions, the pressure waves and hot air. The pain of something ripping into her arm and my crude cauterization.

What happened? Good question.

'We were attacked,' I said. I glanced at Jacobi and Cohen. The prisoner. 'A CalTex jet. It dropped a scattering of bombs, there was shrapnel flying everywhere. Most of them were well clear of us, though. Cohen took a flesh wound, me and Leo are OK.' I stopped, looked at Jacobi's blank face. Then another thought struck me and I said, 'I just cauterized your arm. Best I could do.' I shrugged, more for my own benefit than for the unseeing Amagat.

'What about all the Comtac?' she said, breathing in short gasps. 'It went crazy back there.'

'Huh?' I thought Amagat's circuitry had been completely blown. Clearly not all of it. 'Oh, they were jamming us. Some sort of signal that screwed with the circuits. Didn't it affect your other implants?'

'Oh, uh yeah,' she said. 'Of course. All of them.' I didn't believe her. I could have asked her to fire a zap, or give our reference on the GPS, but I didn't. If she wanted us to believe she wasn't as bad as she was then that was fine by me. Maybe she wanted to fool herself more than us. I left her alone, let her gather herself. I left her stick resting against her leg so she could move if she wanted.

The sun was now climbing rapidly and its heat was

beginning to make me just want to sit out the day. 'We'll have to move on soon,' I told Jacobi. 'Have to get away from this place in case they decide it might be a good idea to gather the bodies.' I grinned but Jacobi looked away. I was suddenly aware of how the walk through the desert had broken him down, chipped away his protective coating. He had always been the hard man.

Him and Plato. I wondered for a moment what had become of Plato. Had he really allowed some trigger-happy Union kids to pick him off in the street? No, Plato was a survivor, always had been. To look at him, nobody could ever think of him as a strong soldier, but he was. Overweight, bad blood, he suffered all the allergies available when we came down to Grand Union, but he fought through it all and came out on top. I wished Plato had still been with us, none of this might ever have happened. But I cut that line of thought: it wasn't fair to blame it on Amagat, we had all played our part. Even Jed the soldier.

Jacobi went and sat at the edge of a bomb-crater. He stared down into it as if he wished it had been his. The ordeal had broken him right down to his constituent parts, like it had done to us all. I wondered how it would put us back together again. If it would even bother.

I turned and Cohen was standing at my shoulder. I don't know how long he had been there. 'How's the head?' I asked.

'Still there,' he said. His blue eyes that had always been so piercing had lost some of their intensity. Until then, he had taken it all better than the rest of us, had only shown a few signs of breakage. There were very few chinks in *his* armour. 'It was from the Alignment,' he said. 'It was one of ours.' He was trying to believe it and having trouble.

'One of your own,' I said. The smoke had stopped

rising from the bomb-holes, but the smell of burnt soil lingered in the air as if to remind us of how close we had been.

'But . . .' said Cohen and paused. 'But why didn't someone tell them that I was with you? Must have been a mistake. Yes.' He directed an almost insane grin at me. 'A horrible mistake.'

He was right on the edge. I didn't know whether to humour him or try to burst his bubble, but it popped of its own accord. Maybe that was best, I was just too exhausted and sore to have to save Cohen's mind as well as my own.

'But they must have known,' he said. 'They'd have found Lyn, seen I wasn't there. And the pilot would have told them. But *Jed*,' he said, 'they tried to *kill* us.'

'They're fighting a war,' I said. 'That's what you do in war.' Images flashed through my head of some of the killing I had done in this filthy little war. Killing that the soldier in me had done. I closed my eyes tightly for a moment. Couldn't spare any fluid for the desert.

'Why do they want to kill me?' said Cohen, still trying to let it sink in.

'Maybe it was easiest,' I said. 'I don't know. Maybe they just wanted to make sure we didn't get through to the Union with you. We're getting close, now.' I shrugged, waved my hands. My throat was sore and dry and my head was hurting. Too much pain for my chip to handle – I seemed to have found the overload point on just about all of my circuits. Maybe my mind, too. 'Maybe they thought you might have given something away. We might have contaminated you, they don't know what techniques we might use on you. I don't know,' I repeated. 'Maybe they're just scared. Making sure.' I shook my head. *I* didn't know.

'How far we gotta go?' asked Amagat in a husky

whisper. She must have got up and homed in on our voices.

I smiled, this was admission that her chip wasn't functioning. 'No more than ten kays,' I said. 'Couple of days if we work at it. If we don't come across any patrols from the CalTex base in Askar Town, that is.'

'You get those directions right,' said Amagat. 'We don't want to end up in the town by mistake.'

'I'll get it right,' I said. Askar Rock, then back into Grand Union. They'd take Cohen, do what they had to in order to extract their information. I glanced at Cohen. He was regaining his composure quickly. He seemed to heal up any cracks almost as soon as they appeared. It would take a long, long time to prise anything from him that he didn't want to tell. I looked away. I might get a few days in hospital then they'd probably assign me to one of the big policing squads. It takes a long time to put together a small tightly-knit squad, they tend to put survivors on to policing duty rather than make new squads. I guess we only got Amagat because Plato needed replacing at the last minute.

Another year and a half until I'd served out my notice. I had no idea how it would end. The only way I could last that time would be to let the soldier in me take over again. I couldn't allow that. Hell, I'd tried to get rid of the soldier, but he just wouldn't budge. I wondered for a paranoid moment if it was my military chip I was fighting – a computer-soldier built into me when I went for surgery. But no, I couldn't divert the blame for the things I had done by pretending it wasn't me. *Externalizing* sounds like what that would be called.

'You feel you could walk a while under that sun?' I said to Cohen. 'We have to get away from here.'

He looked at me, his eyes piercing their way right through me again. 'And what,' he said, 'would you do if I was to say "No"? If I said I wanted to sit right here and wait for them to come find me?'

A surge of fury rose to the surface, but I chipped right down on it. That's how the soldier gets the upper hand in my head. Moments of anger, moments of action. I kept chipping down, let the calmness take me over. Much better than anger.

'You wanna sit here,' I said. 'Then you sit here. I'm getting the fuck out. But if you find that nobody comes to look for you – maybe you don't matter enough to them, maybe they think we're dead. Maybe they make another "mistake". Just you tell me: what you gonna do? Gonna walk in a straight line and hope you hit on the direction of one of the Askars? Gonna hope you can even *keep* a straight line, not just walk in a circle until you drop? Tell me, Cohen, what you gonna do?'

My answer seemed to satisfy him, a grin of achievement showed on his face. I chipped down again, the anger had won that time.

'OK,' he said, wiping his dusty hands down the front of his dusty body-suit. *Gil's* dusty body-suit. 'I'll walk.'

Jacobi was standing, now, facing north. He looked at us. 'Nine kays, I'd put it at,' he said. 'I'm going to get out of this shit-hole. Get me some Union ass. No stopping me, huh?' He grinned at us and it seemed to hurt, seemed to crack the mask that had dried on to his face. He still had that look about him, the look of death.

I wondered if even nine kays would be too much for him. Maybe not if he could force some of his enthusiasm through the surface and down inside him. 'We can *share* some Union ass,' I said. 'They won't know what's hit town, huh, Leo?'

'That's right.' He turned and started to walk. 'I've got point,' he said over his shoulder.

I looked at Cohen, at the bandaged head of Amagat.

'Let's go,' I said quietly. I turned, the sun beating down on me. Burning, even through my body-suit – I wondered if *it* had reached breaking point like the rest of us. The heat seemed to be pressing me into the hard ground.

I kept my eyes on the dusty surface, a few metres ahead of my sore feet. I'm going to get out of this desert, too, I thought. But somehow the thought of 'getting ass', as Leo put it, didn't have much appeal to me right then.

Stay put. What—?

Light. A roaring, crashing sound, tearing through my skull. Pressure, heat, pain. A bomb. The world folded in on me, crushed the breath from my lungs. The Earth seemed to have stopped spinning.

Everything went black.

Chapter Twelve

Extract from the diary of Louis Brindle, recorded on memory block N63a, Grow Coil B.

15 JANUARY 2084

My son is dead. I guess he started to die back in March when they sent his draft notice, but now it's all over.

There's a new person in that body of his. When he's served out his notice we'll just have to see how he fits in back here on Lejeune. He might recover but I don't like the odds.

I've just relayed a long communication from him to the family house. He says what's been happening since he landed on Earth, all the usual things; but it shows the changes the military have made in him, the moulds they've squeezed him into.

The Army does that to people. I should know. It dehumanizes you, turns you into a machine they call a *soldier*. I warned him.

Not long after that *Heroes* trash they showed on the holovision, Jed was part of the biggest single movement of people to or from Earth since Gagarin started the whole show.

Thirty thousand trained killers, and they call it the *Peace*-keeping Force.

The shipment to Earth went on over most of two weeks. Jed says he queued up at a transport bay for three hours before they reached him. Then he had to climb into a micro-thin plastic box. Like an old-fashioned coffin. After another wait, a tech approached. Oily skin, mining accent and a strong smell of hashish. The tech plugged a lead into Jed's suboccipital.

And he woke up with a different tech deshunting him. Small and dark, with a cute ass, is how Jed put it. He comes to the point these days; he used to beat about for ages before actually *saying* anything.

In between whiles Jed had missed out on nearly five days.

Chipped into a semi-coma back in the transport bay, he had been loaded into a transport's cargo hold along with a few hundred others. A slow trip down to Earth-surface to land at Levittown, then they just left them in their plastic boxes. Waiting until they found the time to 'commission the carcases' (Jed's phrase). Jed lay in his box in a New Jersey warehouse for *three days.* Ain't it just plain that there's no humanity left in the Army?

Jed says some of the soldiers are dodging combat duty, using their wits to get into clerical postings. Some even avoided getting sent Earthside. Not our Jed. He always has to do the right thing. Tell him to fuck himself and he'd break his back trying.

There seems to be a lot of confusion about things down there. Jed's squad is now posted in some little town just outside Syracuse – right down on the shore of the Great Lake – but before that he'd been halfway around New England and back. The Army doesn't seem to know where it's sending people. Bad communication with the Frags could explain that, if you really believe all that about the EPs only being there to help.

Sure. They might have been when it all started, but a lot has happened since then.

It's moderate to heavy making out what it's really like

down there. They say there's complete freedom of information up here. Hell, I'm not fool enough to believe any of that, but I did think that maybe they might be letting us know *some* of what's going on.

Nobody else would have noticed, but Jed's HoloGram was censored.

Since they've developed synth holovision – hee-vee animation – they've had near one hundred per cent capability to manipulate the images we receive in the hee-vee arena. But on the large scale required to censor mass communications even the AIs slip a little. Leave a few discontinuities. (I reckon that's the reason for the Comms Blackouts that go down every few weeks – they have to catch up on all the censorship; the latest Blackout lasted three weeks, so we didn't get our Christmas greetings until now.)

If I wasn't rigged up in all the computing power of Lejeune – in a very real sense I *am* Lejeune – I would never have detected the glitches. But, Jeez, I relay the messages: I see them in their *digital* as well as their visual form.

I wasn't fooled for a second.

There's no easy way to piece together what Jed is really saying, but I don't like what I can read between the images. Things sound pretty hostile, even from the natives whose peace Jed is supposed to be keeping. Guerrilla fighting throughout the Grand Union; Jed's been bent to say it's the Callies. Judging from the fact that they felt it was important to stress that it's infiltration from the outside, I have to believe the opposite. The EPs are now an *occupying* force.

Most of Jed's active work is search and secure raids on guerrilla strongholds. That's tough work at the best of times, but Jed is in a good squad so they're being given the worst clean-up jobs available. Maybe that's why they're being moved about so much. Into the trouble spots. We had a lot of that sort of work after the Fight for Freedom, cleaning up the Terran sleepers.

It sounds like Jed suffered a real dislocation. He never was one for change. Training to action, safety to danger, Lagrangia to Earth. He'd never been on a planet before the moon and even then he was indoors all the time. Then suddenly he's flung on to the Earth and expected to fight a war.

There's the physical shock of living in the open and then there's the psychological shock. They say it hits your mind worst but I guess I don't know about that. Born and bred in the colonies, I never expect or want to leave the safety of Lejeune. It's not worth the risk to my drones.

He details the physical shock and some of the cultural shock, but he doesn't really give much away about his state of mind. Jeez, he's so changed I can't really place much weight on any interpretations I make from what he says.

First thing was, before he even left the building they woke him up in, he had to put on a breathing mask. It hadn't rained that day, said the tech, so there would still be some 'pepper' in the air. Then they were marched outside, his squad and several others. The sky was a glaring yellow-tinged white and the cold stung through Jed's uniform. He knocked his mask when he climbed into the back of a gas-fired truck and he says the air burned the lining of his nose.

I didn't know things could still get that bad down there.

Jed didn't say anything about how it actually felt to be standing on the outside of a planet, open sky over his head. *Open sky.* I guess he must be so used to it now, he doesn't think it's worth telling us about.

He's only just getting over some of the physical shock of arriving on the Earth. That first whiff of the air set his nose streaming. He spent much of the first week struggling to see through puffed up eyes, breathing through a sore and blocked nose. He says he fared better than his buddies.

Skin rashes were the other effect of terran air. His hands and face cracked and peeled and aren't fully healed even now.

He says the Army chip they built into his suboxy has a suite of healing programs. Hell, if he's still peeling and flaking now they can't be doing their work all that well.

Some of the sights that Jed has seen made me just a little bit envious. Up here we only have history measured in decades. Jed has seen buildings that are measured in *centuries.* Down in the Latin countries they go back thousands, but I guess that is just too incredible to sink in. I'd settle for the centuries.

Standing on the Atlantic coast, Jed has seen the sun rise behind the remains of Boston. Black rooftops force their way above the sea's surface and break the waves into angry white fangs, ribbons of saliva.

Jed has patrolled what they call the Concrete Curtain. Standing on top of the Curtain, you're level with the fifth floor of the old United Nations. The UN grounds are now grey with the corrugated roofs of the refugee shantytown and 42nd takes the overflow. Manhattan is fighting a losing battle with the sea. The Curtain can't protect it for ever. Jed joked that there's talk of raising Manhattan. Ten metres should do it, he says. At least I *think* he was joking.

When Jed sent his message he had just carried out six days of active duty in a little shantytown called Rubenstein 16. That's probably changed now the town's namesake has been shot through the neck and a new president 'elected'. The town is right on the eastern shore of the Great Lake. Jed says that if you walk out of Rubenstein northwards, after about ten minutes you are faced with an awe-inspiring sight: you come up a rise and from the top you see Interstate 81 dropping away ahead of you. After about half a kay-em the road just disappears under the waters of the lake.

I guess humankind can only ever have control over the power of nature where we created it ourselves. In the colonies. Hell, we even have trouble up here sometimes.

Jed seems quite amazed at the difference in lifestyles between us and Earth. He seemed to think they'd all be shunted into Ents chips and watching hee-vee. It's a very low-tech life down there. With the power cutdowns, the poverty, the rationing, I guess they're lucky for what they manage to scrape together. Jed said he was shocked at first by what he described as 'the flat hee-vee'. Then he came across radio entertainments – just music and talk.

Even further back on the evolutionary tree, he actually came across *live entertainment.* On a night off, Jed and friend called Gil went into a club in Syracuse, not sure what to expect, but probably hoping for some sort of Ents chip to jack. Maybe a piece of Earth ass. There was loud music and native marijuana was being smoked; the smell was too sharp and it made Jed cough. They sat at a table by the wall and ordered drinks from a human waitress. Then a woman came out on to a wide platform and, before Jed knew what was happening, she was singing. Then she started to take off her clothes: a check shirt, high-heeled shoes, jogger trousers. Down to a single-piece thermal undersuit, she slowly unbuttoned the back. She let it drop until it was trapped around her hips and then started to massage her body. Eventually the undersuit slid over her hips and fell to the floor and her massage became more intimate.

Jed says he watched with a curious mix of feelings. He says it might have been a good show on hee-vee, especially if there was a good chip to shunt in tandem. Different. But why was there only a woman? There wasn't a great deal of art to the whole thing and Jed found the thought that the woman was actually doing it in front of a live audience kind of distasteful. He and Gil moved on to another club.

There's a whole grey area of social behaviour that Jed is only scraping the surface of at the moment. He mentions the accents (basically a weird nasal twang in the parts of the Grand Union he's been so far), different customs (like stripping in a nightclub), and a whole new body language of gestures and signals. Jed says it's easy to walk into a bar and, just with your foreign body language, start a fight.

Jed saw this happen in a bar in Manhattan. He was sitting with a quiet drink when an EP walked in and ordered a beer. Hell, all this poor young soldier did was pat the waiter's ass when he delivered the drink, something you might do in any off-Earth bar without a thought. The place descended into a chaos that took a long time to sort out.

It must be a strange war to fight. Confusion about the real reasons, confusion about who is the real enemy, confusion with the citizens you're actually supposed to be protecting. And all of it going on in an environment that none of the young troops have ever even come close to experiencing.

I guess it must have been the other way around in the Fight for Freedom. Terran troops with little experience at the various gees of the colonies. That's one advantage we do have now: we can simulate Earth gravity up here.

Back in '51 they had no way of preparing for low-gee combat without training off-Earth.

On our side we had a quarter of a million people working and living in the colonies, most of them young and fit, and the most experienced people there had ever been in low-gee. It still took near on twenty years of escalating political campaigns and then eventually guerrilla action. With almost the entire population wanting Independence, I guess there wasn't a lot the terrans could do.

We have old Mother Gaia to thank too: the Struggle coincided with the worst years of change on Earth. Icecaps melted and the seas were rising by tens of cee-ems a year. The whole Earth's circulation system was in turmoil, the patterns changed by global warming; the resulting weather changes were causing drought, flooding, an unprecedented number of cataclysmic events. Nobody really knows why there was such an increase in seismic activity, maybe the surface stress of global warming had a more profound effect than anyone had predicted. The result was widespread flooding, massive land movements (like the sinking of Iceland) and enormously changed weather.

And, of course, civil unrest. The pressure from us, coupled with the pressure from Earth, led to the collapse of the imperial forces. Freedom was declared and many of the terran troops stayed on to train the new Defence Militia. And, of course, to avoid the conflict in their homelands.

I guess I was pretty like Jed, once upon a time. Always doing what seemed to be the right thing. My duty. All it took was the shock of Army life to work that out of me, make me realize that I was a human being in my own right. But Jed has a tough hide, it'll take one Hell of a lot to shock him into some independence.

The Fight for Freedom was my own fight for freedom. Once I'd shaken the Army out of my skin I was my own man; the Army had shaken everything else out of me.

I was born when it was still a diplomatic struggle and the only people who took it seriously were the Extraterrans. I grew up in an environment of political radicalism and I guess that made it pretty inevitable that I would join the fight as soon as I was old enough to spray graffiti.

At the age of seven I was running messages past terran soldiers, too naïve to question children. In my early teens I was running weapons on seemingly-innocent school trips. I planted my first bomb at the age of fourteen. At sixteen I was a member of the party that burned out an entire Bernal sphere at L4.

At seventeen Independence came and I was faced with drawing together what I had of a life after a childhood of guerilla warfare. It wasn't much, and I lost myself on lysergine for a time that could have been days but was most likely weeks or months.

Then I joined the Defence Militia.

Four long years in a brand new army. I guess I thought it might be something like what I had known through my childhood. But the war was over, we had no-one to fight.

I didn't expect it to be several months going through pointless training excises. The Militia was trying to find its way from a loose confederation of guerrillas into a genuine Army. The leaders thought we needed 'real training' so we learnt how to drill in nice straight lines, how to keep our shoes shined and have a bed made with neat folds, how to take flak from the officers. The AI generals didn't come along until the early seventies to tidy up what mess was left of Army thinking.

The commanders did begin to sort themselves out after

those first few months, though, and eventually we were something that vaguely resembled an Army. But those few months had wrought the changes in me. I saw that my officers were not necessarily my betters, that the system was not everything.

And over my four years in the Militia my new attitude made me begin to notice the effects that the military way of life had on individuals. *Individual* isn't a word they like in the Army, it smacks of independence. There *are* no individuals in an army, it's just one big machine.

When Jed was called up, Toni was worried about what they would do to his body. I guess she doesn't want him ending up like me. But she was focused on the wrong thing: it's what they do to your mind that matters.

The military is like one big computing system. The generals do the programming and there's one awful lot of equipment to be coordinated. The soldier is the place where hardware and software came together and do their work.

It's where the sparks fly.

Now, when a new recruit heads into training, he has a whole load of software up there in his head that the Army doesn't want. Sure, some of it might be useful, but even that has to be adapted. Just to make sure it fits with the Army's scheme of things.

I saw that happen to the men around me and I felt it trying to happen to me. But, like I said, those first few months of disorder had brought me to my senses and I wasn't having any of it.

I served my four years, never even threatening to move up from Private in a time when all you had to do was serve time to rise the ranks.

I'm just glad I got through it and retained my humanity.

If there was ever a just fight it was the Fight for Freedom, but that still doesn't make it a civilized way to act. It can only achieve the minimum and it tends to leave huge diplomatic battles in its wake. Even now, thirty years on, we have bad relations with Earth. Sure, some of them can't afford to lose our trade, but that doesn't make them *like* us. It's like Milton said in *Paradise Lost*, some 400 years ago:

> Who overcomes
> By force, hath overcome but half his foe.

Punching a guy in the mouth never wins the fight. It just leaves a whole bunch of hard feelings that needs to be patched up later.

I found my way through the Army, preserved what I had of a soul. I maybe even built it up a little, through my rejection of the military paradigm. I'd like to think that God values peaceable souls more highly than others. I have this sneaking suspicion that He would have dodged His draft if they ever had such an obscenity in Heaven.

I find it an almost amusing irony that I should come to worse harm on a farm museum than in my four years as a soldier.

Sixteen years after the fighting ended and guess who stumbles on what was later decided to be an old Terran weapons cache? You guessed it. Felling conifers halfway around from Simpson and a tree landed on what looked like an old stack of logs. But there were boxes under the top layer of wood. Chester Whitney took a look and then fell away yelling and screaming and writhing around like there was a snake in his pants. He was dead by the time I reached him. I backed away and drove to Simpson before it hit me. It was like my arms were on fire, burning from the inside. I don't remember much more for the next few months.

Piecing it together years after, it seems that we found ourselves a weapons cache left for Terran sleepers, agents that would wait until there was an opportunity for a counter-rebellion. No surgery or medicine could do more than make my pain almost bearable. So now I'm wired into Lejeune.

Even in the colonies, some people have prejudices against what they archaically call *cyborgs*. They say we're not human. Well, I reckon it's their right to close their minds if that's what they want. But I certainly don't feel any less human as part of Lejeune. Maybe even a little *more* than human.

If only I could get it through to Jed that humanity comes in a huge variety of forms. Sometimes he shows signs of understanding – Triona has helped him on that – but I think Jed has taken after Toni on this issue.

Toni was a great help at first. She had just had Triona and it was a remarkable thing that she did over the next three years, teaching a baby to use its handicapped body and helping a grown man to do much the same thing. When I decided to wire myself up Toni stood by me. But after my twelve days of surgery, she had changed her attitude. I think she decided that she could never be close to me again. She seemed to think that shedding a body, even a useless, painful one, was the big step away from humanity. No, she never said as much, but a man can tell when his wife is drifting away. She even turned away from my bed drone, wouldn't accept the comfort I could offer through it. Even now, she can barely touch one of my drones without flinching. People take a lot of understanding, sometimes.

Up here in the colonies you can see such a great variety of human forms. People are surgically altered, ranging from the basic suboccipital access to individuals such as myself. There is genetic alteration like that carried out by the miners. Some of them are so changed that they could never even set foot on the moon for fear of being crushed by its light gravity. And then there are the people like Triona, trapped in weak and ailing bodies, sad relics of the accidents of our ancestors, a warning for the future.

What binds these various peoples together under the term *humanity* is the way they *think*, not the way they look. You can be a lot less human in a supposedly 'perfect' body than other people in their 'imperfect' bodies can be.

I guess what I've been trying to say is that humanity is a state of mind more than it is one of body. The great crime that the Army commits against the human race is that it perverts young minds so that they can work as part of its machine.

Hell, it doesn't matter if you're blown half to pieces so long as what comes out of it at the end has a mind that thinks like it is a human being. Mind beats matter every time.

Chapter Thirteen

3 July 2084

Blackness turned to grey, then the violent orange of strong sunlight shining on closed eyes. Pain coursed through my body as if it were a vital constituent of my blood. I chipped down. At least *that* was still working. I was on my back, the sun burning down on me, my ears bouncing loud messages around the inside of my skull.

I moved a little. Regretted it. Lay still a moment or two more, savouring the luxury of ordinary pain as opposed to the pure agony I had felt when I moved. I tried a different tactic, opened my eyes. Dislodged grit and dust from my brow. Bits fell into my eyes and made them sting. Quickly I raised a hand, the pain of movement secondary to the necessity of getting those malevolent little particles out of my eyes. That stinging, scratching feeling, no tears to wash away my assailants. A piece of grit gouging its merciless track across the surface of my eyeball. Multiply that. *Lots* of pieces of grit. And the dust, drying up what moistness had survived almost two weeks of the desert.

I rubbed vigorously at my eyes, forced the grit deeper, increased my discomfort. Stopped. Chipped down again. Forced my hand away and tried to ignore the feeling of my eyes scratching against their lids every time they moved. It would ease, I told myself, it would ease.

I worked my hand slowly down over my face, trying

to cover as much of it as I could with the span of one hand. Found a warm wetness after only a few cee-ems. The wound felt familiar. I ran a finger down its length, about six cee-ems. Hoped the flow of blood would stop – the cauterization I had carried out on Amagat had lost some of its appeal. I felt my hand running down the wound again, recognized the gesture, the source of *déjà vu*. Saw a scythe arcing through the air, its tip slashing at my left jaw, chipping the bone and leaving me scarred for life. For some reason I had never gotten around to having the scar wiped. The look in Triona's eyes, fury turning to a terrible, terrible fear. Hands leaping to her mouth, swallowing a scream. She had thrown the scythe at Lacey, missed and hit me. Big brother. Lacey had been teasing her about her primitive support frame – she had only been fitted into the Amstrad when she had stopped growing. I had been trying to shut Lacey up. But I got too close. Triona had cried all the way home. We told Ma it was an accident.

Now the scar was lost beneath a mess of blood and Jesus knows what else. It was like the desert had finally wiped out the last link with my past. Destroyed the old Jed, left a broken shell of a soldier in his place.

I pulled my hand away. Opened my eyes and saw blood on my fingertips. My eyes hurt and I closed them again.

I wanted to just lie there, wait for the life to slip out of my body. I longed for a gentle afterlife of soft rains and Bernal spheres. One full of forgiveness. A vision of biting into an apple cruelly floated before my closed eyes, the sweet juices running down my chin, leaving their sticky trails. Driving me mad. I forced my eyes to grate open, shattering the image and bringing me back to my own harsh reality.

More of that deathly white smoke clung to the desert

ground, drifted about in the warm breeze. Another bomb. Delayed fuse, maybe just faulty. But no, this was bigger, probably more powerful than all of the others taken together. Deliberate. Maybe it was booby-trapped. Vibrations in the ground, maybe just sound or heat. Maybe one of the rumoured sniffers, waiting for the smell signature of a human to reach its sensors.

The sound of coughing drifted through the clearing smoke. Nearby. Male. Cohen.

Priorities. Get myself together. Get the squad together. *Get the Hell out.* I brought my hand back up and gingerly fingered my wound. It was warm and sticky and the blood seemed to have eased off in its escape, dust clogging up the flow. Maybe that would lead to complications later, but at the time it was a blessing. The wound was tingling, and I realized that my chip was beginning the healing process, playing an electrical field through the nerves and encouraging my body's defences. I ran my hand down over my face. No more holes. I moved again and there was a darting pain in my spine. But it allowed me to move so it couldn't be too serious. The rest of my body seemed OK and I moved into a sitting position, trying to ignore the pain in my back.

Cohen was squatting about three metres away, looking across at me. 'You OK?' he said. 'I ever get back to CalTex, someone gonna hear 'bout this.' He coughed again, his voice was a dry whisper, almost inaudible. 'People worth more'n this.' He trailed off into another fit of coughing.

Politicians. I guess they have to be shot at before they appreciate just what it means to go to war. Maybe we should go back to feudal kings. Let them lead the troops in person. I guess that's the only way to define a 'just war'. 'I'm OK,' I said. I looked back and saw Amagat lying a few metres back, her bandaged head face-down in the dirt. I remembered the attack and the sub's confusion. 'A delayed-fuse bomb,' I said to her by way of explanation. 'Not another attack. We're gonna get out of here. You OK, sir?'

She pushed herself up with her one good hand and settled on her knees. 'As OK as I was before,' she said. 'Where's Leo?'

Shit. Leo was on point, sent back that Comtac. I looked ahead of us, dreading what might be there. The breeze had cleared the smoke and I had no trouble seeing Jacobi's still form. I rose painfully to my feet and took a step.

'There may be more, boy,' said Cohen, his voice regaining some of its strength.

I stopped. What to do? I looked across at Cohen, then at Amagat. If we spread out we would be less likely to blow each other up. But it would also be more likely that at least one of us *would* get blown up. Assuming they were booby-trapped bombs, of course, and assuming that there was more than one. If they were on delayed fuses, then time was the crucial factor.

'Come on,' I said. 'Can you get up? Can you walk?' Cohen and Amagat stood, then Amagat crouched and felt around at her feet. 'Forget the stick,' I told her. 'Cohen'll look after you. Come on!'

Cohen went over and took the sub's arm, brought her up to where I stood. 'Follow me,' I said and turned. Started walking. After several long moments I realized that I was holding my breath and I made myself take a deep lungful of the hot, dry air. We stayed in a tight group, hoping not to trigger anything. I trod lightly, tried to float on the air. I followed what I hoped had been Jacobi's route. The way should be clear, at least until we reached Jacobi.

It was only about twenty metres to Leo but it seemed

like the longest walk of my life. We had to find some sort of a balance between speed – time-delay bombs? The thought sent my pulse racing, despite my chip – and care, in case of booby-traps. I walked at what might be described as a casual pace in other circumstances; a slightly faster beat than a death march. But pace was the only casual thing about that walk. My limbs were rigid, my innards tense. My heart roared as if it had moved up from my chest to my head, jumped there with the shock of the explosion. My back hurt with every step. I stretched, hoping to hear that loud click, but there was nothing. Just the pain.

Halfway and no sign of another bomb. I kept my eyes peeled for any giveaways. Marks on the ground, the glint of metal, a warning sign saying BOMB: PLEASE KEEP CLEAR. Anything. After all, it had not been placed and concealed, it had been dropped from a fast jet, from a height of at least fifty metres. In my head I knew I would be able to see if there was anything, but in my gut I knew that seeing it could be too late.

Jacobi had seen *his* bomb.

As we drew closer to Leo I saw that at least he was still in one piece. He hadn't moved at all.

I looked at him. He was lying on his side, facing the direction we had been heading. His face was black and distorted, but somehow it still had that deathly calm I had seen on Gil's. I couldn't see any sign of his chest moving, but then his position and the way his arm lay could have obscured that. My eyes didn't linger on his chest for long, they were drawn first to the way his arm hung from a few thin strips of flesh at his shoulder, the white glint of bone, and then to the horrible red mess of his abdomen.

I stopped and knelt. Lowered my hand to check his neck without hope for a pulse. And found one. It was weak, but there had definitely been a movement under my finger, then another, a few seconds later.

The touch of my hand must have got through to Leo and he half-opened an eye. His mouth twitched in what I took to be an attempted grin. I drew my hand away. 'Leo,' was all I could say.

His mouth opened a crack and settled in that position. 'Don't try to speak,' I said.

He blinked. 'Heard you . . . talking . . .' he said through a half-open mouth that barely seemed to move. 'Get . . . gone . . .' His mouth slowly closed. I felt for a pulse but there was none. His blank eye stared at me and I reached out and closed it for him.

Plato, Gil. Now Leo. My whole life was slowly stripping itself away, as if it wanted nothing to do with me. I couldn't find it within myself to blame it.

I looked up at Cohen. 'We walk,' I said. I rose to my feet, left Leo with one final look and started walking. After a moment or two Cohen followed, leading Amagat by the arm.

Wrong person. *I* should have been on point. They should have gotten *me.* Yes, that bomb had my name on it, only Leo found it first. All a mistake. Should have been me. I concentrated on the task of lifting each foot and placing it ahead of its companion. The sun beat down on my neck and I realized that I had left my hat somewhere. Just have to walk quicker, beat the sun. I increased my pace. Tried to ignore the complaints from my back, my eyes, my dry throat. And the new pain starting to grind away in my jaw. I brought my hand up and felt the sticky mess. Let it drop.

Just walked.

All those days ago, Cohen had told me that we wouldn't get more than a hundred metres – *yards*, as he said – in the heat of the day. Not under that desert sun. In a strange way, I guess he was right. Back then we would probably have dropped in under fifty. But we walked for nearly a *whole fucking day* after Leo. I don't know about the others, but I just went into a sort of overdrive. It was the state I sometimes found myself in when we were in the heat of some piece of action. My mind detached itself, seemed to float above my toiling body. I concentrated only on the lifting and placing of my feet. Each step was about sixty cee-ems. That was sixty off the target, sixty less to Askar Rock. Another sixty.

My body found its rhythm, my mind found nothing. It worked at the steps until it realized that my body had taken over the job. It lingered for a long, long time over the pain in my body. Everything ached, my head throbbed, my median was still sore, my feet were red and raw. All of the complaints of my body seemed to settle into a slightly off-focus ache in my lower back.

The sun had been hotter on previous days, but then I had been in shelter during the hottest hours of the day. Now I felt tremendous waves of heat breaking on my head, my shoulders. My hair gave me some protection, but its thickness and darkness made an oven of my scalp. Little eddies of wind stirred dust into the air, made breathing difficult. I could have accepted all that if the moving air had brought some coolness to the day, peeled some of the layers of heat away from my body. But the air was hot and dry, just like the rest of the desert.

Thinking about it, I guess Cohen or Amagat, or even both, could have given up at any time that day. I wouldn't have noticed, I just kept my eyes focused on the ground. Guessing the spot where my next step would fall. But they kept going, maybe supporting each other, maybe not. I guess they stuck together. I certainly didn't hear any sound of Amagat falling.

I kept chipping way on down. That kept my mind in some sort of order, helped me bear my load.

The soldier seemed to be keeping well to the back of my head. Maybe it didn't hurt quite so much back there. I cracked a painful smile. Way back, I thought I had him under control. Power of the mind. I was shaking the Army right out of my system. Yeah. Then we hit the road, Cohen got the soldier mad. Rattled him right back out into the open. He had been near the surface ever since, taking over whenever he wanted. I felt like a hee-vee projection, free to play my walk-on part, free to speak my lines. Until somebody changed channels. The soldier was a part of me, maybe a bigger part of me than anything else, now that I had been ripped apart from my old life. Several times that day, I wished that I had been in Leo's place, that there had been a bomb to rip the soldier out of my head. I guess that's the only way he'll ever be persuaded to leave.

Chipping down seemed to keep the soldier at bay, let me be in charge of my own body. Maybe I could spend the rest of my life chipped right down. As low as I could go, then maybe a bit lower.

I worked at that for a while.

Tried to work some spit into my dry mouth. I bit my tongue, but it only hurt; didn't make my mouth water. Not even any blood.

I walked dumbly on.

Hours under that desert sun, I still don't know how we did it. My legs just kept on swinging past each other. The dull pain that had focused itself in my back vanished after a time. Or I just stopped noticing it. I lost all the feeling in my legs apart from an incessant tingling that kept jumping about on the skin. Much as I hated the tingling, I wished it would replace the pain in my head, too. My sweat soon dried up and my skin felt like a husk of plastic. My chip kept my pulse at bay for some of the time, but at others it went racing away too fast to count. Not that I really wanted to.

Memory of a series of lectures, back at the Merc. Symptoms of fatigue, thirst, overheating. From what they taught us I should have been dead with the number of symptoms I had. The way my mind and body were plugging away, totally separate from each other, I Hell as near *was*.

Soldier started to talk to me, somewhere out there in the Dust Bowl Desert. Stop thinking, just *walk*, he kept telling me. That kept going through my head, like he thought he could drum it into me. Maybe he was trying to hypnotize me. Ain't gonna die on Earth, was another one. He kept chanting it like some crazy mantra. Hell, maybe he *was* crazy, maybe I was coping with the desert better than him. The thought crossed my mind that maybe I should stay out in the desert; maybe that would be the way to keep soldier boy down.

Hell. I don't know.

For quite a time all I could think of was that last empty juice carton that I had thrown away, back near that old road. Maybe there had been a few drops left in it. But no, Cohen and Amagat would have been careful about that. Days on end in the desert makes you careful about these things. It had been orange juice, I think. Flashed me a memory-image of an orange Soldier had eaten once before.

Wichita or Topeka or somewhere. South-western Grand Union, anyway. A raid in a nice, comfortable part of town. That was unusual – I guess that's why the memory stuck – the kid rebels in Union tend to be from poor districts. Kids who think they'll miraculously become better off under a new government. Soldier was chewing on an orange as the squad approached the house, threw it away as we passed through a loose ring of Union troops; they were keeping well out of it, as usual. It was getting dark and there was a big shadowy car pulled up on the lawn. Soldier took the back with Jacobi. Comtac. Then we burst through the door, into a side room, where we knew they were hiding. Four of them, Latins, no older than fifteen. Leo hesitated and Soldier shot. We killed three and the last girl ran out, shouting to her mother or grandmother. Soldier shot her at the old woman's feet. A nice, straightforward mission. But they were *kids.* Jeez, I had to be out in the desert before I realized the number of our targets that had been children.

I had to get the soldier out of my head, any way I could. He had done so much that I just couldn't live with any more. Gotta go, I kept telling myself, to the rhythm of my plodding feet. Gotta go.

But that just brought the soldier back. Stop thinking, just walk, he kept on telling me. He was only using me to get out of the desert. Once the going got better, he was going to take over the controls again, turn me back into a fighting EP. Ain't gonna die on Earth.

For a moment my senses climbed back near to the surface. My blurred vision resolved itself in incredible detail. As my foot hit the ground it sent up a little puff of dust. I could almost see each particle, floating amongst the others, playing its part in the scheme of things. Each time the dust would hang in the air and then be dragged away by the irregular breath of the breeze. Sometimes it would be blowing as my foot hit the ground and the dust would be dragged away instantly. I couldn't see much detail when that happened. The particles of dirt began to look the same after a while, even the shapes the dust-clouds took in the air started to repeat themselves. My mind wandered away from my senses again.

A short time later – I don't know quite how long – I was forced back to awareness by a tangled tumbleweed that some unseen enemy had thrown through the air at me. Luckily it was a bad shot and I didn't have to dodge. If my rhythm had been broken then I think I might just have sat down and given myself to the desert. Hell, it had been trying to get me for long enough. The breeze had become cooler and had picked up some grit. It stung my cheeks and I looked back down at the ground, watched my feet, the dust being torn away from each footfall. Kept to the beat of the desert.

Just walk. Soldier had come close to the surface for an instant back there. The surprise of the weed rolling across my path, the surge of adrenalin. Snapping me alert. Soldier's always close when there's the possibility of action. I guess that's what he was put there for.

Back before we ever set foot on Earth, all the soldiers had been convinced of the infallibility of the generals. Everybody calls them Artificial Intelligences; that's not accurate, but I guess the Army is happy enough not to correct people on that. AI sounds a lot more daunting than Sixth Level AI Simulant. They still haven't conquered the final level, maybe they never will. The Church says they won't, says Level Seven equates on a non-parametric basis to the soul. So they say. But near-AI is good enough for the generals, anyway. We used to think that whatever the generals said was unquestionably right. They knew all the answers. But it was orders coming down from a general that threw Amagat on us at the last minute. Orders from a general that planned the whole operation. Something went wrong somewhere. The generals had psyscans of all of us, had all our records. They say they can predict us down to some microscopic area of uncertainty. So what went wrong?

I tried to stop myself thinking along those lines. Externalizing again. My situation wasn't the fault of some fancy computer on the moon or Lagrangia. It was all the fault of Soldier Boy, sitting in my head and pissing on my life. I shook my head as if that would dislodge him, but it just hurt more and the world spun dangerously until I felt I would collapse in a ragged heap on the ground. It spun for a moment longer, then began to level off.

My rhythm went on, unbroken.

Some time, late that day, a stab of Comtac brought me back to the surface. Nonsense. Undecipherable. I began to sink again. Then I snapped right back. Jamming?

But no, there was just that one message, nothing more. I glanced around for the first time that day. Cohen and Amagat were about fifty metres back, walking slightly apart. Amagat appeared to have found some sort of a stick again and was using it to guide her. Cohen limped by her side. A heat haze cut the short distance between us, made the two of them appear to be walking on a flickering mirror. I kept to my rhythm.

A short time later – seconds, minutes, not as much as an hour – I felt a faint jabber of Advance Warning. AW never sends a message, just dances in your head. With experience you find you can recognize patterns that tell you what sort of warning it is, which bursts to ignore, which ones are telling you to run like Hell and cover your ass.

This faint AW was the sort to ignore. Atmospheric, maybe, or animals. But I couldn't just fall back on experience and let it go.

I stopped walking, felt an instant stab of stiffness and

soreness in my limbs, my back, my head. Looked around. Late afternoon, I decided. The sky was dark in the east, some of the heat had been taken from the air. Another burst of AW hit my head at the same time as a gust of grit stung my face. Some landed in my dried-up eyes and renewed that horrible scratching feeling. The AW was just atmospheric interference, static or something, I decided.

I looked back. Cohen and Amagat were still walking, although they seemed no closer. They didn't appear to have noticed that I had stopped.

I turned round and started again, trying to regain that elusive rhythm. I knew it would only come if I stopped thinking about it, left it to my body, but I couldn't drag my mind away. One foot, then the next. No, the rhythm wouldn't come. I looked back to my right, the greyness of the approaching dusk. I had never noticed before how sharply defined it was, the break between night and day. A dark grey wall spreading along the horizon. I had always thought it would be less distinct, diffused and scattered by the intervention of the planet's atmosphere between sun and surface. I enjoyed, for a moment, the dancing of the cool breeze on my cheeks. Turned my head back to the direction I was following.

I checked our position on the GPS and my mind map. Only about four kay-ems to go. I didn't think I could make it without a break. Needed to rest for the night, set out again at dawn. If my body didn't just seize up overnight.

I was working my way up a rise and I lowered my head and decided to get to the top before thinking about when to stop. Eventually I could see horizon over the top of the slope. The band of ground I could see grew with each step. Dry, hard ground, a few saguaro cacti, a little patch of scrub, a farmhouse, an old fence blowing stiffly in the wind.

A farmhouse.

I dropped to a stiff crouch, lost sight of the building. Advanced up the slope until I could see it again. We had come across several ruins in the previous two weeks. Big farmhouses, wide apart. I guess the farming can't have been too good in this region if the buildings were so isolated.

None of the farms we had found were more than shells. Broken-down out-houses, lines of brick where walls had been, maybe just a great big heap of rubble. Cohen said the farmers had remained until a decade or two ago, then they had finally been forced off the land. 'The New Okies', he called them.

But this farm was different. It had a roof, to start with. And walls that went right the way up to *meet* the roof. Windows that still seemed to be intact. The one door I could see hung awkwardly from its frame, wobbled in the wind. There was a huge barn standing just beyond the farmhouse, just as intact as its companion.

I heard a sound, a bang. Someone had slammed a door. Soldier leapt to the front of my mind, tried to take control. This was a job for him, he seemed to be saying. I took a deep breath and chipped down.

It was about eighty metres to the farm. Down a gentle slope, over a small ridge and into the yard. There wasn't much cover on the slope, nothing until the ridge. I looked back. Cohen and Amagat seemed to be hurrying in the dimming light. I hadn't known the nights to draw in so quickly before. I looked at the grey wall of dusk and it was much closer than before.

I stood and forced my tired body to half-walk half-trot down the slope. The sound of feet slamming into hard ground drove itself up through my body to my sore head.

My breath came in dry, sobbing gasps. I kept my eyes fixed on the low ridge ahead of me. As I moved, the stream of nonsense-Comtac increased, the random, patternless AW thundered in my head. It was like the jamming had been, but not as distinctive. A crazy jumble of static playing with my circuits.

I reached the ridge, dropped myself against it. Using the momentum that remained, I crawled a short distance so that I could see over the ridge to the farm. Drew a long, painful breath, let it out in an equally painful manner. Looked at the farm. Only a small front yard separated it from me. A cold wind tugged at my hair. Grit peppered my head from behind as I surveyed the scene.

Another bang of a door. A movement in my vision: it was the ill-fitting front door that had closed. Strange that I hadn't seen the person that slammed it.

A mad chuckling sound from nearby. I twisted sharply. Painfully. Grabbed for my non-existent zap. Looked for the source of the sound.

A ragged hen tumbled away from the other side of my ridge in a frenzy of chucklings and cluckings. A gust of wind caught it and turned it in a wild somersault before depositing it by the door. The bird gathered itself and looked around before slipping between the door and its frame. Seconds to calm my raging pulse, then the door swung slowly outwards. I waited, my breath dragging at the air. The door was wide open, nobody there. Then the wind tore at it, flung it shut in a wild fury that I wished was my own.

The wind. It had been the wind all the time. Looking at the house, it was old and worn, the windows broken, wooden boards coming away from the walls. A piece of guttering hung from the roof, dancing madly in the wind.

The wind. Playing tricks on me. The door opened and slammed again.

I buried my head in my folded arms, held it tight. It hurt so much. The wind. My body started to shake with tired, dry sobs. A pitiful whine hung in my throat; I don't know if it escaped or if I held it under some sort of control.

I don't know how long I lay like that, just that all the physical suffering I had gone through over two weeks wasn't as bad as those few moments of grief. It was the purest emotion I had ever felt.

I came back to reality with a hand resting lightly on my shoulder. Cohen. 'Better get inside, son,' he croaked. 'There's one great big mother of a storm coming. Come on.' He gave me his hand and somehow had the strength to help me up. 'Amagat's inside already.'

Chapter Fourteen

News feature from the New Union Journal, *14 April 2084.*

The fight to clear our nation of CalTex-backed terrorists has turned once again in favour of Grand Union. More terrorist bases have been located and sterilized in the past month than over the entire preceding year.

In response to a growing number of attacks on the citizens of Grand Union our allies, the EPs, have stepped up the pressure. The results have been impressive. Last week, in just two days EP forces raided thirty-four terrorist bases throughout Grand Union. Our own over-stretched national police service raided a further three.

The largest operation was down in Oklahoma City, Okla. Local services cooperated with EP strike squads to coordinate raids on six separate terrorist safe-houses.

The raids in Oklahoma City were based on information received from Jackie Trentnor, a Texan, captured a week earlier in an attempt to plant a lysergine-based psy-chemical bomb in Enterprise Square on the Christian College campus (Memorial Rd and Bryant).

Operation Jackie, as it was labelled, was spearheaded by a four-man squad, led by Sublieutenant Thom Sorakin, known as 'Plato' to his squad. The main terrorist base in Oklahoma City was a third-floor flat. The building faced on to a small yard, just off May Avenue, guarded by city police, armed with automatics and knockout grenades. The terrorist flat was quiet, but an EP technician was keeping electronic tabs on the four killers inside.

Privates Leo Jacobi and Gil Lohmann appeared momentarily at a window above the target flat and then there was a blur of action. The four EPs leapt out one by one. Cables snapped taut against the window frame and the troops were swung violently back into the flat below. Plato led the way, holding a square shield in front of him to ensure that the window broke evenly and there were no dangerous shards of glass left in the way.

Plato landed on his feet in the middle of the lounge. Moments later, he had the rest of his squad behind him. According to a pre-arranged plan, they went after their targets. The terrorist who had been guarding the door stormed into the room and Lohmann shot him through the stomach with a quick burst of laser gun.

Jacobi and Corporal Jed Brindle ran past the twitching body, crossed an entrance lobby and kicked in the bedroom door. A shot came out of the room, the troops taking cover by the door frame. Jacobi, with his laser gun on wide spread, stepped into the doorway, aiming low. Brindle fired over his colleague's shoulder, high-intensity bursts picking off the two naked targets with perfect accuracy before the woman with the gun had time to let off another shot.

Meanwhile Plato had headed for the one other target. Bursting into the shower room, laser gun at the ready, he made the only live capture of the raid. Plato found nineteen-year-old native of Oklahoma City Maria Chinzo standing opposite the door.

Dressed in a robe, her hair a black and white lather of soap, Chinzo eventually revealed the secrets of the flat. Communications equipment, documents that led to the subsequent arrest of many others, including high-place city businessman Sam Hilary. The most valuable find was a disk, which was disencrypted to reveal details of three major import routes from Texas into Grand Union. These routes have been broken and massive arms shipments confiscated (*see p.9 for full story*).

The results of the two days of action include the neutralization of thirty-four bases, capture of fourteen terrorists, death of 127 terrorists, confiscation of GU$28 million worth of weaponry. Many of the weapons are of African and Thai origin. Many of them were still in crates that bore import stamps from ports on the western seaboard.

Rapid follow-up on some of the items found in the raids has had a crippling effect on the terrorist organizations. EP and state security forces have interrupted arms imports, arrested key figures, cut lines of funding and traced many previously unsuspected branches of the terror industry. Investigations are still producing new advances in the fight to make Grand Union a safer place for its citizens.

These latest victories in the war against terrorism point to the great success of our cooperation with the Extraterran Peacekeeping Force. The opponents of democracy cannot hope to last under the combined onslaught of EP and local forces.

The latest achievements in the fight against terror provide strong support for the claim made by President Sanchez in his acceptance speech. Yes, President Sanchez, the democratic principle *is* close to victory within the borders of Grand Union.

Excerpt from Voice of the People, *printed on 15 April 2084, distributed throughout Grand Union by the youth section of the People's Underground, 16 to 17 April 2084.*

Citizen of an Advanced Nation. You watch TV, or if it's a power-down maybe you read the paper. *New Union*? Would you read that? It's been a bad day at the factory, the out-of-date machinery is trying to break down and secure its retirement. Your baby's screaming because you can't afford to keep your house warm. The screams crack your head, each one a nail in the coffin of your human pride.

And you see a story about the new president. Elected by his buddies in the White House and now living in a palace with a piece of everything he wants, and spares just in case.

They say they can't *afford* national elections; they say the president was elected *democratically*. By a vote among his forty friends. They say Grand Union is the greatest upholder of human values since old USA.

They say a lot.

You sit there watching TV and the power goes down: they have their own generator in the White House.

You sit there reading the *Union* and your last candle flickers and dies in a pool of molten wax: they only use candles for state occasions in the White House. In candelabras.

You hold the baby, sharing your precious body-heat: they have integral heating in the White House, log fires for decoration. They have child-minders too.

You sit at home in the cold and dark, your day at an end. Your freedom never even started. Maybe a tear runs down your cheek. You scratch it away. It's cold.

You sit in your poverty, the poverty the aliens want

to preserve. Maybe you've read this much of the leaflet, maybe you threw it away in fear, scared an EP might see you reading subversive literature. Maybe you say *What can we do?*

We can rise up. We can oppose the EP dictatorship.

We have the power, we just need the will of those people who sit at home and ask what can be done.

Brothers, sisters, we need *you.*

Selective Reality. You sit in your warm apartment. Maybe it's in the city centre to save on the inconvenience of travel. You watch the news bulletin you've recorded from earlier. You watch with the lights down to save power like they tell you on TV. Maybe the darkness makes you feel cold so you turn the heating up.

Your breathing steadies and a few of the tension lines drop from around your eyes, your mouth. The news is good. EP raids on terrorist bases. Hundreds of rebels killed, a handful captured, weapons found. And didn't our own Grand Union security forces do well? Look: they're actually shown in the same shot as an EP, they *must* be doing a good job.

Oh wow, and you believe it. Just like they want.

Isn't it good that those generous EPs have been finding more and more terrorist bases? That they are killing more and more young freedom fighters?

But don't you just stop and wonder, sometimes? No?

Well maybe you should. Maybe you believe the Press: soon all the terrorists will be wiped out.

On the other hand, maybe you just begin to wonder if perhaps the reason they are finding more terrorists is the obvious one. *They find more terrorists because there are more terrorists.*

If more of the young people of Grand Union are taking notice of the call for freedom there is one inevitable result. There are going to be more inexperienced young people calling themselves freedom fighters. More young people for the EPs to catch.

Have you ever noticed something about the 'terrorists' we hear of on the news? The ones that have been killed or captured? They all tend to be young.

Don't you find it a little strange that there are never reports of the capture or murder of experienced freedom fighters? Maybe the EPs can't catch them.

The young ones are more fun anyway. They're fun to shoot to pieces.

Some of them are fun for other reasons. There are very few freedom fighters captured alive. Those that are have all been female. And young. Strange, huh?

The EPs are aliens, with alien minds. Maybe it's unfair of us to demand basic human decency from them.

The news reports tell us a lot about the successful raids, but they never mention the failures.

Sitting there in your comfortable apartment, you may feel slightly less at ease if you knew about the number of EP raids that have been aborted, the number that have ended in death to the EPs and not even a scratch for a freedom fighter.

And, strangely enough, they don't mention raids by freedom fighters on alien targets. They don't report the EP transport tug we blew up on the launch pad at Levittown. Or the truck-load of comatose EPs whose carcases we decommissioned with an acid bomb shortly after they had been taken off a transporter.

No, successful action against the alien invaders does not get a mention. Maybe it's just not newsworthy. That's the only reason *we* can come up with.

Maybe we've removed some of the comfort from your apartment, brought some of the real world back into your life. Maybe next time you see the news you might just look out for that smack of insincerity, the story that doesn't quite ring true.

Maybe you'll begin to select your own reality rather than let your leaders do it for you.

Creative Reality. You sit in your seat on the crowded bus that takes you into your comfortable warm office. Others stand, the ones that work on the factory floor, the ones that are on social security tabs. You sit because you are a yup-man, secure in your job, secure in your home. Secure in your fit with the world.

And you read in the *Journal* or maybe the *Times* about a bus. A bus just like the one on which you have a seat. A bus that blew up. Terrorists, the story says. A bomb made in Phoenix, or maybe Albuquerque. Anywhere so long as you all know it was supplied by the Alignment.

It's always close to you, too close for comfort. A bus carrying commuters: just like the one you are in. Forty-eight dead, regardless of whether they were sitting or standing: there must be about fifty people on your bus. There was no warning: well, nobody's told *you* anything.

But it's always in another city. It's always somewhere at a safe distance. Too far for rumours, for eye-witness accounts other than those the paper reports. But it could still happen to you.

The paper says so.

It's weird, the stories papers tell. You see it's all part of the war that is being fought around you.

Ultimately, war these days is fought by and through the people.

We, the freedom fighters who claim to represent your interests, try to win you over; with the people on our side there is nothing the government can do. Not even with the EPs behind them.

The aliens, and the cartoon leaders who claim to represent your interests, need to keep you on *their* side; with the people behind them, there is nothing *we* can do. Not even with the force of justice behind us.

So when the *New Union* gives you the grisly details of a terrorist strike on a café, or on a school. Or on a crowded commuter bus. When they tell you we are blowing up the citizens of Grand Union.

Think for a minute. Ask yourself what purpose these acts would serve.

Maybe we have hidden goals, maybe we want to rule the world. But I don't think you believe that. All we want is a free country.

A free country for you, a free country for us. A free country for anyone who wants it.

So we blow up the citizens in callous acts of barbarism. Hmm. Well, it must be true.

The papers say so.

The Best Form of Defence. We have always pursued the policy of taking the fight to those who want to fight.

We have no fight with the people of Grand Union. So we don't attack them.

We fight the aliens. We fight those citizens of Grand Union that are aiding the aliens. We fight the aggressor.

But we can only fight them on the ground. Although our support is high and growing, the EPs are a brutal and well-equipped force. A straight confrontation is beyond our capabilities. All we can do is carry on in the underground. Fighting in the only way that is available to us.

We have connections, though. Since the EPs stepped up border operations the CalTex Alignment has come into open confrontation with the alien aggressor. They could not just sit back and watch their border being eroded, with enemy military forces massing and threatening invasion.

We can happily announce that the resources of the Alignment permit the fight to be taken to the aliens. It is now more than a year since CalTex first struck out beyond the atmosphere. They have destroyed several EP satellites and threaten much worse. There are now weapons available that could strike the aliens in their homes, from the surface of our planet.

Not surprisingly, the EPs are worried by this latest development. For the first time they are scenting the possibility of defeat.

Our actions here in Grand Union are turning that scent into a very definite smell. With the people actively behind us we can make this whole place smell so bad to alien noses that they'll have to hightail it back up to their tin-cans in the sky.

Join us in repelling the aggressor.

Kick up a stink!

Excerpt from the journal of Trixie Solenstadt.

22 MAY 2084

Wow, I just got to write this down, you know: put it on paper before it starts to slip away from me. I'm lying in my bed writing this and I'm not going to leave it until it's lost Jed's warmth. His body heat.

Back to the start of the story. I got to get this down right.

I was on early evening slot down at Cherevano's, skipping my way between the tables, doing my best to 'Get the drinks and make it snappy'.

The main lounge at 'Vano's is a low, wide room in the basement below a supermarket. The tables are packed close together and they always seem crowded, even when we've just opened the doors. The whole place is dark except for the bar that runs the length of the north wall. Lights dance on the liquor bottles, sparkle off the glasses, shine off Santo's bald head. 'Fuck the power,' says Santo when anyone mentions energy shortages; 'The bar stays lit.' Santo is a big man. Big in height, big in width and big in the mouth. No-one argues with Santo. He doesn't exactly *own* 'Vano's, but he runs it for whoever does.

I was wearing my uniform and not liking it. High shoes, stockings and a red one-piece crotch-and-camisole. When I started the job three weeks ago I loved the uniform. It made me feel really *something*. But it's quick to lose its appeal. Shit, you can't be out there for more than half a minute before there's a hand on your ass or your tit or your crotch. And you can't be rude to the customers.

Well maybe. Last night I was on early evening, seven to twelve. Past eleven I had just about had enough. Some grubby old bastard was pawing pussycat, wouldn't let go of me. He must have been about sixty, with a purple face and skin flaking off his bald head and neck. 'Do you want lemon and soda in your bourbon again, sir?' I grated through a face frozen with disgust. 'Or do you want me to piss in it?' 'We-e-e-ell,' he seemed to drag the word out of the depths of his huge stomach. 'I reckon as how I should just think on that one, just a little while longer.' His thumb slipped inside the high leg of my cammy and slid its slippery way down. I let it reach the first tight curls and then I'd had enough. 'Fuck this shit-assed job!' I yelled and ground my right heel into the bastard's instep. He jerked his thumb away, tearing my cammy and knocking over his empty glass. I punched him in his sagging jaw and he rolled off his chair into a heap on the floor.

When I turned away there was a loud cheer and a round of clapping. I suddenly realized what I had done: thrown my only hope of a job away on some brainless lump of meat and a fit of temper. The people around me had enjoyed the spectacle but I knew someone who would not be joining in the applause. I tried to resist it but my eyes seemed drawn towards that brightly lit bar like a houseplant grows towards a window. Santo's eyes burned into my forehead. I started to walk dumbly towards him like some automaton.

'Hey!' I looked around for the source of the cry that had broken my trance. It was an EP. I stopped. 'I saw all that and it was a pleasure to watch,' he said. 'I'll have an Irish Turn-up and get whatever you want.'

I looked at Santo. The murderous look had gone from his face and he was all smiles. I approached the bar nervously. 'Two ITs,' I muttered, staring at Santo's multiple chin. 'You better not fuck up on the aliens,' he said, grinding the words out through a fixed grin. I took the drinks and headed back.

The table was crowded with seven or eight EPs and I tried to pick out the one that had spoken to me. One grinned and I had me a good look at Jed for the first time. *Ricky-Dicky!* as they say on *Laugh or Cry*. He was a coloured guy with a fantastic body. He was sat on a padded bench, leaning back and looking me up and down. His gaze paused in its journey and I realized the extent of the damage that fat bastard had done to my cammy. I put the drinks on the table and looked into his big brown eyes. 'Gimme a minute to go change this?' I said. 'No,' he said. 'Just come and sit here.' I sat. The tone of his voice made me want to do anything for him.

I sat by his side and felt the hard iron of his thigh pressed against mine. He slipped an arm around my shoulders and I settled into his big chest. Somewhere at the back of my mind was the thought that Santo wanted to encourage the EPs in for business, wanted to be on the side of whoever was running the city. Maybe I could save my job, after all.

I spent the rest of my slot sat on Jed's lap, letting him get to know me a little better. I knew all I needed to know about *him.* At twelve I reluctantly slid off my mount and went into the back room to pick up my things. Once I was away from Jed's aura I was suddenly scared, my foundations removed. I expected Santo to come in at any moment as I threw my long coat over my uniform and picked up the bag that held my clothes, but he didn't appear. I went back to Jed and we slipped out into the hot, dry night. We don't get the worst of the weather, a safe distance from the coast and not quite into the Dustbowl, but the summer nights of St Louis feel like desert to me. I was glad I only had my uniform under my coat.

We headed down Fourth and passed one of the stainless steel stumps of the old Gateway Arch. I'd watched them cut it down when I was a child. Scrap metal, they had said. We went down to the river and wandered over the short grass; it grew well on the mud that used to be part of the river. The river that was always a disappointment when you got to it, not much more than a stream. But it wasn't a disappointment *last* night. Jed hadn't said much since we left the bar. We stopped on the bank. 'What's your name?' he said. 'Mine's Jed.' 'Trixie,' I said, 'Trixie Solenstadt.' Formalities out of the way, he turned and kissed me. Long and hard. And then he lay me on the grass and finished the job of ripping the uniform from my body. He was wild, like some sort of animal. His frenzy couldn't last long and it was over soon for both of us.

I lay back, my long coat open to the stars, my uniform lost somewhere in the dark. Up to that moment I can say with certainty that I had never had it so good. Not until later that night. 'Where do you live?' he said, and we went back to my room.

It was incredible. No other word. Every time he was wild and rough, like there was no tomorrow. He didn't care a gram how I felt about it all, I was just a vessel for him to come into. But he didn't need to care, he satisfied everything I could ever have wanted from him. Even today, there aren't many men like that around.

Lying here in my bed, the sun has broken through the two holes in my draw-blind and is shining on to the pillow beside me. That was where I lay my head until Jed left. Now I'm in his warmth, trying to make him last.

Maybe it's futile, trying to make someone so wild and fast hang on for any time. Like last night, it was wild and now it's gone.

I'll have to get out of this bed soon. See if I've still got my job or something. But I can smell him on the sheets, smell him on my body. I think I'll just lie here a little longer, feel his warmth. Hmmm.

Chapter Fifteen

3 July 2084

This old house gives me a weird mix of feelings. Wind whispering through glassless windows, the irregular drumming of a distant door, the creaks as it settles into another desert night. It makes me feel that I should be on edge, the atmosphere should be spooky, should send shivers racing up and down my aching spine.

But this is the first place I've felt comfortable for months. *Really* comfortable.

It has the feel of age. Cohen says it's well over a hundred years old. It's lasted better than the other farmhouses we've seen; from its good condition I guess the last occupants had tried to stay out here, fighting the spread of the desert longer than their neighbours. Soon we will be free of the desert, too. We leave the farm tomorrow, and hopefully the Dustbowl, as well. The soldier reclaims his body.

Right now I'm just enjoying these moments of freedom. Peace, right through to my seventh level, I guess.

Cohen's hand on my shoulder brought me to what senses I have. Hell, if he hadn't come back for me, I'd probably still be out there. That was one mother of a storm, as Cohen said. It's settled down since then, only the occasional gust of wind rushing past outside, slamming that old front door. Cohen said there won't be another storm on the heels of this one. I guess he's right, he seems to know quite a lot about this land. He says it was like this in Arizona and it's all coming back from his childhood.

I climbed slowly to my feet, still not quite sure of the world. The wind tore at me, tried to drag me away from the house. Cohen, satisfied that he had done as much as he could, limped away quickly and stood in the front doorway, looking back out at me.

I stood a few seconds more, let the wind bring me round. I could claim to have been disoriented by the static of the storm, sending confusing messages through my Comtac and AW, and there is at least a small element of truth in that. But a larger element of that truth is that I was fixed to the spot simply through the strain of our escape from the plane. My feet had grown roots.

Wind whistled in my ears in an eerie disharmony with the *basso* roar of the approaching storm; wind-borne grit felt like it was gradually scraping the skin from my face. Maybe I would have moved sooner, been stung into action, if I had been facing the other way and the wind had been attacking the wound on my jaw. Dumbly, I turned to face the storm. Dust and grit tore into my eyes and I looked through the narrowest slits I could make. The blackness that I had stupidly thought was the approaching dusk was now nearly upon us. I was suddenly aware of how cold it had become. The cloud stretched from horizon to horizon, its darkness tainted by amoeboid stains of brown that seemed to swim around, spreading their vile intent. The horizon was a narrow band of fire, blurred by a swirling filter of greyness. Somewhere beyond the storm the sun was setting an angry red.

The fiery band grew narrower.

'Come on, son. You can't fight it on your own.' Cohen. I turned my head. Took a step. Recoiled from the burst of pain from my foot, my back, my median, my head. Forced another step. The pain was less this time and I took another. Adjusted my stride and climbed the two steps to the veranda. Paused. Met Cohen's eyes. *Come on, son*, they told me. Clearer than Comtac.

The whistle of the wind and the storm's roar came together in a bellow and it seemed as if the earth was shaking beneath my feet. Cohen stepped back through the door and I followed him, the sounds of the storm diminishing as I entered the house. Immediately I was overtaken by a sense of safety. The world could throw whatever it liked outside and this house had stood up to worse in its long past. My pains were lost as I moved deeper into the dark security of the old farmhouse.

The corridor was dark and smelt of ancient dust. The only light came irregularly from the entrance, occasional draughts stirring the air as the door moved in the wind. The half-light gave the corridor a faintly brown hue, but this was the brown of ages, rather than the malevolent tone that swam in the storm-clouds. Several closed doors lined the corridor and through an archway I could see a dark lobby area, with extravagantly wide stairs forming the centre-piece.

Cohen ignored the arch, the doors, and headed down to the end of the corridor. He half-turned before a door at the end and opened it, letting me pass him and enter first.

Amagat's dirty head-bandage looked almost luminous in the darkness of the room. She was sat on the floor just to one side of the doorway, moving her head as if she was trying to look around. Weak light squeezed through gaps in the boarded windows on the far wall. The room was no brighter than the corridor and I realized just how dark it had become outside. I could still hear the sounds of the storm, pick it up on my circuits, but somehow it seemed more remote from within the sanctity of the farmhouse. The room was a large country kitchen. There was a tarnished metal sink hanging at a rakish angle from the far wall and I could see marks where there had been fittings. Cupboards, washers, cooking equipment; I stopped myself from adding consoles, autochefs and other basics to the list. This was Earth.

A loud crashing sound snapped me to a semblance of alertness and I looked sharply around. 'The storm,' said Cohen. I let my shoulders sag. Leaned against the wall and sank down next to Amagat. The comfort of a *real floor*. I grinned. My first genuine smile for some time. Somehow the house seemed to inspire good humour in its occupants. Maybe that was why its owners had stayed there longer than most other Okies.

There was another crash, followed by an angry stream of clucks from a hen. Cohen shut the door and leaned against it. 'I hope this old place can stand up to one more storm,' he said.

I looked up at him, said, 'It will.' I knew it would. The house had inspired confidence in me. We've been here a few hours, now, and I can feel that confidence coursing through my body like a new drug. Things are starting to take shape in my mind, sort themselves out a little, you know? Soldier hasn't paid me a visit since I've been in this old house. I think he's scared.

Lined up against the wall, we sat for a time. The sound of the storm intensified and icy draughts sent up clouds of dust from the concrete kitchen floor. The light vanished from the cracks between the boards as the storm closed on us.

I savoured the tingling needles of pain as life returned to my numb limbs. Felt the stiffness settling into my muscles, felt my back begin to seize up. I moved a little every so often, fearful that my body would lock in position and leave me trapped in this old kitchen. But that was just a precaution. I knew the house would do me no harm.

In a way, Jacobi had saved our lives. If we hadn't marched blindly through the heat of the day we would still be out in the desert, maybe five kay-ems back-a-ways. In the dust storm. I lingered for a long moment on the question of whether the wind would have torn us apart with scalpels of sand and grit, or if it would simply have picked us up and broken us on the ground. Like rag dolls.

A burst of AW and Comtac, followed shortly by a crash of thunder, dragged my mind away from that question. Another roll of thunder, more gentle this time. There was no precursory flash; the lightning must have lost itself somewhere in the darkness of the clouds.

I wondered for a moment if it was going to be a storm of rain and not dust. But no, that was just a desert-bred fantasy.

The bomb that killed Jacobi had driven us to shelter. A fair price? That was an unfair question, but the peace of the house somehow made me feel that it deserved an answer. If there had been no bomb, Leo would certainly have perished with the rest of us in the desert. In balance-sheet terms it was a fair price. But not a price I would have chosen to pay. I think I would have chosen the honourable option of dying together. Nobody could pay the price of another person's life.

There was a loud tearing sound and the storm had ripped a board from one of the windows. The kitchen was filled with a swirling mass of dry, stinging dust and grit. I began to cough as I leapt to my feet and staggered under the burst of pain from my sore body. Cohen swung the door open and I dragged Amagat out on her knees.

Cohen shut the sounds of the storm into the kitchen

and said, 'Are you *sure* this old house is going to stand up to it?'

I nodded and sat against the wall, let Amagat sink down silently beside me. 'Just gotta sit it out,' I said. 'Here'll do.'

Cohen sat on the floor and we waited in silence.

The storm lasted for what seemed an eternity, but Cohen put it at closer to thirty minutes. 'They don't last long,' he said. 'Never more than an hour. They just kick up a mess and then move on.'

The house survived the onslaught. Throughout the storm there were sounds of breakage, sounds that told us another part of our refuge had been broken into. Chipping away at our defences, edging closer every minute. But the violence of the storm passed us by, went on to wreck someplace else. The silence that followed was an emptiness that made me wonder if I was deaf. But there was the husky breathing of Cohen, the occasional sound of the house settling again after the disturbance. The crowing of a cockerel shattered the illusion of peace and I climbed slowly to my feet. 'Gonna look around,' I said. 'Who knows how to roast chicken?'

Cohen's eyes took on a fevered glint. 'I'll eat it *raw*,' he said.

I turned away. Didn't tell him that he'd be a fool to eat anything, especially protein. It'd just make him need to drink even more than he was needing it then. I needn't have worried, though. In the hours we have been in this house the best view I've had of a hen was when I was lying outside, oblivious to the approaching storm. Since then I've heard them, but never seen them well enough even to shoot with the instant reflex-control of a zap. Not that any of us had a zap to shoot one with.

I pushed at the door of the kitchen and it swung open, slowed by a drift of sand. The boards had come away from all of the windows, dragged off by the wind, except for one that clung stubbornly by a corner to its frame. It was dark outside, the sun long set. It was as if the storm had dragged a blanket of darkness over the world, left it behind for the sun to pull back with dawn.

I walked slowly over to the sink, the only reminder that this had once been a kitchen. It was full of sand from the storm and there was only one tap. I was struck motionless for a moment by the crazy thought that the previous owners had taken the other one. Maybe they needed it in their new house. I reached for the remaining tap and tried to turn it. It wouldn't move. I twisted harder and it gave a little. Twisted even harder and it came away in my hand, dislodging an avalanche of dust and sand into the sink. Another crazy thought: maybe this was just part of some colossal training programme. Maybe someone who had done this course before me had broken off the other tap. What would the next guy do?

Cohen had followed me into the kitchen. I turned and saw him trying to force open a door; I walked over and he stepped aside. It looked like a built-in cupboard. I pulled lightly at the handle but, as Cohen had found, it wouldn't open. Then I pushed and the door swung easily, almost as if someone had just oiled the hinges. Illogical. Cupboards shouldn't open inwards, but this one did. I stepped back, let Cohen through to investigate his find. I guess we shouldn't have expected logic.

A muffled 'God*damn*' drew my attention back to the cupboard. Cohen emerged shaking something in his hand. 'Look at this!' he cried. 'Look what they've left us!'

I tried to look, but he was waving his hands about too

much and I couldn't focus. He disappeared back into the cupboard and I followed. It was more a small room than a cupboard. It was too dark to see much, but I could guess the size from the echoes of Cohen's delighted cries. There was slightly more light by the door, trickling in from the kitchen, and I could see that the nearest wall was lined with deep shelves. On these shelves there were dark shapes. Tentatively I reached over and felt one of these shapes, picked it up. It was cold and surprisingly heavy, hand-sized.

'Food,' said Cohen from some dark recess. 'Tinned *food.*'

The image of the object in my hand resolved itself with the memory of tinned food. Another primitive, centuries-old process still in use on Earth.

'Let's get some out,' said Cohen. 'See if we can read the labels.' He pushed past me, his arms full of tins. I followed with some more and we spent the next few minutes trying to read tattered labels in the low light of the kitchen.

The knowledge of what lay in my hands took some time to sink into my understanding, but I found it took far less time to reach my subconscious. By the time we had deciphered a handful of labels my mouth felt moist for the first time in two weeks. My stomach hurt like it was filled with fire. I swallowed, hoping the juices might extinguish some of the flames, but the pain only intensified.

I heard a shuffling sound behind me and turned to see Amagat crawling towards us. She tipped her head up and said, 'Did I hear the word "*Food*"?'

'Sure,' said Cohen. 'I'll get you something.'

Several of the tins contained meat and I put them aside. *Apple and Apricot in Special New Recipe Low-Sugar Syrup.* That would do. We had to remember that our stomachs wouldn't take much yet. Energy and liquid were what we needed.

'How do you open these things?' I said.

Cohen stopped, looked at me. 'You . . . you use a can-opener,' he said slowly.

'Right. Where's that?'

Cohen didn't say anything and the truth began to sink in. It was a quicker process than the realization that there was food. And it hurt.

'What *is* it?' said Amagat, her voice wavering slightly.

I ignored her. 'Can we break into them?' I said.

'Don't know,' said Cohen. He sat down in a gesture of resignation.

I took my can and hit it against the concrete floor. Cautiously at first – I didn't want to lose my meal in the dust – then more violently. Finally I threw it down as hard as I could.

It didn't even mark the floor.

Just as I began to think that maybe this house wasn't such a Godsend, after all, I was struck by an idea. I picked up my can and headed back to the front door. 'Won't be long,' I said over my shoulder.

The night air was dry and dusty, but there was something new about it since the storm. It was mild, for a start. Not the usual cold that descended with the darkness. I looked up at the sky and there were curious blanks in some of the places where there should have been stars.

Clouds.

The desert weather had broken. For some reason I credited the house with the change. A big new ally.

I headed round the corner of the house and stopped outside the barn. There was a small, man-sized entrance set into the huge double doors of corrugated metal. I stepped in. It was dark inside and I fumbled around until

I could open the bigger doors, let in the slightly better light from outside.

A wild clucking greeted this action and I heard angry flutterings of feathers from the darkness. There was a strong musty smell in the barn and I began to be able to make out the shapes in the dark. Looked like sacks, maybe grain. That would explain why there were so many hens.

I looked down at my feet and just to one side I saw that magical glint of metal. I kicked at it with my feet then bent and picked it up. Hefted it in my left hand, switched it to the right. A scythe.

I stepped out into the night, put my can on the ground and knelt. Swung the scythe down in a graceful sweep and struck the top of the can. The blade lodged and I worked it loose. There was a hole in the tin. A lighter blow and a few twists of the blade opened the hole up and I dipped my finger in and sucked the juices from it. Perfect. I ate the rest of the fruit more and more greedily, drained the remaining juices and threw the can away. An angry flutter of hens in the barn. My stomach protested at the sudden onslaught of food but at the same time it cried out for more. I laughed crazily and turned back towards the house and the kitchen.

Before I had taken more than a few steps, I felt the light touch of rain on my face. I stopped in pure wonder. Tipped my face up to the sky and waited for more. A few moments and I thought it must have been my imagination. I opened my eyes and the stars were completely blotted out of the night sky.

Another drop hit my chin. Then quickly there was another. Soon I felt the delicious patter of rain on my face. Suddenly the world seemed a much, much better place to be.

I stood for several more minutes before going back to the kitchen to fetch the other two.

We re-emerged, carrying armfuls of cans and sat in a small huddle in the front yard. I scythed open several cans, warned Cohen and Amagat not to let themselves be overcome by greed. Cohen took it easy, but Amagat was soon retching violently, bringing up all that she had pushed down so quickly. She went easy after that.

After a time the rain became heavier and the ground turned to little muddy rivulets. Funny how the only thing you want for days can be some form of water, yet when it comes you find you can't take it for more than a few minutes. You get wet. Cold. Your clothes, impregnated with blood and two weeks of desert dirt, start to feel extremely uncomfortable.

I exchanged a glance with Cohen and we went back into the farmhouse, leading the sub.

We went through the archway and sat Amagat against a wall in the large lobby area. It was difficult to make out anything in the murkiness of the house. By then it was completely dark outside. The stairs were picked out from their surroundings in a faint light, although I guess it would be more accurate to say that they were bathed in less darkness than the rest of the room.

I walked into the middle of the floor, then over to the stairs. Looked up and saw that there was no roof over my head. That explained the light. The rain was softer again and, for some reason, it felt more acceptable in there. I sat on the stairs and Cohen joined me.

We were silent for a long time, then I said, 'A little under four kay-ems to go. We'll do it tomorrow at dawn.'

'Then it'll be some prison in the Union, huh?' Cohen stared into the darkness ahead of him. 'And you'll go back to soldiering.' He looked at me. 'Are you ready for that, Jed?'

I glanced at him for an instant. My eyes had adjusted to the light levels and I could just about make out his features. There were lines set hard into his face that I had never noticed before. Like a rock formation. Cooling lava. 'They'll take care of you,' I said, avoiding the second question. 'They need you.' The rain seemed to have stopped. I looked up and saw the glimmerings of one or two stars.

'Lyn was in the Army, a few years back,' said Cohen. Staring off into the darkness again. 'That's unusual down here, you know. They had a women's corps, based in Ukiah. That was where I met her – State Rep. visiting local installations, you know the sort of thing.' He chuckled quietly. 'A little subversion and she let me buy her out. She was my bodyguard for nearly five years.'

He paused and I realized that this 'Lyn' was the great hulk of a minder that I had shot on the plane. Mosander was her other name. Lyn Mosander.

'You have to hold some of yourself back from the Army, Jed. They want it all. Jesus, you have to hold some of yourself back from *every*thing, there has to be something that's still your own. Lyn kept herself. Underneath it all she was one of the tenderest human beings I've ever had the privilege of knowing.'

It seemed that I should say something, give Cohen an exit. Maybe in the light of day he might regret saying all this. 'The Army can't take everything,' I said. 'There's a level it just can't reach.' I was having trouble picturing Mosander in the light in which she had been portrayed. Perhaps I began to see a little. It's what goes on in your head that counts.

Cohen took the exit and we lapsed into silence for a time. 'It's the Thais and the Southern Africans that bother me most of all,' he said eventually.

'Huh?' The different tack caught me unawares.

'They always have,' he said. 'We don't need the squabbles with Grand Union, you know. We have a lot more in common with our neighbours than we do with anyone else in this world. The greenhouse has split us, destroyed our bases of production. The rains in Africa, the east Asian techno-booms – all the changes seemed to push the old US off its pedestal. Now that we're in such turmoil, fighting amongst ourselves, they could take us at any moment.'

'Invade, you mean?'

'Yes,' he said. 'Secure our downfall. Make it permanent. The Zambezian Alliance has been making threatening noises recently. The Thais don't need to. The whole situation drives me to despair.'

It was strange to see Cohen reverting to CalTex politician as the end of our journey drew near. I held my breath, half expecting to detect signs of Soldier struggling to the surface. No, he would wait until he was ready. Let me finish the work. I shivered violently, put my head on my raised knees, felt the bones grind against my forehead. Tried to calm myself. I had come this far without breaking. Just a few more kilometres.

I raised my head and Cohen was looking at me, a strange – almost pained – expression on his face. 'Not long to go, now, son,' he said. 'You'd better decide just who you are.'

I lowered my head again. Breathed slowly.

That was three, maybe four hours ago. I'm sitting in an upstairs window, now, looking out at the starlit desert. There's glass in this one, that's why we chose the room. Cohen and Amagat are asleep on the floor. In each other's arms, unconsciously keeping up habits formed in the cold desert nights. I'm keeping guard.

The veranda roof is just below me. I could step out

on to it if I opened the window. It might even take my weight, it looks sturdy enough. I can see dark shapes moving about in the low scrub that encroaches on the yard. Hens, taking advantage of the new moistness in the soil. What a simple life they must lead, none of the complications we humans make for ourselves. Oh, to be a mere hen!

I guess this room must have been a master bedroom at one time. There are still some of the fittings: the fancy cornices, the huge blades of a colonial-style fan suspended from the ceiling, tattered shreds of a wall-hanging that might actually have gold leaf set into it. I could believe anything of this grand old building. For some reason we all automatically assumed that to sleep we must find an upstairs bedroom. Maybe the other two feel, like me, that we have to do right by the house. It saved us; the least we can do is treat it with some respect.

Sounds crazy, huh?

Sitting here, I find it easy to just drift off. Hear laughter, sounds of clinking glasses, the popping of corks. The thunder of hooves comes from outside and a carriage pulls up at the door. A black servant steps out and holds the door wide for the powder-pink ladies to strut out on to the veranda. Hey, maybe that was my great grandfather. Better than picking cotton.

Yeah, it's easy to drift. I've hardly slept in the last two weeks, yet I don't feel tempted to lie down with Cohen and Amagat. I want to savour the night.

A strange melancholy has descended on me since the two of them fell asleep. Maybe it's the thought of going back to the Army tomorrow. Soldier taking over again. I know that's not necessary, but what is the alternative? Deviate by a few hundred metres and walk into Askar Town. Get shot by CalTex soldiers; if they didn't shoot me they'd imprison me, torture me. Maybe those rumours of the interrogator chip that scrambles the brain are true. What then? Jed the vegetable.

It would kill Soldier, though.

Maybe I would do that. But what about Amagat? I can't let them get her – I've been responsible for too many deaths already.

Eyes closed, I press my head against the window until I fear the pane will break. It's cold and hard. Traces of sweat lubricate the join between skin and glass. I haven't sweated for days.

I wonder, is an AI troubled with conscience? Maybe that's one of the functions of the uncharted seventh level.

My left hand finds the hardened wound on my jaw. Runs delicately along its length. It feels different to the old scar, lacking the familiarity. The family connections. I grin a little. Only a little.

Amagat said tonight that her face was feeling a lot better. Cohen peeled away the bandages. It obviously hurt, but Amagat kept quiet. In what light was available I couldn't see a lot, but I *could* make out that she looked almost normal. The swelling that had closed her left eye had vanished. There was bruising, but not a lot else. 'I . . . I can *see*,' she said tentatively. A grin broke on her face. 'I can see.' Not very much, just a blur of dark and less dark, but, Hell, that wasn't a lot worse than I could make out in that light. We left the bandages off for the night. See how she is in the morning. The bright desert light might just make her want to put the bandages on again.

The desert looks at peace in the starlight. Almost benevolent. The house creaks. *Heard you talking*, it says. *Get gone.* I nod slowly. Yeah, we'll get gone. In the morning.

I should really stay here at the window. On guard. But that's Soldier talk. Nothing to guard against.

Right now, I think I'll go down and join the sleepers. One good night's sleep. That's what I need.

I leave my post and get down on the floor by the two shadowy forms. Lie down, loop an arm around a body, I don't know which one. It's warm and comforting. Yeah, I chip right down, feel myself begin to drift. Sleep beckons and I hold back for an instant. Just to show who's in charge down here. I drift a little more.

Chapter Sixteen

Transcript of counselling interview, 9 June 2084.

Subcolonel (Med.) Hugo Vax sits behind his plaz desk. 'Who's next?' he asks his console in a tired voice. He is mid-forties, bearded, head topped by a coarse stubble of steel-grey hair. His thick black eyebrows join in the centre and cast a dark shadow that makes his eyes appear to shine out of deep cavities. He is chewing a gum that gives his small office the reek of an Eastern bazaar.

A synth voice comes from a speaker panel built into the desk's monitor. Synth: 'Mr Thom Sorakin is next, Sub Hugo. He is waiting outside, with an orderly.'

Vax: 'Give me some data, then give me a minute before you call him in.'

Synth: 'Sir.'

Vax leans back and feels the chair giving slightly under his bulk. He stretches and puts his hands behind his head. A list of details scrolls slowly over the monitor and he sits forward again. Thom Sorakin. Born in Independence Year, 2051. A New Londoner, hence his squad nickname, Plato. Blood imbalance, kept in check by a marrow-implanted biomonitor. Was a sublieutenant, in charge of a high-rating four-man squad until 30 May. On Earth for six—

A knock relays its message from the outside of the door to the ears of Vax and he breaks away from his scrutiny of the monitor. Vax: 'Yeah?'

The door opens and a man in a soldier's uniform enters the room as if he has been pushed from behind. An orderly in a crisp white uniform follows him in. Orderly: 'This is Sorakin, Subcolonel Vax.' She folds her bare arms and stares at a spot on the wall just behind and above Vax's head.

Vax: 'Hi, Thom.' He glances up at the orderly for a moment and continues: 'OK, Julia, that's it for now. I'll beep.' The orderly looks as if she is about to argue but thinks better of it. She lets her arms drop to her side and then leaves the room. She closes the door behind her with a heavy thud. Vax: 'Have a seat, Thom. Can I call you Plato?'

Sorakin lowers himself into an ice-blue chair. He is average height, stocky with a tendency to excess around the jaw and abdomen. His loose curls of rusty brown hair frame his round yellow face, the jaundice being one of the few symptoms of his blood disorder not suppressed by the implant. Sorakin: 'I'd prefer it if you didn't, if that's OK, sir. Plato's gone away and I don't want him to come back.' Sorakin's left eye twitches and he flicks violently at a lock of hair over his eye as if it was to blame for the tic.

Vax flinches at Sorakin's sudden movement. Then: 'Sure, Thom. I'll call you whatever you want.' He reaches for the free end of a lead that protrudes a few cee-ems from the edge of his desk. He pulls at it and it stretches itself out. Vax: 'Please excuse this, it's just part of the procedure. You know how it is.' He smiles kindly and raises the lead, locating the central socket of his suboccipital interface with his free right hand. He plugs the lead in, shunting the Psychan Interview Prompt. Vax: 'Now, Thom. Let's begin.'

Vax: 'You've been up here three days now, Thom. How are you settling in?'

Sorakin: 'I'm settling in just fine.' He looks around the room with a vacant gaze.

Vax: 'Are you feeling any better, Thom?'

Sorakin: 'I'm feeling just fine, now, Subcolonel.' His gazc settles on his left foot. He covers it with his right foot and then extracts it to cover the right.

Vax: 'You're an experienced soldier, Thom. A volunteer, nine years in service. What do *you* think your problem is?'

Sorakin: 'I don't have any problem, sir.'

Vax: 'No? How do you explain your circumstances then, soldier?'

Sorakin looks up from his feet and fixes his glassy eyes on Vax. Sorakin, his voice breaking slightly: 'I *did* have problems. Jesus.' He flicks violently at his hair as his eye resumes its tic. 'I had problems so big they filled my whole head.' He looks down again. Quietly: 'But not any more. I'm out of it now, no more soldiering for Thom Sorakin. No, *sir*.'

Vax moves in his chair, recognizing that the interview will be a long one. He scratches at his jaw and shunts a message via his suboccipital. *Record Pink Sox versus the Menelaus Marauders. Put fifty on the Sox.* Sorakin is fidgeting at the split plastic of his chair, pulling at the filling. Vax: 'Why did you want to get out? What was so bad about the Earth?'

Sorakin: 'It was what I had been training for since I joined up. But it's not the same, action's never what you think it's gonna be. I guess a lot of us still have the romantic notion that it's going to be like Crimea or something. Grape-shot in your musket and a warm flask in your pocket. But it isn't.

'I guess we paid the price of success: they wanted us *everywhere.* We landed in Levittown. Our first action was an assault on a terrorist base in Providence. We patrolled for a time in Manhattan, stopped an attempt to blow a hole in the Concrete Curtain. We were based near Syracuse for a time, then I lose track of it. Policing in Cincinatti, Des Moines, Davenport, Peoria. Raids in Topeka, Pittsburgh, St Louis, Tulsa. Jesus. I remember the names but all I can see is a crazy mess of images. Concrete towers, grand bridges, seedy tenements, kids on the streets seeing who can be the rudest to a soldier and get away with it.

'My *mind.*' Sorakin puts his hands to his head and screws up his hair. He stops and looks at Vax. 'All that change – it was too much for me.'

Vax: 'Was it just the moving about that upset you, Thom? That confused you, so you couldn't take it any more? Or was there more to it than that?' Vax hopes it was just the moving. Maybe he can still catch the Sox on hee-vee.

Sorakin: 'I . . . I guess there must be more to it than that.' Vax settles back into his chair with a loud creak of vinyl. Sorakin: 'I was just travelling from one city to another, taking a piece of action and moving on to the next place. Raid a third-floor flat in Oklahoma City, shoot someone and maybe capture someone else. Raid a basement in Tulsa, shoot dead four terrorists. Patrol the Curtain in Manhattan, shoot dead a kid carrying a bomb.

'The only thing it all had in common was the killing. The one constant in my life was the fact that most days I shot someone. Syracuse or St Louis, Tulsa or Topeka. The settings didn't matter, they all just blurred into one. There was one stable thing in my environment: killing.'

Vax: 'But surely you didn't kill them all? Your record says you had a high rate of capture, sometimes you risked your own life just so you could take someone alive. If you'd survived to the end of it all, you'd probably have been given a medal for bravery.'

Sorakin: 'No, we didn't kill them all. Usually you come on them by surprise – that's almost the definition of a raid. If they don't have a gun to hand then what's the point in shooting them? They're usually kids. Kids that might be too young to be called up if they were on *our* side.

'Sometimes I think it might have been kinder to kill them right away. Save them from what came later.'

Vax, leaning forward and resting his elbows on his desk: 'What do you mean by that, Thom?'

Sorakin: 'Well, there were rumours.'

Vax: 'Rumours, Thom?'

Sorakin: 'Yeah. The squads hand prisoners over to the specialists and they get out any information they can. Then they're handed over to the Frags. To the Grand Union police. Torture, rape, buggery, mutilation. These kids, fighting a war they probably don't even understand, and this is what they get! And *my* job was to hand these kids over.

'Oh no. I didn't *shoot* them, sir. I couldn't shoot a kid without a good reason. So I handed them over, skipped the responsibility. I guess I must have sent twenty or thirty kids down that line. All of them practically young enough to be my children.' Sorakin rubs at his twitching eye.

Vax notes that his monitor says the time is 14:23. Three minutes into the game. The news window in the top left corner flashes that the Marauders have gone six points up, with a possession penalty on Brubecker. Vax sends a rapid command down his suboccipital lead to close down the monitor. He only wants to find out the result when he can sit watching it in holo in his own room, maybe smoking a joint of Irish Gold.

Sorakin doesn't have any children and Vax decides that it is best to skirt around any paternal feelings for the young terrorists. Vax: 'They were only *rumours*, Thom. You've got to expect there to be all sorts of untrue rumours going around in a conflict situation.

'What effect do you think all this had on you, Thom? The guilt over the prisoners, the killing, the constant movement.'

Sorakin: 'It didn't have *any* effect on me, sir. That was what struck me first. After maybe three or four months I suddenly realized that I had been killing people, witnessing the most horrific scenes of violence, I had been responsible for so much destruction. *And it wasn't having any effect on me.* That scared me worst. What had I become?

'Then I began to notice the people around me. I looked at what they were and wondered if I was like them. That scared me worst.'

Vax: 'What was it that worried you about them, Thom?'

Sorakin: 'They were just ordinary guys. Ordinary guys that had been ripped out of their homes and pushed through a great big machine. They were ordinary guys that killed for a living and didn't give it a second thought. They didn't need reasons, all they needed was to be told by someone in a military uniform with those insignia that magically made them your superiors: "This is what you must do." That was the only reason they needed to kill people, and I was just the same.'

Vax: 'But that's how the Army works, Thom. It needs lines of command.'

Sorakin: 'Yeah, I guess so, sir. But what I saw was *individuals*. They were taken into the military and chewed up so they could be fitted into their rôles better.

I saw the nicest guys turned into monsters. Like my corporal, Brindle.'

Vax: 'What happened to Brindle, Thom?'

Sorakin: 'Jed was a really nice guy. He was conscripted from one of the Lagrangians, then he became one of the top recruits at the Merc. He was excellent physically and a good steady learner. A really nice guy. Everyone liked him, he had a sort of magnetism. People who'd never met him before would tell him things they'd never told anyone in their life.

'But that was Jed's one weakness, from a military viewpoint. He needed sharpening, needed to be given a killing edge.'

Vax: 'So you worked on that in your squad-training.'

Sorakin: 'Yeah, we sharpened him up. It all started to pull together in the final simulations on the Disc, but Jed didn't really lose his "weakness" until we went into action in Grand Union.'

Vax: 'What was he like, this new Brindle?'

Sorakin: 'Scary. As I said before: I didn't see what was happening at first. It was all just action, action, action. No time to stop and think. But when I saw what Jed had become it frightened me.

'There's one scene that just keeps on going round and round my head. It was a raid. Tulsa, Wichita – *I* don't know where it was. I just keep getting this scene played through my head. A comfortable house in a comfortable neighbourhood. A real gas-fired Buick, all shiny and clean, parked on the front lawn.

'Passing through a loose circle of Grand Union troops, hiding a safe distance away, we pull our gas masks on. It's dusk and a mockingbird yells at us from the shadows. There's a light patter of Comtac in my belly and Lohmann kicks in the front door. I follow him in and hear the sounds of Jacobi and Brindle's forced entry at the rear. Lohmann and I throw three gas canisters up the stairs and I leave Lohmann on guard. The pre-raid scan had told us there was nobody up there, but mistakes are not unheard of. Lohmann was a precaution. Screams come down the passage as Brindle and Jacobi locate their four targets in one of the back rooms. A door to my left is open and I burst through, still early enough for surprise to be on my side.

'A candle feebly lights the room, a flat TV lights the face of an old woman. My target. Her hair pulled back from a face of folds and lines and liver-spots. Her tiny circular eye-correction glasses reflecting the flickering image of the candle against the dancing pattern of the TV screen. I stop with my PT11 aimed at her chest. She waits a while before she looks up at me. *Shoot me if you're gonna shoot me, then*, she says and returns her flickering spectacles to the TV. The old woman is fidgeting with a tangle of string on her lap. Then I realize what it is: she's *knitting*. Not even with a machine, just two sticks and a tangle of some sort of yarn. I move slowly into the room, searching its dark corners for signs of life. Looking back over the old woman's head I can see the TV screen. It's showing a public execution, the three kids that shot President Sanchez. They used the finest weapons: manual PT11s, stolen from some luckless EPs. They're being executed by a very old weapon: the guillotine. I look away. I guess the killing's the same, no matter how you do it.

'The bubble bursts, the moment is dragged out of my grasp and I become a soldier again. A screaming girl, thirteen or fourteen, Latin features, comes rushing into the room with her blue-black hair flailing around her shoulders. *Gramma! Gramma!* she cries. *Man gonna shoo' me!* Man comes running in after her, sees her, shoots her. A gasp comes from the crowd on TV as the guillotine descends on some kid's neck. Brindle looks up at the old woman, his eyes glinting in the darkness. He raises his gun. *Leave her!* I say, and he drops his gun to his side and heads back out. The kid lies in a spreading pool of blood that looks like oil in the weak light of the room. The pool reaches the old woman's right foot. I look up at her but she is watching the TV, her needles working away in an unbreakable rhythm. Adverts now. A policeman comes in and as I leave a single tear finds its channel down a fold in the old woman's left cheek.' Sorakin begins to cry freely, his face in his hands, his elbows in his lap. He rocks slowly back and forth.

The game will be into its third quarter, now. Vax tugs at his mat of hair and presses it down. Vax: 'Did Brindle act incorrectly, Thom?'

Sorakin: 'No. I don't know. ''Following Orders'' – you know. But that look in his eye.' Sorakin shudders and forces himself back in his seat. Sorakin: 'One of my first assessments of Jed was that he was *solid.* I reckon there's no such thing as a solid person. Some just have higher breaking points than others. They're *brittle*, not solid. They can let the pressure pile on, then it'll get too much and they'll blow. They'll do something crazy.'

Vax: 'Is Brindle going to ''do something crazy''?'

Sorakin: 'We're all gonna do something crazy eventually. Yeah, Brindle will break. It's like gravity: it always pulls you down in the end.'

Vax: 'What made *you* finally break, Thom?'

Sorakin: 'I dunno.' He looks around the small room as if searching for something, then: 'I guess it all just built up. It started when I realized what was happening to me and it ended when I went on my last leave.'

Vax: 'How did it end, Thom?'

Sorakin: 'It was Kansas City. We'd just shot up some

kids in Lexington and they downloaded us in the nearest city for our thirty-six hours standard. *You coming out to burn up the town?* asked Brindle. I just tore away. Couldn't get away from him fast enough. He'd begun to give me the creeps. I hit the first bar I found and collected a lot of verbal from the drinkers. Some places are like that in Grand Union: no mixing with the aliens. They usually get away with it. The next place I found was friendlier. Four bourbons friendlier. I moved on.

'Eventually I came to a basement bar, somewhere off Southwest Boulevard, I think. The sounds and smells of sleaze were fighting their way out on to the street. Through my blur of liquor that seemed to be just what I wanted right then.

'There was a big black guy on the door. He stood in front of me when I tried to get in. *Wha'chou lookin' for?* he says. *Don' wanna no mudcrushers here.* Then he looks at me. *Juz wanna drink*, I say. Maybe he senses that I'm not looking for trouble – at last: communion between EP and Frag. He lets me in. *You wanna some tuskie, go see hammer man in the corner*, says the guy on the door. There was a little black guy sitting where he pointed, all jewels and leather. He had a diamond set between his eyes and a sapphire nose stud. I walked over. Shit, *I* didn't know what "tuskie" was. Maybe I thought the hammer man would buy me a drink, maybe I wasn't thinking at all, you know what I mean?

'I was stopped two tables away by a guy even bigger than the one on the door. *I think you wanna sit over there*, he says, pointing to the other end of the room. *But I juz wanna see Mr Hammer*, I say. I guess I *wasn't* thinking. The bruiser steps towards me, but the little guy says, *Let him through, Julius, let him through.*

'Well it turned out this little guy was a pusher and he didn't have to push very hard. I don't know what it was but it wasn't like anything I'd hit before. I guess it was cruder, everything is down there.' Sorakin's story seems to have run out of steam and he goes back to stacking his feet.

Vax checks the time. The game will be coming to an end, now. Vax: 'What happened next?'

Sorakin: 'Next I remember was a hospital ward and feeling like I'd rented my body out to a circus. As I came to my senses I began to realize that somewhere on that leave I'd made a break with my past. Yeah, I've been feeling real shaky, nervy, ever since, but I've been chipping down on that since even before I blew myself in Kansas City. It helps a lot, you know? I got to feeling that I had shaken the Army out of my system for a time, and now I just didn't want to let it creep back in. My soldiering was finished.

'A few days later, they shipped me up here to this place, a high orbital base, they tell me. And now I'm here, waiting to see what happens next.'

Vax shunts a summoning bleep to the orderly. Vax: 'What happens next? We'll try to patch your life together again and see how you feel *then.* I reckon that if you still want to quit the Army then you'll be allowed to buy out.

'Of course, we'll have to take your suboxy away from you, Thom. You realize that?'

Sorakin's mouth opens and then closes again. The door opens and the orderly walks in, her crisp white uniform making slicing sounds as her legs swing past each other. Vax: 'OK, Julia, you can take him away. Confine him and boost him eighty mils chlorprimazate. He won't be any trouble then, for a time.'

Orderly: 'Yes, sir.' Sorakin has stood up and the orderly grabs him by an arm and pulls him roughly out of the room.

Vax, quietly: 'Fucking nut-case.' An endless stream of cowards and nut-cases is Vax's lot in life; he spends most of his working hours wishing he hadn't majored in Psychiatry at the Academy. With a heavy hand he reaches up and deshunts his suboccipital lead. Vax: 'Any updates before I go and watch the game?'

Synth voice, from the panel by the monitor: 'Fifty has been debited from your account, Sub Hugo. Pink Sox lost one-twenty-eight to one-ninety-four and they're now out of this year's play offs.'

Vax tries to swipe the OFF switch at the base of his console as soon as he realizes what the synth is telling him, but he is too late. Vax: 'Shit.'

Chapter Seventeen

4 July 2084

Ground shaking. Shoulder pulled about in all directions, feels like it's coming loose. Amagat's voice drifts into my consciousness: 'Jed. Jed, wake up.'

I climb to the surface, break through. Open my eyes. Room bathed in blood-red light, face leaning over mine. Sink back into muzziness. The shaking stops and I open my eyes again. The world is drawn sharper this time and I manage to keep my lids apart, let the picture resolve itself.

Amagat is kneeling, sitting back on her heels. Looking down at me. *Looking.* 'Thought you'd never wake,' she says. Her face is a patchy vermilion, partly a result of the light but partly her injuries. There is no eyebrow above her left eye, its place taken by bubbled, cracked skin. Her eyes are small and watery.

Cohen is lying a short distance away on the floor. I guess we must have moved apart in the night.

'Jed.'

I look back at Amagat.

'Jed,' she repeats. 'The light . . . it's too much. My eyes are hurting.' She moves an arm slightly and I notice that she has a length of bandage in her hand.

The message is clear and I sit up, move to my knees, crawl over behind the sub. Take the bandage and start to wind it around her head. Not as much as before, just enough to protect her from the light. At least she can see, doesn't need more implant surgery to fix her up.

Working behind Amagat's head, I wonder at how she has changed over these two long weeks. How it has affected her. Jeez, I've been with her twenty-four hours a day, yet I've only just begun to notice the change. The Amagat of two weeks ago would just have woken up and wept, maybe even screamed when the light got too bad. Maybe some of Cohen has rubbed off on her. Maybe just experience. Hell, she's had more experience in the last two weeks than in all the rest of her military career.

'Is the world really that red?' she asks, as I try to figure out how to fix the bandage. I've wound it too far to tie a knot.

'Huh?' I say. 'It's the light. Sun's rising.' I take back two turns and tie a knot.

'Good,' she says in a far-away voice. 'It was so beautiful; I didn't want it to be just my eyes. Thanks,' she says as I move away, the job done. Then: 'All I could see were vague red shapes. I could make out *some* things, but it was really just a mass of shape and colour. It was surreal. I wish I could paint.'

This is a completely new Amagat. How had I missed the changes? 'Anybody can paint,' I say. 'Use a holo-wand.'

Amagat has her head turned to the window, as if she can still see. 'No,' she says, 'I mean *paint.* Flat, on canvas.' I stand and she tips her head towards me. 'Will you tell me what you see out of the window?' she says.

'Sure.' I walk over.

Incredible. It's as if someone has dug up the desert overnight and replaced it with Eden. Where before there was hard-baked mud, dust and a few ghostly saguaro, there is now a luxuriant carpet of greenery. The sky is a fiery mass of yellows, oranges, reds, even a delicate hint of green mirroring the glory of the ground. Shading off into a pastel blue in the west. A blue that will spread and deepen as day takes over the burden of the night. The rains have revived the life of the Dust Bowl, brought it bursting through the newly softened soil, reaching for the sun in a wild frenzy of life and procreation. Our journey will be at its end before the withering of death has swept across these lands. The return to desert. Looking closer I can make out pin-pricks of yellow and blue. Flowers already.

I glance at Amagat. 'Same old desert, out there,' I say. 'Sun's getting hot, ground's getting hard again. A few flowers, is all.' I see her mouth form the word *flowers* but she says nothing. In the few instants that I have looked away the blue of the sky has taken over, deepened; the sun is just a white-hot atoll in a sea of blue. Maybe I imagine it, but it seems that a few more flowers have opened to greet the day.

'Come on,' I say. 'We gotta go. Don't wanna be walking in the middle of the day again.' I walk out of the room, leave Amagat to wake Cohen. Down the wide sweep of stairs. For a moment I hear high-pitched laughter, the clink of glasses. Ghosts from the last century.

The scythe is where I left it, on the kitchen floor. I open a few tins of fruit, drink the juices from one as I wait. Sounds, then Cohen emerges leading Amagat. 'Come on,' I say. I pick up an open tin and head out, throw it away empty by the time we are clear of the yard.

I hear the word *flowers* as I slow to let the other two catch up. Amagat is walking with the aid of a stick.

Looks like half a broom handle. Cohen is talking. '. . . night's rain,' he says. 'There's green everywhere. Flowers opening up, too. There's plants I've never seen before, some I have. Can you smell the *change* in the air? It'll all be over by the end of the day, the sun will dry them out and the only life that will be left will be in the seeds and roots. They . . .' I let him tail off into the background, absorb myself in the new day. Sure it looked spectacular from the house, but down here you can see the desert trying to reassert itself. It's only cosmetic, the green, trying unsuccessfully to cover up the hard, cracked grey-brown of the ground. Already I can see dust forming drifts at the bases of the plants. The desert doesn't stay beaten for long.

The house is still in view behind us, an oasis of calmness, but already I feel its influence dissipating. Earlier my body felt almost repaired, but now I can feel the aches returning. The pain. My body is settling back into the desert faster than my mind. I notice that my feet have fallen into that old rhythm. A smile twitches nervously at my mouth. Stop thinking, just *walk*. The smile flees. Returns. But it's not mine: Soldier put it there. I force it to vanish. Ain't gonna die on Earth.

I chip right down. Soldier's not got long to go. I'm gonna keep him down for as long as I can. Keep the juices down, keep Soldier down. I find myself repeating this liturgy to the undying beat of the desert.

Yeah. Just have to keep him down for a little while longer. Less than four kays.

You know, I feel like I've finally come through something. Like waking up. You fight your way up, maybe hang there for a time. Then you break the surface tension, grasp the world and try to keep your grip.

I've got a hold, now. Just have to hang on for a little while longer.

I don't know how long we've been walking. Must be more than an hour. Travel's slow in the Dust Bowl, you have to fit yourself to its rhythm, let it pull you along. Keep chipped down.

We're more than halfway, now. The vegetation doesn't look as green, but it has more permanence to it. Like we're finally leaving the desert. That's an illusion – the Askars are just an island in a vast ocean of dust – but it means we're getting close. GPS tells me it's a little under a kay and a half.

Death's been hanging over us, this last fifteen or so minutes. Saw it drifting, a dark speck against the deep blue of the sky. Circling. Cohen says its a turkey vulture. Like I say: Death. Scanning the sky, I can't see it. Maybe it's given up on us. Maybe not.

I've kept Soldier down for some time now. I guess he's happy with the pace I've been setting. It's not me, it's the desert; I just keep to the beat. A smile bursts on to my face and I stifle a fit of the giggles. Cohen and Amagat are a short distance behind and they don't notice. I chip down just a little more. Got to keep it back a while longer.

The body's been holding out well. The pains of the desert came back and hit me hard at first. But I realized that it only seemed hard after the respite of the farm-house, it was really a whole lot better than I had known it. The aches jostled with each other for a while, then they found their places and settled back in with a cosy familiarity.

Now it seems that I've never known anything else. I can't imagine life without that knotted ache in my stomach, those arrows of pain that my back sends out with each step. That throb in my head. I guess I've finished the job the Army started on me. I've wiped out all traces of my existence before the transience of 'now'. A man without a past, without a future.

I am nothing.

But I guess it's a pleasant sort of nothing. Debts no longer exist because they were incurred by another person. Soldier. It's all over, all I have to do is walk. Chip down on Soldier. I let the grin burst on to my face, suppress all else. And walk.

Stop thinking, just walk. I chip him away.

A dark shape has appeared in a shimmering haze on the horizon. Askar Rock. The Union base is at the bottom of the craggy hill, all I can see is the rocky summit.

We walk on.

The town appears on the horizon. An untidy cluster of corners and straight edges stuck on to the landscape. Standing out from the desert in complete contrast to the way the farmhouse had blended in as if it grew there naturally. They should know we're here, soon. Both sides. The desert between the bases will be full of detectors. Hidden cameras, sniffers, microphones. They can probably hear our footsteps. Hear the rhythm of the desert.

Waves of unease threaten to swamp me. I lose the rhythm and stop. Cohen and Amagat catch up and I start again without a word. It's like the desert has stolen back its rhythm, aware that we are about to abandon it. These last few unsteady metres hurt more than any that went before. The sweat dries on my brow and I chew at my lower lip. Have to keep going. A few more metres. Left foot then right, but it's hopeless: the rhythm has gone.

The view alters as we approach. Suddenly an image

flashes into my head, like the subconscious view from a zap. The posters, the pictures on the video networks, back in the Union. This was the cliché image of the war. The two bases at Askar, one kay apart, yet the gulf between them so huge. That's what we're told by the posters, the news reports, the speeches.

I can see a cluster of mobile cabins and a few vehicles at the foot of the Rock. Still can't make out anything unusual about the town. Another few steps and I see the movement of a khaki van amongst the houses. Like the map says, the bases look about a kay apart. We are about a kay from each of them.

Soldier tries to leap into the driving seat but I am ready. I keep him chipped away in oblivion. This is *my* show. Not any of my past incarnations.

Hell, I feel more me than I've ever been.

I stop and my two companions stop beside me. Amagat senses something. 'How far?' she asks.

'Not far,' says Cohen. He looks at me, stays quiet. *I'm not going to lead you*, he seems to be saying. *You gotta decide just who you are.* On my own.

I turn slowly to Cohen. 'I'm sorry about Mosander,' I say. Unexpected. His face breaks its hard lines for an instant and he looks away. Then back at me. Still not a word.

I wave a hand. 'Town's that-a-way,' I say. I turn away, stifling something. I don't know what. 'Get gone.'

I lower my head, my eyes squeezed painfully shut. Open them and the world is a blur of swimming spots of light as my vision readjusts. A faint gasp from Amagat. But she says nothing. I wonder again at the changes the desert has wrought in the sub. Dust lifts and settles amongst the woody stems of the desert plants.

No sounds, then a vague shuffle. The sound of

retreating footsteps. I imagine the dust stirred up by his feet, falling in a unique pattern that could never be repeated.

'They'll string you up for this one.' Amagat. But she doesn't sound angry. Resigned. Something else, that I can't quite put a name to. Maybe there isn't a name for it yet. Finally I raise my head, look around. Cohen has already created quite a distance between us.

Amagat's head is facing me. Viewing me blindly through her bandages. I walk over, put my hands on her shoulders and turn her towards the camp at the foot of the Rock. 'Askar Rock's that way,' I say. 'Flat and scrubby, like we've just been going through. Looks like it gets a bit uneven towards the end. Can you manage with the stick?'

'Yes,' she says. 'But what about you?'

'I just need some time to think,' I say. 'Time on my own. You know?'

'Yeah,' says Amagat. 'I think I do.'

She begins to walk. She sure has changed. Grown. Walking seems slow in the desert, but somehow Amagat's figure diminishes quickly. In the other direction Cohen pauses and looks back. Sees me, Amagat walking away. Hesitates, but I can't see the expression on his face. Turns and starts to walk again.

My debts are settled as far as possible. I've turned everything back as far as it will go. That just leaves Soldier.

I turn and start to walk. Not to the Rock. Not to the Town. My route runs equidistant between the two.

Yes, walking seems slow when you are doing it yourself. Maybe it's the sun, the way it tries to grind you down. Maybe just the pain of movement. Maybe it's the way Soldier is starting to protest. Creeping through the back-routes of my head. He knows something is wrong. Can't quite figure it out.

I let the grin take over my face as I walk. Let the laughter escape from between my lips.

But I don't let Soldier take control. *Just walk*, I mimic in my own head. The laughter threatens to run away with me. Have to keep walking. My head rolls about on my neck and I let it for a time, then snap it alert. '*Tenshun*, I tell it. And giggle just a little more.

I look around me and the sun throws burning daggers into my eyes. I tell it to fuck off. Release a yelp of laughter. Snap back to control.

No good chipping down now. No need, Soldier's too scared.

I can see the two camps. Guess I must be on the line between them. About five hundred from each. See a rock just ahead. Nice size to sit on, so when I reach it I sit. It has a hollow that could almost have been cut for me. I look around.

Funny how the desert looks now. Almost tame. Why would that be?

I can't see Cohen or Amagat any more. Don't really want to. They're part of the past and I don't have a past no more so I guess as how they just don't exist any more. What a crazy world it is. I take a long, dry breath.

Yeah, this is the place.

I chip the other way. Right up. Let all the juices flow. Adrenalin, testosterone, endorphins. All the juices there are.

A wild surge rips through my body. I catch it and ride it, feel Soldier being dragged out of my skull. Open my mouth and let a shout break on the crest of the wave.

'*I'm out here! In the middle of the desert!*' Pause for

another surge to rip to the surface. '*Come and fucking well get me!*' It's a wild feeling, you know? Screaming can be fun when you're a complete nothing and all you have to do in the world is SCREAM. I tip my head back, raise my arms to embrace the sun. Let my final shouted *me* twist itself into absolute craziness.

And scream.

THE END

THE PEOPLE COLLECTION
by Zenna Henderson

Once you have read their story, you will never feel at home on Earth again . . .

Zenna Henderson's *People* novels, *Pilgrimage* and *The People: No Different Flesh*, are among the most acclaimed classics in science fiction. They are published here in one volume for the first time, together with the previously uncollected *People* stories, *The Incredible Kind, Incident After, The Walls* and *Katie-Mary's Trip.*

'The People are the descendants of the survivors of a spaceship from another planet which crashed on Earth long, long ago. The People were scattered, and their children have lost the knowledge of their origins. Since they possess special powers of telepathy, telekinesis, etc., which would be regarded with horror and terror by normal terrene natives, their's is a story of the conflict between their desire to conform to Earth standards, and their slow recognition and acceptance of their special identity'
Alfred Bester, *Fantasy and Science Fiction*

THE UNFORGETTABLE SCIENCE FICTION MASTERPIECE OF STRANGERS AMONG US.

0 552 13659 X

DESOLATION ROAD
by Ian McDonald

Miles from anywhere, but only one step short of Paradise, somewhere on the line from here to Wisdom where the trains never stop, there's a town that shouldn't exist at all, even in the Twelfth Decade when miracles happen every day. In fact, it's so tiny and faraway that it's only known because of the stories they tell about it.

It all began thirty years ago with a greenperson, you see. But by the time it all finished, Desolation Road had experienced every conceivable abnormality on offer, from Adam Black's Wonderful Travelling Chautauqua and Educational 'Stravaganza (complete with its very own captive angel), to the Amazing Scorn, Mutant Master of Scintillating Sarcasm and Rapid Repartee, not forgetting (as if anyone could) the astounding Tatterdemalion Air Bazaar, Comet Tuesday, and the first manned time trip in history . . .

'The most exciting and promising debut since Ray Bradbury's . . . here's a first novel brimming with colourful writing, poetic imagination and outrageous events. A magical mystery tour, hugely readable.'
Daily Mail

'A master for a new generation of Science Fiction'
Analog

'The kind of novel I long to find yet seldom do'
Philip Jose Farmer

0 552 17532 7

BATTLE CIRCLE
by Piers Anthony

In this visionary trilogy of a world based on superstition and a warrior culture, master science fiction writer Piers Anthony creates a legend of savage power, of primitive and brutal laws where all disputes are settled in the battle circle, and the vision of a new empire is decided by the might of their primitive weapons.

'Anthony's story of men fighting for mastery of wandering tribes, with sword, club and rope in the ceremonial Great Circle, has its own internal conviction – its own grandeur, even . . . a rigorous masculine power, rare in any kind of novel nowadays'
The Observer

0 552 13549 6